THE EMERALD SHAWL

LOUISE DOUGLAS

Boldwood

First published in Great Britain in 2025 by Boldwood Books Ltd.

Copyright © Louise Douglas, 2025

Cover Design by Alice Moore Design

Cover Images: Alamy, iStock and Shutterstock

The moral right of Louise Douglas to be identified as the author of this work has been asserted in accordance with the Copyright, Designs and Patents Act 1988.

All rights reserved. No part of this book may be reproduced in any form or by any electronic or mechanical means, including information storage and retrieval systems, without written permission from the author, except for the use of brief quotations in a book review. This book is a work of fiction and, except in the case of historical fact, any resemblance to actual persons, living or dead, is purely coincidental.

Every effort has been made to obtain the necessary permissions with reference to copyright material, both illustrative and quoted. We apologise for any omissions in this respect and will be pleased to make the appropriate acknowledgements in any future edition.

A CIP catalogue record for this book is available from the British Library.

Paperback ISBN 978-1-83751-661-2

Large Print ISBN 978-1-83751-662-9

Hardback ISBN 978-1-83751-660-5

Ebook ISBN 978-1-83751-663-6

Kindle ISBN 978-1-83751-664-3

Audio CD ISBN 978-1-83751-655-1

MP3 CD ISBN 978-1-83751-656-8

Digital audio download ISBN 978-1-83751-658-2

This book is printed on certified sustainable paper. Boldwood Books is dedicated to putting sustainability at the heart of our business. For more information please visit https://www.boldwoodbooks.com/about-us/sustainability/

Boldwood Books Ltd, 23 Bowerdean Street, London, SW6 3TN

www.boldwoodbooks.com

For Sarah: friend, editor, partner in crime. With love x

'My first child, my darling.'

— ISAMBARD KINGDOM BRUNEL, SPEAKING
OF THE CLIFTON SUSPENSION BRIDGE.

1

TUESDAY, 25 OCTOBER 1864

The woman was standing beneath the sign of the inn, holding the ends of a green shawl to her throat with one hand and a wicker basket in the other. The wind was gusting, the sign was swinging, and leaves were scuttering across the cobbles.

The *Courier*'s first female reporter, Nelly Brooks, was glad to see the woman. That morning, she had found a note posted in her pigeonhole in the foyer of the newspaper offices.

A dreadful murder has been done. If you wish to know more, meet me at the Llandoger Trow at 5 p.m. Come alone. You will recognise me by my green shawl.

Nelly had wondered if the note was fake – a trick being played on her by one of the other newspaper staff, for it was no secret that she longed for the chance to investigate and write a story of significance. But there was the note's author, good as her word, exactly where she'd said she'd be, outside one of Bristol's more notorious watering holes.

The day was coming to its end. The wheels of laden carts and carriages leaving the docks rattled over the cobbles on King Street. Dogs sniffed around the corners of buildings. The destitute were queuing outside the doss house and costermongers were packing away their wares. Lights were glowing behind windows and smoke puffed from chimneys.

And beneath the sign, the woman huddled in her shawl, and waited, a picture of disquietude.

She was about forty years old, wearing a plain brown dress, an old-fashioned bonnet and shabby boots. Everything about her appearance – except the shawl itself – indicated that she was not wealthy, but that she was respectable.

She looked constantly about her, in a most furtive manner.

Nelly caught the woman's eye and raised a hand in greeting.

'Good afternoon,' she said. 'I'm Nelly Brooks from the *Courier*.'

'You came!' the woman said.

'I could not resist your invitation. May I ask your name?'

'Eliza Morgan. You may call me Eliza.'

'Shall we walk by the harbour while we talk?' Nelly suggested.

'I cannot abide the water.'

'Somewhere else then?'

'I'd rather be inside where we cannot be observed. Let's go into the inn.'

The *Courier*'s crime reporter, Will Delane, had warned Nelly against interviewing contacts in pubs, because usually all they wanted was to be bought drinks. But Eliza was already opening the door and Nelly had no choice but to follow her into the gloom of the Llandoger Trow.

They went into the saloon bar, a long, narrow room. Paintings of ships and seascapes hung on the walls. There was some nautical ephemera, and mirrors reflected back what little natural light came through the windows.

The two women seated themselves in a quiet spot close to the fire. Nelly took her notebook and pencil from her satchel and asked the serving maid to bring two glasses of port.

'And a nip of gin to see it down, if you please,' said Eliza.

She put her basket on the floor, took off the shawl and laid it over the back of the chair. Her features were pleasant, but there were dark shadows beneath her eyes and her fingernails were bitten to the quick. She was twitchy, nervous as a kitten.

In the old days the Trow, an Elizabethan inn within spitting distance of the river, was renowned as a hangout for press gangs. Nelly had heard rumours of tunnels beneath the street where men too drunk to understand what was happening to them were hustled to the docks by the gangs and boarded onto waiting ships. When they woke, they were at sea, on their way to war, and it was too late for goodbyes or regrets.

Nowadays, the inn was popular with sailors and dockworkers, who came to spend their money and find female company. Nelly could hear raucous laughter in the public bar but they were the only customers in the saloon apart from an elderly man, dour in expression, who was drinking alone, and another fast asleep on a bench, with a hat over his face.

The serving girl brought their drinks and placed them on the table. Eliza took the gin and drank it neat.

'I needed that to steady my nerves,' she said.

'Your note said you feared there'd been a murder,' Nelly prompted.

'I didn't say I feared it, I said there *had* been.'

'Who has been killed?'

'The wife of an important man,' said Eliza. 'Her newborn infant has been done away with too. I didn't know who I should tell. I don't trust the police, and I've heard awful tales about the gentlemen of the press. "A woman reporter is what I need," I told myself. That's why I came to you.'

'I appreciate you entrusting me with the story,' Nelly said. 'Tell me, who is this important man?'

'I'm not ready to say.'

'But I can't do anything without the names of the man and his wife.'

'I won't tell you their names unless I am paid five pounds.'

Nelly inhaled sharply. Five pounds was more than she earned in a month.

'I don't have anywhere near that amount of money with me,' she said.

'We don't have a deal, then. Perhaps I should approach a different newspaper.'

There was an uncomfortable silence. Nelly tried to think what Will Delane would do in this situation.

'Eliza, we're here together now, so you may as well tell me what you know,' she said reasonably. 'If, when you've told me, if I think it's worth five pounds to hear the names of those concerned, I'll find it, somehow.'

Eliza leaned down to take a drink while she considered this proposal. Her hand trembled so badly that she spilled some onto the table.

'Very well,' she said. 'Where should I start?'

Nelly tried not to reveal her relief.

'Tell me, when did you find out about the deaths?' she asked.

'Yesterday.'

'And how did you come by this knowledge?'

'I am a seamstress by trade. I went to collect a coat from the gentleman that required alterations. I knew his wife was expecting, and I thought the baby might have made an entrance. I'd made a little gown for it, as a gift, and some dear little socks. But when I got there, the clocks were stopped, the mirrors covered, the curtains drawn shut. "Whatever has happened?" I asked the gentleman's stepdaughter. "Who is it as has passed?" but, do you know, Miss Brooks? I knew even before she told me. I knew it was the wife and her child! And she, God bless her heart, was little more than a girl herself!'

Her eyes filled with tears.

'What were you told had become of them?' asked Nelly gently.

'That the wife had given birth the previous afternoon and bled to death during the night, and the infant was feeble and didn't last the twelve-hour neither.'

'But you didn't believe that explanation?'

'I did not! He wanted her dead, you see.'

'The husband?'

'Yes! She'd heard him speak of it. He intended to suffocate her, while she lay sleeping in her bed.'

Nelly's heartbeat quickened. If this was true, what a story it would make!

Eliza continued: 'She wrote his exact words in her diary, which she gave to me for safe-keeping lest anything untoward should become of her. When I read them, it made my blood run cold. And now she's dead...' She shook her head as if in utter despair.

'Do you still have the diary?' Nelly asked.

'I do, but not with me.'

'May I see it?'

Eliza Morgan drained her glass and narrowed her eyes.

'You may. But only after I have been paid.'

2

Since taking up her post at the *Courier*, Nelly had spent most of her working days writing about those topics the editor, Mr George Boldwood, perceived as being appealing to women. She had nothing against knitting patterns and tips for a healthy complexion, but she wanted more.

For eighteen months, she'd been frustrated. Whenever an opportunity to write something more meaningful had arisen, the story had been snatched away and given to Will Delane, chief correspondent Duncan Coulson, or one of the other reporters, all of them men.

But this might be everything she had dreamed of: a chance to prove herself and to make a difference.

She was anxious to keep Eliza Morgan talking, to harvest as much information as she could. Outwardly, she remained composed; inside, her thoughts were tumbling over one another.

'When did you first meet this young woman, Eliza?' she asked.

'Two summers ago. I altered the gentleman's first wife's wedding gown to fit the second.'

'She didn't have a dress of her own?'

'He was too tight-fisted to pay for a new one. He never loved her, see. Not even at the beginning. He needed a wife because he wanted a son. And to stop people speculating about his mistress.'

'He has a mistress?'

'A married woman from Chipping Norton.'

Eliza looked disappointedly at the empty glass in front of her. 'All this talking's dried my throat something dreadful,' she said.

Nelly signalled to the barmaid to bring more drinks.

Eliza continued. '*She*, the young woman, was available. She was pretty, and bright and young enough to bear him as many sons as she could manage.'

'And, after their marriage, you used to visit her at his house?'

'More of a mausoleum than a house. Grand as a palace, cold as a tomb. But yes, I always met her there. She used to call for me when he was away so we could have a good talk without him breathing down her neck.' She sighed. 'I watched her change. She became a shadow of the girl she used to be. Oh, she tried to put a brave face on it, but it was plain for all to see that she was miserable.'

The door opened, and Eliza jumped, but it was only a man bringing a tray of mugs to the bar.

'Are you writing all this down?' Eliza asked Nelly.

'Yes,' Nelly said. 'You were saying that the young wife was unhappy.'

'That's correct. Then, one time, about six months ago, there we were, me and her, in her dressing room. I was pinning up the skirt of a new dress and I commented that she was looking well and she told me she'd got herself into a situation...'

'A situation?'

'I could see how it had happened. There she was, locked up inside that great gloomy place like a princess in a fairy tale, while he was gallivanting about on his so-called "business" travels with his fancy woman, leaving the door open behind him and inviting trouble to step in.'

'What kind of trouble do you mean?' Nelly asked.

'The usual kind,' Eliza said.

* * *

They were interrupted by the barmaid bringing more drinks. Eliza waited until she'd moved away, then picked up the story again.

'She, the second wife, was such a good-hearted soul. I admired her emerald shawl once, and she said: "Oh, Eliza, it's much more your colour than mine, you take it!" That's what she was like. She treated me like family because she didn't have family of her own.'

'You mentioned a stepdaughter?'

'A mousy thing, the daughter of the gentleman's first wife.'

'What happened to the first wife?'

'She died of a weak heart some years back.'

'But the stepdaughter continued to live at the house?'

'For a short while.'

'You said she was there yesterday?'

'She'd returned to help when the baby was born.'

'I see. And I suppose the gentleman is older than his second wife?'

Eliza thought for a moment. 'By thirty years, I'd say.'

'My goodness.'

'He is a dour man, a *grey* man. Grey inside and out.'

She leaned across the table. 'Shall I tell you how I *know* his wife was murdered, Miss Brooks?'

'Please do.'

The log on the fire crackled, sending sparks across the hearth.

Eliza's voice dropped almost to a whisper. 'It's because last night, when I was sleeping, she came to me.'

'Who came?'

'*Her! The murdered wife!* She was standing beside my bed. I couldn't see her clearly, but I knew it was her.' She glanced about her then said: 'She leaned down and she whispered in my ear. "I did not die, I was killed, Eliza. And I will not rest until the truth is made known." I could feel her sadness, Miss Brooks. It almost broke my heart.'

Eliza sat back and stared hard at Nelly as if challenging her to doubt this account.

'Goodness,' said Nelly. 'How frightening that must have been for you.'

'My sister died in childbirth, Miss Brooks, and she and I were close as peas in a pod, but she never came a-whispering to me. That's proof that my instincts are right.'

'But even if he didn't have any feelings for his wife,' said Nelly, 'why would any man kill his own child?'

Eliza finished her second glass of port, and wiped her lips with the back of her hand, leaving a blood-red smear on the skin.

'I already told you,' she said. 'He had good reason to kill them both.'

3

Will Delane had once described to Nelly the feeling he had when he came across a good story. 'It's like you're a dog catching the scent of a deer,' he'd said. 'It might be faint, but it's irresistible. You have to give chase. You don't have a choice.'

What Nelly was experiencing now, she realised, the keenness, the compulsion to find out more, was the sensibility he had described.

'Is there anything more you can tell me about the deaths?' she asked Eliza.

'Only that, before I left, I saw the bodies removed; shrouded and loaded into the back of a carriage.'

Nelly wrote this down.

Eliza continued talking. 'After I'd done the measurements for the coat, the gentleman said I was to ask Mr Lilley – that's the tailor on Park Street what I does some work for – to come and see him. He wanted adjustments made to his dark jacket and trousers so he might wear them as a mourning suit, and a black band fitted to his hat. So, I came directly back to Mr Lilley's and told him where I'd been and what had transpired. I said I was certain the husband was responsible for both deaths. "The alterations to his clothes is all for show," I said, "it is all an act, and I know it is for his appetite was not diminished one bit. I watched him eat three pieces of toast with my own eyes."' She fell silent for a moment, then said: 'Mr Lilley told me I should not speak about his best client in such an impolite manner.'

She sighed, as if the effort of the telling was draining her spirits. 'Are you sure you don't want none of this port, Miss Brooks?'

'No, no. Please, take it.'

'Thank you.' She drank. 'Trouble was, I was in such a lather, I didn't know when to stop. I didn't realise there was a customer behind the curtain, in the fitting room, and I kept on with my accusations. The customer heard it all. As soon as I saw his face, I knew him.' She shuddered. 'He was an acquaintance of the bereaved husband. I'd seen them together. But it was too late by then to take my words back.'

'Oh dear,' said Nelly.

'Oh dear indeed. When Mr Scarr—' Eliza collected herself, 'the customer left, Mr Lilley told me to finish the alterations to the coat. He said he would honour his payment to me for that work, but that would be the end of our business together. He wouldn't employ anyone who belittled a tragedy by her tittle-tattle. Thing is, Miss Brooks, the work I did for Mr Lilley was my main source of income.'

Ah, thought Nelly, *that's why you need the five pounds.*

She felt a rush of pity for the woman.

'It is a most disturbing story, Miss Morgan,' she said. 'I would be glad to pay you for the names of those involved.'

Eliza became immediately alert.

'How quickly can you get the money?' she asked. 'By tomorrow?'

'Perhaps, but—'

'We should meet again tomorrow then. Early. Then I shall go directly to the railway station. I have to leave Bristol. I can't stay here now they know that I know.'

'Who are "they"?'

'The gentleman and his friends.' She leaned closer to Nelly. 'I am being followed.'

Nelly smiled as reassuringly as she could. 'I think it unlikely,' she said gently.

'You don't believe me?'

'You've had a shock, Miss Morgan. You are unsettled, and it's perfectly understandable that your imagination is running away with you.'

'Last night, I saw a man outside my lodgings. He stood beneath the lamp, looking up to my window.'

'I'm sure he just happened to be there.'

'No,' Eliza shook her head. 'I've seen him before. I know he works for them. And this morning, I found a playing card outside the house! The ace of spades. You know what that means, don't you?'

Nelly shook her head.

'It means death is coming.'

She was becoming agitated. Nelly did not know what she might say to calm her.

'He might be watching me even now!' Eliza finished, wide-eyed and pale.

Nelly looked up and around; the elderly man was staring into the bottom of his glass, and the other man was still sleeping. Nobody else was present. Yet Eliza's fear was palpable. It seemed almost infectious. If she was right, and she was being followed – if her pursuer *knew* she was in the pub, wouldn't he also know that she was with Nelly?

'What time is it?' Eliza asked suddenly.

Nelly looked at the clock on the wall. 'Almost six.'

'I have to go. I need to get the coat to Mr Lilley before he shuts the shop. I'll see you tomorrow morning, Miss Brooks, outside the *Courier* offices, at eight o'clock.'

'And you'll bring the diary?'

'I'll bring it.'

Eliza almost toppled forward as she leaned down to grab her basket, and when she had picked it up, she headed back through the bar, bumping into chairs and stumbling in her drunkenness and her haste to leave. Nelly noticed the green shawl puddled on the floor.

'Eliza...'

The woman ignored her, hurrying forward.

'Eliza, wait! You've forgotten your shawl!'

The serving maid stepped in front of Nelly. 'Begging your pardon, miss, but someone needs to pay for the drinks.'

'I will pay,' said Nelly. 'Just one moment.'

'I can't let you leave until you've paid.'

Nelly took a handful of coins from the purse in her pocket and dropped them onto the tabletop. She looked up just in time to see Eliza go through the door. By the time Nelly reached it, she was gone.

4

During the walk back to her lodgings, a hurried walk, entirely tainted by the fear that she might be being watched, Nelly's head was full of Eliza and what she'd said. The circumstances of the deaths of a mother and child brought back memories that Nelly was constantly trying to forget.

This is something that has happened to someone else; it is not my experience; not my pain, she told herself, but the trauma of her past, never far away, crowded around her. This story felt personal. If a terrible wrong had been done to the cruel gentleman's young wife when she was at her most vulnerable, then Nelly vowed to disclose it. She determined that she would make things right.

Her immediate problem was that the answers to her questions about the identity of the murdered woman would cost her, and she couldn't think how she could acquire five pounds before eight o'clock tomorrow morning, unless she asked for the money from Mr Boldwood himself. That would mean explaining what it was for, and even if Mr Boldwood agreed to give Nelly the cash, she knew that as soon as Eliza had given her the names the editor would take the story from her. He would make her tell what she knew to Will Delane, or one of the other male reporters, and they would continue the investigation and Nelly would be back in her women's page cubbyhole, offering household advice from the best hair pomades to the polishing of glassware.

It would be the ultimate capitulation to concede a story about which Nelly felt passionately, as a woman, to a man.

And all that was assuming that Eliza remembered the arrangement and turned up as she'd said she would. She'd been so inebriated when she'd left the pub that it was quite possible she would wake in the morning with a headache, and no recollection of the last part of their conversation.

Had the story Eliza told even been genuine?

Nelly could picture Will, who was her friend, shaking his head in disbelief.

'Most likely she was regurgitating the plot of a penny dreadful in an attempt to extort you,' he would say. And perhaps he would be right: the popular scandal sheets were full of stories of cruel husbands, murdered wives, mousy stepdaughters and 'trouble that came calling'.

Will was a quiet, self-effacing, superficially anxious man, although Nelly suspected that he wore his hapless persona, along with his spectacles, as a disguise; to put people at their ease so they would think him harmless; incompetent even. Naturally self-deprecating and thoughtful, he had been a foundling, taken into an orphanage as a young boy. At the age of nine, he had been selected for a scheme designed to give street children the skills they needed to pull themselves out of poverty. By twelve, he was working as an errand boy for the *Courier*, and lodging with Maud Mackenzie, the graphic artist and the only other woman employed editorially at the newspaper. By eighteen he was a reporter; by twenty-eight he was crime reporter and had bought a small house of his own, although he remained close to Maud.

In contrast to some of the older reporters, who were bumptious, self-important and chronically cynical, Will Delane was kind-hearted, and inclined to see the best in people. But even he would be wary of Eliza.

'Drunks,' he had once told Nelly, 'are the most sincere people you will ever meet. Never trust them, least of all when they're swearing on their mother's life that every word they've told you is God's honest truth.'

Nelly knew her desperation to investigate a big story of her own was almost certainly colouring her perception of Eliza's credibility, but there had been real fear in Eliza's eyes and conviction in her words. Nelly found herself looking over her shoulder almost constantly as she hurried up the hill on the last part of the walk back to the house in Kingsdown, where she lodged. The lamps were being lit, and carriages clattered past. The chill of a late autumn evening was settling over the city. Nelly was out of breath when she turned into Orchard Hill and utterly relieved when she reached the front door to number 12.

The door was painted a glossy moss green, with a semi-circular window divided into three segments above it, and a brass knocker. The steps were clean and the warm glow coming through the stained window glass assured Nelly that the lamps had been lit inside the house. Smoke issued from the chimney pots in a most friendly manner. She opened the door and stepped into the familiar hallway: ornate tiles on the floor; a sideboard beneath a grand mirror; matching coat and umbrella stands and a large, leafy aspidistra in an elevated pot. The hallway smelled of beeswax with an undertone of turpentine.

The tabby cat, Flossy, came to greet her, winding her little body around Nelly's skirts.

Downstairs, in the basement kitchen, Nelly could hear the cheerful sound of the cook, Sarah Kerslake, laughing with the housemaid, Ida Cox, and the clinking of cutlery against crockery as they prepared for dinner.

Nelly was one of three lady lodgers here. She liked the house very much.

It was her home and her safe haven.

5

Nelly took off her jacket and bonnet, hung them up, then checked the mail lying on the lace doily on the polished surface of the sideboard to see if there was a letter from her aunt Angel, but there was nothing for her.

She petted the cat, then climbed two flights of the wooden stairs. Hers was the only room on the top floor, in the eaves of the house, with an attic above.

Ida had already been into Nelly's room to light the lamp, sweep the floorboards and refresh the water in the jug on the washstand. A fire was burning in the grate, softening the chill, and in the vase in the centre of the table were a few lacy, dried hydrangea heads, a reminder of the summer that had recently slipped away.

Nelly shut the door behind her, unbuttoned her boots, pulled them off her feet and left them by the wall. She took the green velvet shawl out of her bag and hung it over the back of one of the two plain wooden chairs on either side of the small round table.

Then she sat on the bed, with the pillows stacked behind her and a blanket around her shoulders; she peeled off her stockings, wiggled her toes, which were grateful to be freed, lay back, and did what she always did at this time of day: she thought of Harriet.

Nelly had seen her daughter more times in the last few months than she had in the preceding twelve years.

For most of Harriet's life, Nelly had been locked up in Holywell Asylum for women in Essex, where she had been committed by her parents soon after Harriet's birth. Mr and Mrs Brooks had not known what else to do with their daughter. She could not remain at home, because she had refused to disown the baby, and her parents could not risk their friends, neighbours and associates discovering the truth: the prospect of the shame this would bring was unbearable to them. Furthermore, it would seriously impede the marriage prospects of their two younger daughters, for what respectable, middle-class parents would allow their sons to marry the sisters of a ruined young woman? Nelly's fall from grace had the potential to destroy her sisters' reputations, and their futures too.

Far better, Mr and Mrs Brooks believed, for them to keep the baby as a foundling they'd say they'd taken in from the goodness of their hearts, and to send Nelly away, to a place where she would never encounter anyone they knew; somewhere where even if she told the truth, it would not be believed.

They told the family, and the neighbours, and Nelly's younger sisters, that Nelly had gone to visit a friend and died while she was away. As far as Mr and Mrs Brooks were concerned, their elder daughter *was* dead.

Promiscuity was a valid reason for having an unmarried girl locked up in an asylum. Nelly had encountered other young women in similar predicaments in Holywell. Some of their stories had been more traumatic than her own. And every time she heard about the way women who did not follow the proscribed societal rules were regarded and treated, the shame that had originally threatened to destroy Nelly transmuted into anger. Shame was soft and sad and useless, but rage was hard and strong and powerful.

She had remained in the asylum for ten years, from the age of fifteen to twenty-five, when she was released thanks to her aunt Angela, who everyone called Angel. Angel had returned from Argentina on the death of her lover, and had been horrified to learn what had happened to her favourite niece after Mrs Brooks let slip about the asylum to a mutual acquaintance. Angel had volunteered to act as Nelly's sponsor and threatened legal action if Mr and Mrs Brooks refused to give Nelly over to her care. Nelly's parents had not been enthusiastic about Mr Brooks' bohemian sister taking charge of their elder daughter, but the asylum fees had become burdensome and, having obscured the truth for so long, the last thing they'd wanted was a scandal, so they had capitulated.

Nelly was duly collected and moved into Angel's house on the outskirts of the city of Wells, far enough from Colchester, where Mr and Mrs Brooks lived, for it to be unlikely she would ever have to encounter them. There, in the Somerset countryside, she began the long, slow process of recuperation.

It took more than a year. By then Nelly's hair – shaved in the asylum – had grown, and she had gained some weight. Exercise, fresh air, good food and kindness had brought the roses back to her cheeks. Outwardly she looked 'normal', but inside she was still a mess. It took the slightest thing – Angel dropping a pan in the kitchen, a door slamming, the sight of a woman slapping a child – to summon all the horrors of the asylum. Sometimes Nelly could manage the panic that ensued; other times she sank to her knees, shaking violently, feeling that she could not breathe, that her heart, this time, would surely stop.

She was free, but she would never be truly liberated.

Angel, however, was persistent in her efforts to rehabilitate Nelly.

It was Angel who persuaded Nelly to consider becoming a professional writer, having watched her drafting countless letters to her daughter; letters that she would later burn in the fire.

'You like writing,' she said, a gentle hand on Nelly's shoulder, 'so why not make it your career?'

Angel was a firm believer in women having careers, even though very few did. She said one only ever had agency over one's own life if one had financial independence. She was self-sufficient thanks to money she earned translating letters and other documents from English to Spanish, and vice versa. Angel had left home when she was seventeen and stowed away on board a ship, pretending to be a man. She had supported herself ever since.

'You have to stand up for yourself in life, for those you love, and for what is right,' she told Nelly, when Nelly asked why Angel was doing so much to help her. 'I'm standing up for you now, and, in the future, I expect you to do the same for someone else, someone who needs you.'

At that exact time, the first few women were beginning to be appointed to roles in the press. Angel's friend, Maud Mackenzie, worked for the Bristol *Courier* and told Angel that the editor, George Boldwood, was not averse to employing a female reporter, if the right one came along. Nelly knew her writing wasn't as skilled as it could be, nor her research as thorough as it should be, not yet. She kept practising, copying out by hand the articles written by the best magazine and newspaper correspondents of the day, to get a feel for how to write well-constructed sentences, and making it her business to investigate small mysteries, so that she might become proficient at uncovering secrets. When she became more confident in her abilities, she began submitting her work to magazines and periodicals, with some success.

Eventually, she sent a selection of cuttings of her published work, together with three unpublished articles, to the *Courier*, which was the biggest and best-selling newspaper in the southwest. These were a news story, a women's interest feature and an interview with a young woman who had been sent to an asylum after giving birth to an illegitimate child when she was fifteen. For this, Nelly had effectively interviewed herself.

During the subsequent meeting, during which Angel had told her to omit certain facts about her life, Mr Boldwood told Nelly that the asylum article was one of the best things he had read in his thirty years as a newspaperman.

'Heartbreaking,' he said. 'Moving, compassionate, shocking, compelling and completely unsuitable for publication. Respectable women don't wish to read about such difficult matters.'

'Respectable women find themselves on the wrong side of the asylum door more often than you might imagine,' Nelly replied, the rage that she'd nurtured for ten years threatening to reveal itself.

Mr Boldwood frowned. 'I assume you went into an actual asylum to research this article?'

'Yes, I did.'

'How did you gain access?'

'I pretended that I was mad,' Nelly said.

'How did you do that?'

'It was not difficult. It doesn't take much to persuade men that a woman is unstable.'

'For how long were you there?'

'Several weeks.'

Mr Boldwood looked at Nelly for a long time. She held his gaze. She had learned to feign confidence while she was at Holywell. She had determined never to let the cruellest of the wardens see that she was afraid, or weary, or cowed. Now, her resilience stood her in good stead.

The editor blinked first.

'I respect your courage and commitment, Miss Brooks,' said Mr Boldwood. 'That must have been quite an ordeal.'

'I was glad to get out again. The smell will stay with me forever.'

She had not described the smell in the article: the salty, sweaty, bloody reek of the female body combined with the stink of the sewers; the foul cleaning liquid that was swilled daily over the floors, the disgusting slop that had been the main component of her diet for a decade.

George Boldwood, a large man in every way, sat back in his chair and held his chin between his thumb and forefinger.

'If,' he said, 'I were to offer you the role of women's page editor for the *Courier*, Miss Brooks, which I am inclined to do, I want your assurance that you will stick to writing about cheerful and uplifting topics.'

'Cheerful and uplifting?'

'Exactly. I don't want any political nonsense. None of your women's emancipation or suchlike and nothing about illegitimacy or asylums or... or the *messiness* of life. Do I make myself clear?'

'No asylums?'

'Absolutely none.'

Nelly had concurred, of course. Writing about the asylum

had won her the role at the *Courier*. It had helped lance the boil of her anger. She did not need to think of it again.

It pleased her still to remember how happy she had been that day, although several times subsequently, when she'd had a strong desire to write about subjects that were neither cheerful nor uplifting, she had regretted the indecent haste with which she had accepted Mr Boldwood's terms.

When Nelly was ready to take up the position at the *Courier*, Angel had helped her find her lodgings in Mrs Augur's pleasant and comfortable house in Kingsdown. Mrs Augur had let out three rooms after her husband's death, so that she and her daughter, Eveline, could afford to stay in their family home. Nelly had a room of her own, with breakfast and dinner provided daily and the laundry taken away once a week. Mrs Augur and Eveline were delightfully friendly landladies, who made no secret of the fact that Nelly was their favourite lodger. Within an hour of Nelly moving in, she found herself in their private drawing room, drinking tea and being regaled with stories about the house's history. The most memorable of these was that it was supposedly haunted by the ghost of a woman murderer who had once lived there.

The ghost, apparently, showed her face in mirrors, or reflected in the window glass. She could be heard pacing the attic, where she had hidden after committing her crime, and occasionally, a violet-scented perfume was noticed – one that was not worn by any of the living women in the house.

'But you mustn't be afraid, dear,' said Mrs Augur, leaning across to pat Nelly's hand. 'She only makes herself known when trouble is afoot.'

'Or danger,' said Eveline.

'Or danger,' Mrs Augur agreed. She paused a moment and then added: 'Or death.'

* * *

It was a half-hour's walk from 12 Orchard Hill to the *Courier* offices, downhill there, and at least an extra five minutes uphill back, but that was fine: Nelly liked walking.

And she loved her work. She had her own little cubbyhole in the editorial office, and Maud, who knew about Nelly's troubled past although she never alluded to it, kept an eye on her, and was always there if Nelly needed her, but Nelly managed perfectly well. She had always been the kind of person to eschew attention. She kept herself to herself. She had little patience for foolishness, although she never sought to quarrel and, after a while, most of the male reporters, even those who had initially been affronted by her appointment, came to tolerate her presence. Some, like Will and Duncan, Nelly regarded as friends.

Others, more entrenched, made it clear they regarded Nelly as a token female, employed because of her sex, not her skill. They mocked the feminine topics about which she wrote, and were scathing about her writing.

At first Nelly had been embarrassed by their contempt but she'd soon come to realise that her discomfort was what they wanted. She had learned to deflect comments denigrating women with a mixture of humour and sarcasm, but never to ignore them. Mr Boldwood observed her. It was important she comported herself with grace, if she was to keep the door open for other female reporters to follow in her footsteps.

Nelly was happy. But she was happier still on the day she found out, by chance, that her daughter who she had not seen since the day of her birth, was also in Bristol.

Maud had loaned her a novel, *The Female Detective*, and Nelly had found a letter from Angel tucked inside its pages – Maud had been using it as a bookmark. It revealed that Nelly's parents had named her daughter 'Harriet'. It also detailed Harriet's move to Redfield House Reform School for Girls, and the reasons why she had been sent there.

Why can't my brother and his wife celebrate Harriet's strength of character and independent spirit, instead of trying to mould her into a meek and obedient young woman?

The letter read.

They complain she is becoming 'less malleable' and developing 'rebellious traits' which they want 'knocked out of her'. Good for Harriet, say I!
Not a word of this to Nelly! It would be too much for her.
My brother and his wife are unaware that Nelly is living and working in Bristol. It pleases me that she and Harriet are in the same city, even if each must remain unaware of the other. Despite my brother's efforts to keep them apart, fate desires them to be close. We must wait and see what transpires.

What transpired was that Nelly read the letter, and that very evening walked to Redfield House school, to loiter outside the grounds hoping to catch a glimpse of the pupils, and, when she did, wondering which was her daughter.

Since that day, she spent at least two evenings a week in the vicinity of the school, watching the girls when they were let out to exercise. She observed and she listened, until one day, in the garden, a girl called: 'Harriet! Over here!' and another girl turned, and Nelly saw that she was the one; she knew her as if she had known her all her life.

Harriet believed Nelly to be dead, and Nelly could hardly tell her the truth – she would never do anything that might cause

Harriet pain. So, two or three times a week, she stood at the railings at the perimeter of the Redfield House school garden, and watched her child at play, and each Sunday she went to the same church the pupils attended, and sat in a pew several rows behind her daughter, comforted by knowing she was inhaling some of the same air that Harriet might have just breathed out.

Once, at church, Harriet, thin and pale in her hooded cloak, walked right past Nelly, brushed against her, and Nelly looked down into her daughter's serious little face, and smiled.

'Hello,' Nelly said gently.

Harriet was not allowed to speak to strangers, but she gave the smallest smile in return and afterwards, Nelly found a hair, honey-coloured and fine, stuck to her sleeve. It became her most precious possession. And then, the next time Nelly was at the railings outside the school garden, Harriet ran over and gave her a daisy that she had picked. Nelly felt the warmth of Harriet's skin as she passed it over; this child, who Nelly loved more than life itself.

'Oh, Harriet,' Nelly whispered, as she sat on the bed in her room at Mrs Augur's lodging house. She let her head drop back into the pillow, and held the locket that contained that one single, precious hair from her daughter's head, and the small flower that Nelly had pressed in a book to preserve it. 'Oh, my darling girl.'

* * *

Later that night, clouds hung above Bristol reflecting a murky orange light over the rooftops and chimneys and the rippling wavelets on the surface of the water in the floating harbour. Nelly could only glimpse the harbour from her window. Much of it was taken up with the masted boats, having unloaded their cargoes of sugar, rum and tobacco, and waiting now for the right combination of daylight, wind and tide to take them through the Cumberland lock, back out along the River Avon and into the Bristol Channel.

Nelly Brooks sat at the table in her room, with her notebook before her, and, by lamplight, she transcribed the scribbled notes made during the meeting with the seamstress, Eliza Morgan. She did not know if she would see Eliza again, nor if she would be able to beg, borrow or steal the money she needed to pay her to obtain the missing pieces of the story. But she wanted to be prepared for whatever the morning brought.

6

WEDNESDAY, 26 OCTOBER

The fire burned down in the grate and Nelly's room grew cold.

She was engrossed in her work when she was interrupted by a sound from the street outside. Tentatively, she looked out from behind the curtains, but saw only the hint of a shadow disappearing behind the wall on the other side of the road below. The reflection of her own, tired face stared back at her from the window.

She put more coal on the fire – the scuttle was empty now – and returned to the table, gazing at the words she'd written with eyes that were struggling to stay open. Around her, the old house creaked and sighed.

Nelly heard something in the attic above her: was it a footstep? No, only the mice scuttering. In the old wooden beams, deathwatch beetles tapped out their sinister rhythm.

Eventually, Nelly went to bed and fell asleep, but it was a fractured rest, full of nightmares.

* * *

Dawn was breaking when she awoke, a dull yellow light coming through the thin curtains at the window. Outside were the first sounds of the city coming back to life.

Nelly put on her dressing gown and slippers and went down the stairs to the basement kitchen. Sarah, the cook, was already up and about. She had lit the stove, and a pan of milk was warming. She was measuring oats for porridge, and a new loaf of bread was steaming on a cloth on the table beside her. Flossy was patrolling the tabletop.

'Good morning,' Sarah said cheerfully. 'I trust you slept well.'

'Very well, thank you,' said Nelly, accustomed to giving the answers people expected of her.

'There's coffee in the pot. Give me five minutes and I'll have a meat pie ready for your lunch.'

Nelly poured herself a cup, and one for Sarah, then she curled up in the old easy chair in the corner of the kitchen while she drank it, savouring the pleasure of being free to do as she wished; thinking she would never take her freedom for granted after so many years when every mouthful she consumed, and every movement she made, was controlled by someone else.

Nelly left 12 Orchard Hill earlier than usual that morning. She must be outside the *Courier* office before 8 a.m., to meet Eliza, if Eliza came. And if she did, Nelly had decided, she would take her into a coffee shop and make her wait there, while she went to Mr Boldwood and asked for an advance on her wages. She needn't say *why* she needed the money. Mr Boldwood trusted Nelly. He would give her the cash, and she would pay Eliza when Eliza gave her the names, and if the story turned out to be nothing, well, then Nelly would just have to scrimp and save to make up what had been lost.

And if it turned out to be true? Then, once Nelly had investigated and written the whole story, she would come clean to Mr Boldwood, and he would write off the money he'd advanced her as a legitimate business expense. He would be annoyed with her for pursuing a subject that did not fall within the women's page remit, but it would be such a compelling, important story that she would soon be forgiven.

Outside the house, Nelly stood still for a moment, looking about her. The streets were morning-busy, nothing was out of sorts. Certainly, nobody appeared to be watching her. She took a few breaths of the chilly, late autumn air, then turned right, taking her usual route down towards the city centre.

Nelly was entirely lost in thought as she walked down St Michael's Hill, keeping close to the buildings in order to avoid the heaviest of the foot and horse-drawn traffic. She wasn't concentrating on where she was stepping, until she slipped on a pile of dung.

'Damn!' she muttered. She held onto the side of a wall while she wiped her boot on a clump of straw.

'That's bad luck, that is,' said a young lad, heading the other way. He was about sixteen, wearing a ragged jacket and a cheeky grin. 'You want to be careful, today, miss.'

'I don't hold with superstition,' Nelly said.

'It's your prerogative. Don't say I didn't warn you.'

He tipped his hat and walked on. Nelly tried not to take any notice.

It was the kind of autumn day she had always loved. A hint of gold shone through the yellow of the boughs of the trees, and when the breeze rippled, a scatter of leaves fell onto the dusty road. Spiderwebs hung with dewdrops sparkled in the hedges of gardens, and the air was refreshingly cold.

The effluent stench of the river was strong, polluting a city of contrasts. To one side were grand edifices of architectural merit, paid for with fortunes earned through the trading of slaves, sugar and sherry. On the other were slums where families existed rather than lived; where disease and death were commonplace, and children played in filthy, narrow streets.

Nelly's commute through the grander part of the city was accompanied by the cooing of pigeons; the clip-clop of hooves on the cobbles, the calling of the cart drivers and the voices of children en route to school. She walked through bright patches of light and dappled shadows, past houses with plants at the windows, where well-fed cats dozed in patches of sunlight, and the smoke was drawn from high chimneys, and dispersed away to the hills.

At the bottom of St Michael's Hill, Nelly had to negotiate the Christmas Steps, a steep passageway cut between buildings. In the past, the precipitous footpath was the main route from the old Bristol prison up to and down from Gallows' Acre, the place where criminals, including the woman whose ghost was said to haunt 12 Orchard Hill, were executed. More recently the condemned met their fate in relative privacy within the walls of the New Gaol on Cumberland Road, crowds having become so raucous at the Acre that it was decided public hangings represented a danger to life and limb, and should be banned.

The route Nelly took each day down the Christmas Steps was dangerous. Robbers and prostitutes lurked in the shadows; vagrants sought out the darkest corners and slept there, curled on their newspaper mattresses. During the winter of 1863, after one poor old tramp froze to death on the Steps, the *Courier* had run a campaign calling for better facilities for the destitute. Nelly had been proud to be part of the newspaper that cared about issues affecting Bristol, and was establishing itself as the mouthpiece for the city.

7

At the foot of the Christmas Steps, Nelly excused her way through the queue gathered outside the shop that sold boiled potatoes with pigs' trotters, and headed towards the docks beyond.

The water in the floating harbour, contained by locks, was always at the same level. But Nelly knew high tide must be imminent in the river because a small flotilla of ships, sitting high in the water now their cargoes had been unloaded, was preparing to leave the harbour. The sailors on deck were heaving ropes, raising sails, and preparing the vessels for the less flat waters beyond the lock.

As she hitched up her skirts to keep the hems away from the dirty cobbles, Nelly noticed that a crowd had gathered on the harbourside. An ominous dark trail leading from the harbour wall indicated that something had been dragged from the water.

Nelly hurried towards that spot.

'Excuse me,' she murmured, manoeuvring herself through the men, women and children who were leaning over one another trying to obtain a better look. Nelly soon saw what it was that had drawn their attention.

A woman in middle-age, slender, and with gingery hair webbed around her face and over the grey stones of the dockside, lay lifeless on her back. Her clothing – a sturdy brown dress with a modest brooch at the throat – was soaked and streaked with filth.

Nelly crouched beside the woman she knew at once to be Eliza Morgan. Her eyes were closed but her lips parted so that Nelly could see, to her horror, the river water pooled inside her mouth. Her expression was peaceful, but her skin had an awful greenish-grey pallor. It was clear to Nelly, as it must have been to all the bystanders, that the woman was beyond help, although the young policeman squatting beside the body was looking at it anxiously as if wondering what he should do.

Nelly knelt on the cobbles and took Eliza's hand. It was ice cold and waxy.

'God bless her soul,' said the woman to Nelly's left. She had bushy grey eyebrows and only one tooth in her mouth. 'She'll have came out the pub after one too many gins and slipped on the quayside. One gulp of that water and... ugh!' She shuddered and pulled her shawl, ragged as an old dishcloth, over her lips and nose.

Nelly turned to the crowd. 'Did anyone see this woman fall into the harbour?'

There was a shaking of heads, and a mumble of 'No's.

'Excuse me, miss,' said the policeman.

Nelly ignored him. 'Who spotted the body?'

'It was a docker,' someone volunteered. 'He noticed something stuck under the propeller of the steam packet.'

'How was she retrieved?'

The policeman said, 'Miss, beggin' your pardon, but it is I as should be asking the questions.'

'Let's work together,' Nelly said. 'Are you taking notes?'

The officer was so young that he still had spots on his chin. Belatedly, he took a notebook from his pocket and licked the end of his pencil.

A different man took up the story. 'We took a rowing boat out to the packet,' he said. 'Close up we could see it was a woman. We had to push her down with a pole to free her, then hook a rope around her ankles to pull her up.'

'Took three of us to drag her out.'

'She'd been in the water a while,' said someone else.

'Overnight at least.'

'It's a shame nobody was looking out for her.'

Nelly felt the blood drain from her face. She had known how drunk Eliza Morgan was when she'd left the pub, and should have insisted on accompanying her. Letting her stagger out in that state, was tantamount to leaving a child playing alone by an unguarded fire.

In the next breath, she remembered how frightened Eliza had been. 'I am being followed,' she had said.

And she'd also said she hated being near the river.

Nelly's heart pounded uncomfortably.

Her eyes scanned the crowd. Everyone was looking towards the body.

The police constable turned to Nelly. 'Do you know who this is?'

Nelly was conscious of the green velvet shawl inside her satchel. She'd intended to return it to Eliza. Now what was she to do with it?

Perhaps she should confess to its presence, but the complications that would come with revealing the shawl, and explaining how she had come by it, were too numerous to contemplate.

'I don't *know* her, but I had a conversation with her yesterday,' she said. 'Her name is Eliza Morgan and she is a seamstress. She does some work for Mr Lilley, the tailor on Park Street.'

The young policeman wrote this into his notepad.

'May I take your name, miss?'

'My name is Nelly... *Helen* Brooks.'

'The Helen Brooks who writes for the *Courier*?'

'Yes.'

'My mother reads your page avidly, Miss Brooks. She likes the household tips very much.'

A murmur ran through the assembled crowd. Someone muttered, 'Reporters are drawn to tragedies like flies around rotten meat.' But others looked at Nelly with interest.

'I didn't know there was such a thing as a woman reporter,' one said, and another, a woman, asked tentatively if she knew Duncan Coulson and when Nelly said that she did, the woman's eyes widened in awe.

* * *

Nelly stayed with Eliza until the ambulance came to remove the body and take it to the mortuary.

She watched as the corpse was loaded into the back of the vehicle, water dripping from the skirts of the dress and into the spaces between the cobbles. The two porters treated the dead woman respectfully, but in a matter-of-fact way. They had seen it all before. The big black cob harnessed to the ambulance turned to watch, blowing air through his lips as if in sympathy. Eventually the porters climbed up to their seats, the driver flicked the reins and the cob heaved the vehicle forward. The ambulance began to move, bumping over the cobbles, leaving a faint trail of drips in its wake, the horse tossing his head as he clopped away.

With this, the assembled onlookers started to drift in different directions.

Nelly, with the dead woman's shawl folded in her satchel, headed, at last, to work.

She stopped every few minutes to look behind her, to see if anyone was following; but, as far as she could tell, nobody was.

8

The *Courier* offices were based in a grand three-storey building, purposely constructed to house the newspaper and its employees, in a courtyard off Old Market, with the printing works behind. Nelly could hear the steam-powered presses working as she approached, and smell the ink. Both sensations never failed to thrill her. Carts were already lining up to collect the first bundles of newspapers to distribute them throughout the city and the outlying villages and towns. Porters were hefting clean rolls of paper into the print-hall and men whose palms were blackened with ink brought the finished products the other way and loaded them onto the backs of the carts. Nelly walked past the business end of the works and went through the revolving doors into the reception area, where staff were clocked in and visitors welcomed.

A thin man called Mr Snitch sat behind the reception desk. He was tall, in his late forties, and wore an old-fashioned suit and waistcoat with a pocket watch on a chain. His hair was scraped over the dome of his bald head and his eyesight was poor, his expression mean. Mr Snitch was always there. He prided himself on knowing all the comings and goings of the editorial staff.

Also in the reception were a man and a woman Nelly had never seen before, their clothes ragged and their boots worn, sitting side by side. The man was twisting his cap in his hands; the woman was dandling a toddler on her lap. She was wearing a shabby grey bonnet on her head and the little one's clothes were worn and dirty. The couple looked up in unison when Nelly entered, staring at her with expressions of desperation.

Nelly nodded to them politely and went to the desk.

'Good morning, Mr Snitch,' she said.

The man frowned over his spectacles at Nelly, then turned to the clock on the wall.

'Might I enquire why your arrival is so tardy, this morning, Miss Brooks?'

'I was unavoidably detained,' Nelly said, 'by a fatal accident at the docks.'

Mr Snitch raised his eyebrows.

'Was it any of your business?'

Nelly opened her mouth to say that, actually, it was, then thought better of it. She watched as Mr Snitch wrote Nelly's name and the time of her arrival carefully into his ledger. Beside it, he made a dot with the red ink he used to signify that an employee was late.

'Are these people waiting to see someone?' Nelly asked, nodding towards the couple with the baby.

'They want to speak to a reporter.'

'I am a reporter.'

Mr Snitch did not say *'A proper reporter'*, but Nelly knew full well that was what he was thinking.

'I've sent the errand boy to find someone,' Mr Snitch said.

The child, bouncing on the woman's lap, reached out his

hands. Nelly took a step towards him, smiling at the woman. 'He's very handsome,' she said. 'How old is he?'

'Two,' said the woman. 'Nearly three.'

The child looked about nine months old. He was all skin and bones and his belly was swollen beneath his shirt. Nelly detected evidence of rickets in his bandy legs. His tiny feet were bare.

She took his hand: cold and sticky. 'What's your name?' she asked him.

The child murmured something and wiped his nose with his sleeve.

'Archie,' the woman translated.

'He seems a happy little man.'

'Most of the time. Right now, he's missing his mama, our daughter.'

'Oh? Where is she?'

'She has disappeared.'

Nelly felt a sensation in her chest, as if someone had plucked a violin string and made a vibration. Here was another story concerning a woman who had possibly come to harm. Another story someone else would write.

Someone male.

'Have you come to put an appeal for information in the newspaper?' she asked.

The woman nodded sorrowfully.

Nelly considered for a moment, then unhooked her satchel from her shoulder, and removed the napkin that Sarah had given her earlier, containing her lunch. She unwrapped the pie and offered it to the woman.

'Archie is welcome to the food, if he would like it.'

The woman looked unsure.

'I'll leave it with you,' Nelly said, placing the napkin on the table. 'It is up to you whether or not you take it.'

She turned to go towards the stairs that led up to the newsroom but the pull of the story compelled her to turn back to the couple.

'May I ask your names?'

The woman glanced to her husband, who stared at the wretched cap he was still twisting between his hands, the skin engrained with dirt, the nails blackened. Some kind of labourer, Nelly guessed, who did not have access to clean water.

'I'm Mrs Skinner and this is my husband, Albert.'

'And your missing daughter?'

'Gerty. She works in the tobacco factory,' Mrs Skinner said. 'On Friday last, she went out to buy some medicine for our Archie, who had a dreadful cold, and she never came home.' She paused to cough, an awful, hacking, phlegmy wracking of her chest. 'We weren't too worried at first, were we, Albert? She's done it before, Gerty has. Taken off when things got too much for her. Gone on a drinking spree. She's only young. You can't blame her.'

'Of course not,' said Nelly.

'We hoped she was staying with a friend somewhere...' Mrs Skinner paused again, 'then one of our neighbours told us about the article in the *Courier*.'

Nelly pulled up one of the spare chairs and sat on it, close to the couple, her head inclined towards them. She was aware of Mr Snitch's disapproving stare behind her, but paid him no heed.

'What article was that?' she asked gently.

The woman passed the child onto her husband's knee and delved into her skirt, pulling a folded piece of paper from her pocket. Nelly opened it. The headline read:

Dead Woman Still Unidentified

She read the text, recognising that it had been written by Will Delane.

Someone must be missing a wife or daughter!

The body of a young woman found by a chimney sweep's boy in St Nicholas Street remains in the city mortuary, as yet unidentified. The coroner has examined the corpse, and declared it to have belonged to a woman of around eighteen years of age of average build, who died of a malfunction of the heart. The woman had dark hair and brown eyes and in life was fair-skinned with a pleasant countenance. The authorities wish to return the body to the family, so that the unfortunate young woman may be given a decent Christian burial. The key identifying feature is a crescent-shaped scar on the chin. Please come to the mortuary with letters confirming your name and address if you recognise this person.

Accompanying the copy was a helpful engraving of the lower half of the dead woman's face, complete with the scar, like a waning moon, beneath her lower lip. The illustration would have been made by Maud Mackenzie.

Nelly read the article again, then passed the piece of paper back to Mrs Skinner. The child was trying to catch his grandfather's filthy finger in his skinny little hand. Snot was issuing from both nostrils.

'We don't read,' said Mrs Skinner, 'but we know what it says. That's our Gerty's chin, no doubt about it.' She pointed to the illustration. 'Never seen another like it with that exact scar. It has to be her.'

Nelly did not doubt her.

'I'm so sorry,' she said. 'The article says that if you recognise the description of the woman, you should go to the mortuary. It's down by the dockside, on Whipping Boy Wharf. That's where the body is being kept and where it can be claimed.'

'Yes, but that's why we're here,' the woman said. 'We've been to the dead-house first thing this morning, haven't we, Albert?'

'Yep.' The man nodded.

'We showed the attendant the picture of our Gerty's scar and said we'd come for her and he said we was too late, didn't he, Albert?'

'He did.'

'Some people came yesterday, collected our Gerty and took her away. They said she was theirs. But she wasn't. She's ours. And we want her back!'

And with that she collapsed into tears. The child reached out to pat his grandmother's shoulder. Her husband put his arm around her, but nothing would console Mrs Skinner. She cried as if her heart was breaking, coughing in between sobs.

In the midst of this, Will Delane came trotting down the stairs.

He came to Nelly first, pushing his spectacles up his nose, looking anxious, a notebook and pencil clasped in his hands.

'Good morning, Will,' Nelly said. 'These are Mr and Mrs Albert Skinner and their grandson, Archie.'

Mr Skinner nodded his head. Mrs Skinner tried to calm herself.

'And this,' Nelly said, indicating Will, 'is my colleague and friend, Will Delane. He is a good man, and you can trust him. You'll be in safe hands.'

9

Leaving the Skinners to tell their story to Will, Nelly went up the stairs that he had just descended, one hand on the banister. To one side was a fine, large window, looking out over the city, decorated with stained-glass images of ships, the Avon gorge and famous moments from Bristol's history, as well as modern developments such as Temple Meads railway station. To the other was a wall, hung with portraits of the men – they were all men – who had written for the newspaper, or edited its pages. One day, Nelly hardly dared to hope – but nonetheless she did! – that her image might also hang on that wall.

As she ascended, a familiar face leaned over from the first-floor balcony.

'You're very late, Miss Brooks,' said Duncan Coulson, otherwise known as 'The Bristolian' because that was the name by which he wrote reviews and opinion pieces in the *Courier*. Duncan was a man who was the polar opposite of Nelly in terms of personality. He was flamboyant and witty, thrived on attention, loved being recognised, and was one of Bristol's most famous children. Duncan was regularly invited to theatrical performances, to attend parties, open new shops and suchlike and he lapped up his celebrity. Right now, he was tapping the face of his gold pocket watch in a mock-scolding manner.

'Today you are the princess of late,' he said, 'if not the actual queen.'

'And you're the king of stating the obvious,' said Nelly. 'Are you on the way out?'

'I'm off to meet our venerable member of parliament to discuss plans for the official opening of the new Clifton Bridge.'

'Sir Edward Fairfield?'

'The one and only.'

'Good luck.' The MP was renowned for his punctiliousness. Then she asked, 'Is Mr Boldwood vexed that I missed this morning's editorial conference?'

'He's rueing the day he was talked into employing a woman against his better judgement and the advice of all his colleagues.'

Nelly knew he was teasing. She gave a wry smile, brushed past Duncan and went through the double doors that opened into the newsroom.

It was a large room, filling the first floor of the building and divided into two. The reporters took up half of the floorspace. They did not work in enclosed offices, but rather cubbyholes divided by wood and glass partitions, without doors. On the other side were the tables used by the subeditors to cut and paste the handwritten copy to make it fit onto pages, and to devise the headlines, before the compositors set up the lines of type in hand-held sticks. They worked in silence, their brows furrowed in concentration as they selected the correct metals to form each letter and grammatical symbol. Nelly was in awe of their skill.

One corner of the editorial space was divided off into two grand offices: one occupied by George Boldwood, the other by his secretary, Mr Jeremiah Bagnet.

The Emerald Shawl

The door to Mr Boldwood's office was closed, which meant he had someone with him, or did not wish to be disturbed, so rather than going to apologise for missing the daily meeting – there was no greater sin in Mr Boldwood's eyes – Nelly went directly to her cubbyhole. As she passed through the office, she nodded or said 'Good morning' to those of her colleagues who looked up to acknowledge her. Maud, leaning over her drawing board placed by the window to make the most of the light, held up a hand in greeting.

Nelly took off her jacket and hung it amongst the men's coats on the rack, then she went to her desk. Hers was the smallest, darkest, and least desirable cubbyhole, but she loved to be there. A wooden plaque nailed to the side of the opening had the words 'Women's Editor' and, below them, 'Miss H Brooks' painted in black. The H was for Helen, Nelly's given name, and the one used for her byline. Her heart swelled with pride each time she saw it.

That morning, she looked around to make sure nobody was paying her any attention, and then she removed the green velvet shawl from her satchel and placed it in the drawer of her desk, hiding it beneath a pile of letters submitted by readers. After that, she took her seat. She straightened the spike on her desktop, and the inkwell, her pile of notepads and a selection of gifts she'd received from various shops in the hope that she would write favourably about them – mostly beauty creams, small items of haberdashery and household gadgets.

Also on the desk were a couple of potted ferns, gifts from Maud, who was very fond of flora, enjoyed tending to her garden and longed to write a gardening column in the *Courier*. George Boldwood was not yet convinced that readers would be interested.

Nelly's responsibility was to fill the women's page each day with stories that could be loosely categorised as 'one of the four Fs': Fashion, Food, Family and Furnishings.

It was enjoyable enough, but it was not *real* journalism. Real journalism, in Nelly's opinion, was writing about subjects that mattered. Done well, it could change opinions and effect social change.

And here she was, her mission today to produce a list of hints about how to destroy bedbugs, an advertising puff for lambswool bootees, and an opinion piece on the importance of maintaining good relationships with one's servants.

Nelly opened her notebook and stared at the pages before her.

She had three women on her mind: Gerty Skinner, Eliza Morgan and the young wife and mother whose name she did not know. All three from entirely different backgrounds, united only by their sex, their city and their deaths.

These women mattered to Nelly.

The bedbugs could wait.

10

Nelly Brooks began to write; quickly and efficiently adding the events that had taken place at the dockside that morning to the notes she'd already made about the meeting with Eliza Morgan.

Could it be coincidence that Eliza had come to such a dreadful end within such a short time of talking to Nelly?

Hadn't she been so afraid of the consequences of speaking out about the deaths of the woman and child that she'd been planning on leaving Bristol today?

And if Eliza had been right about the sinister intentions of the man she had crossed, and his influential circle of friends – and after all, she was now dead – that must surely mean that Nelly herself would be in danger if she pursued the investigation?

The thought was terrifying – and also thrilling.

'Might I steal a moment of your time?'

Nelly nearly jumped clear out of her skin.

'Will!' she cried. 'Don't creep up on me like that!'

'I didn't creep!' he said, mildly affronted. 'I approached in my usual manner. You weren't paying attention!' Will Delane put a finger on the bridge of his glasses to stop them falling off and peered over Nelly's shoulder. 'What's that you're writing?'

She snapped the notebook shut.

'Nothing of consequence. How did you get on with Mr and Mrs Skinner?'

Will perched on the corner of her desk. 'It's the most tragic story but the only assistance I can offer is to write a second article, this time requesting information about the missing Gerty.'

'You could go to the mortuary and ask for the name and address of whoever it was who claimed Gerty's body and then propose it be returned to the rightful family.'

'But how do we know that the deceased *was* Gerty Skinner, and not some other unfortunate soul who also happened to have a scar on her chin? And why would anyone falsely claim a corpse? To what end?' He took his pipe from his pocket and looked into its bowl.

'To sell it to the medical school?' Nelly suggested.

'Body-snatchers?' He raised an eyebrow. 'It's conceivable, but I've never heard of such audacity. Walking into the mortuary and falsely claiming a corpse is simply unheard of.'

'Nonetheless, it has happened.'

Will put the pipe back into his pocket.

'I feel so sorry for the Skinners,' Nelly said softly. 'They clearly had so little to start with and now they've lost their daughter, who was at least bringing in a wage to the household...'

'I spoke with them at length,' said Will. 'I encouraged them to consider the possibility that the body at the mortuary was not their daughter at all – in which case, Gerty may yet be alive.'

'I hadn't thought of that, but you're right.'

'Gerty aside, we have other business to discuss, Nelly. At the conference this morning, Old Boldwood announced that the

Courier is to produce a twelve-page special edition to commemorate the opening of Mr Brunel's new Clifton Bridge. I suggest you start coming up with bridge-themed women's article ideas if you want to get back into his good books.'

'Bridge-themed women's articles?'

'Might women faint should they attempt to cross the bridge? Are they going to lose their parasols over the parapet if the wind blows? That sort of thing.'

Nelly sighed. She glanced regretfully at her notebook.

'Parasols,' she echoed. 'Parapets. Thank you, Will.'

He looked at her intensely. 'Is everything quite all right, Nelly?'

'Yes, yes,' she said. 'Everything is as it should be.'

11

Nelly drafted a list of ideas for features she could write for the bridge supplement, so she was prepared if she was nobbled by George Boldwood.

As soon as that was done, she went into the *Courier*'s archive.

A copy of every edition published since the *Courier* was first launched as a single-page news-sheet in 1799 was kept in this room. Reporters could go back in time to search for historic articles, or to look up certain events. In addition to this, stories were cut from the papers and stored in envelopes, filed alphabetically. If a reporter wanted to check to see what had ever been written about a certain dignitary, for example, or a convicted criminal, all they had to do was locate the relevant envelope.

Nelly removed the previous day's newspaper from the archive and took it into her office. She sat at her desk, turning the pages to the notices of births, marriages and deaths, searching for any mention of the young wife of an important man who had died at home somewhere in the vicinity of Bristol.

She found nothing. She started again, reading through the obituaries, and the inquest reports, just in case, but to no avail.

The death of a woman in childbed was so commonplace that it would not make the news pages, unless there were particularly unusual circumstances. And if the cause of death was given by an attending doctor of reputation as haemorrhage, there wouldn't normally be an inquest. But if the husband was as high in status as Eliza had implied, surely there would be *something*.

The fact that there was no obituary, no death notice for any young woman fitting the criteria Eliza had described, was odd – but only if what Eliza had told Nelly was true. And of course, it may be that the husband or his staff had simply not had the opportunity to submit an announcement yet.

Nelly was about to return to her desk when she had another thought. She gathered together a number of newspapers and looked through the inquests, searching for cases where the cause of death was given as 'smothering' or 'suffocation'. She was not looking for anyone in particular. She wanted only to familiarise herself with the signs the coroner used to make his judgement in such cases.

Within a short while, she knew that the symptoms that might be observed were distinctive red and purple spots in the eyes, and on the skin of the face and neck, caused by ruptured blood vessels. Often swelling and bruising was present around the mouth and throat, 'foamy' fluid in the facial cavities and bluish skin around the lips.

It was not a pleasant topic. Nelly felt a deep sorrow for the young mother who Eliza Morgan believed had died in this manner, and an aching for the poor infant too – the innocent child who had been allowed to live for only a few hours.

'I shall stand up for you both,' she promised as she replaced the newspapers into the slots in the racks. 'I shan't let your deaths go unnoticed.'

That promise was meant for Eliza Morgan too.

* * *

When she had written enough to fill the women's page in the next edition, Nelly left the office and walked to Bristol's police headquarters in Bridewell Street.

Inside, she asked if she might speak to someone in authority and, shortly after, an inspector came to talk with her. He was in late middle age, portly, with grey hair and rheumy eyes, yet he had an arrogance Nelly associated with younger, better-looking men. His name, he said, was Inspector Vardy. Nelly introduced herself and told him she was concerned about the death of Eliza Morgan, the woman whose body had been dragged from the harbour that morning.

'Ah, yes,' the inspector said, 'the drunkard. What is it about the matter that concerns you?'

'I do not believe Miss Morgan's death was accidental.'

Inspector Vardy laughed.

'I don't see any humour in the subject,' said Nelly.

'Miss Brooks, if I was given a penny every time it was claimed someone had been pushed into the docks, when the truth was they'd had a bellyful of drink, slipped and fallen, then I would be a wealthy man.'

'Miss Morgan disliked the water,' Nelly said. 'She wouldn't have willingly gone close to the harbour edge.' She took a deep breath. 'She also told me she feared for her life.'

'Feared whom, precisely?'

'Men of standing and influence.'

Even as she spoke the words, Nelly knew they sounded irrational: as if Eliza's fear had been the product of a paranoid imagination.

'"Men of standing and influence",' the inspector repeated.

'The kind of men who would loiter around the harbourside waiting to push inebriated women into the water?'

'I did not come here to be ridiculed,' Nelly said. 'I came as a responsible citizen because I fear a grievous crime has been committed.'

Inspector Vardy nodded and when next he spoke, his tone was devoid of sarcasm though no less dismissive.

'Generally, Miss Brooks, the most obvious explanation for any scenario is the correct one. Miss Morgan, God rest her soul, was drunk and stumbled. The weight of her petticoats dragged her under the water. That's all there is to it.'

'So, you don't intend to investigate?' Nelly asked.

'I'll make a note of your concerns,' the inspector said, 'but there's not a shred of evidence of foul play.'

'What evidence could there be?'

'A witness. Unless somebody comes forward prepared to attest to seeing Miss Morgan being pushed, there's no reason to pursue this matter further.'

12

After she left the police station, Nelly bought a hot potato from a street vendor. She sat on a bench in Queen Square to eat it. The daylight was fading, and the temperature was falling. Starlings murmurated in their thousands above the city, before disappearing from view to roost on the enormous arched roof of Mr Isambard Kingdom Brunel's Temple Meads station train shed.

Nelly sat alone, a small, reserved woman with her brown hair pulled back from her face; her sharp, dark eyes observing. She watched the smart women in their crinolines and fur-collared jackets taking their little dogs for their evening walks, gloved hands holding the leashes, the heels of their buttoned boots tapping on the paving stones. She observed the bearded, behatted men strolling in pairs, discussing trade, the nursemaids chatting as they pushed their charges in their perambulators. In the far corner of the square, a woman with a fancy hat and a barrow was selling copies of that day's issue of the *Courier*. Nelly heard the voices of the people as they passed; she picked up snatches of conversation; she noticed where there was tension between companions, and where there was not. From the fragments of information they shed, she constructed, in her mind, their relationships. She could not help herself; she was attracted to people's situations as magpies were drawn to shiny objects. She gathered knowledge about these strangers, harvested it and stored it for future reference, and they never even noticed that she existed.

It had been the same in the asylum. Nelly Brooks – the quiet woman, the collector of stories.

In the late autumn, fading light, with the fallen leaves dappling the lawns beneath the trees, and the elegant houses around the square as a backdrop, the magnificent statue of William III on horseback on the podium in the centre, that part of Bristol seemed tranquil and lovely. It was hard to believe that the Bedminster slums were only a mile or so distant; that, not far away, Mrs Skinner would be preparing a meal for her family with whatever bits of food she could scrape together, while Mr Skinner perhaps wandered the streets with his grandson, searching for his lost daughter.

Dear God, thought Nelly, let them find her; drunk or injured or with amnesia; it didn't matter, just let her be brought home.

She knew how it felt to miss a beloved daughter. She would not wish that pain on anyone.

Nelly finished her meal, scattering the remaining black and burned pieces of potato for the pigeons, and stood up, stretching her spine so that her head was erect on the top of her neck, and she felt a little taller. She walked towards the statue at the square's centre, where the paths radiated like beams from a star. As she walked, she thought of Eliza, who would have almost certainly crossed this square on her way to meet Nelly at the Llandoger Trow the day before.

How unpredictable life was, thought Nelly, how precarious.

Nobody should ever take anything for granted, because one never knew when everything might be taken away.

Everything could disappear in a heartbeat.

Mostly, people had no command of their fate. But sometimes, a person had to do something to effect change.

Nelly Brooks adjusted her bonnet, put back her shoulders, raised her chin and headed off towards Redfield House school.

* * *

Redfield House was a small, privately run reform school for girls, renowned for its commitment to discipline and for setting firm boundaries for its pupils. Nelly knew this from the brochure that she had requested some time ago as an excuse for going inside. This stern ethos, which repulsed her, was almost certainly what had commended it to her mother and father when they were seeking a place to send Harriet.

Nelly had been to the school many times now, though she'd only managed to talk her way through the front door twice – once to ask for the brochure, and once on the pretext that she felt faint and needed a drink. A cup of water had been provided and Nelly ejected from the premises as soon as she'd taken a few sips. Now she imagined herself to be like a ghost, hovering around the edges of the place; sometimes walking past more than a dozen times, hoping for a glimpse of Harriet – often not even being rewarded with that small prize.

But even on those times when she did not see her daughter, at least she was close; close enough, Nelly hoped, for Harriet to sense her presence, and to know that somebody was nearby who loved her.

The school was part of a brick-built terrace and had originally been three houses, now converted into one, its façade dulled with soot. An external perimeter wall enclosed the ground floor and basement, making it impossible to climb in, or out.

Nelly stopped at the end of the street. A cold wind was gusting, blowing the smoke from the chimney pots hither and thither. The air smelled of coal and was gritty on her tongue. A carriage rattled by, the horse's hooves clopping. From inside one of the private houses came the sound of raised voices: a man and woman arguing.

It did not feel like a good omen.

Dark grey clouds rushed by overhead.

Gulls screamed as the wind carried them.

Nelly straightened her jacket. She glimpsed her reflection in the glass of one of the windows overlooking the street, and, although it was more of a shadow than an accurate picture, she could see that she looked respectable.

Each time she came here, she was afraid of being challenged. Her parents must not find out that she was in Bristol, or that she knew where Harriet was, for if they did, Harriet would be snatched away again, sent somewhere where it was impossible for Nelly to find her.

She walked to the front of the school and stood on the other side of the street, as was her ritual. She put a hand on the crown of her bonnet to stop it falling off, and gazed up at the windows above her, all of them securely barred.

Beyond the school, in the pale evening sky, the planet Venus was shining, although it was not yet dark enough for stars.

Suddenly the door opened. A large woman stood on the threshold, her face a mask of hostility.

'What business have you here?' she called to Nelly. 'You've been seen before, loitering outside the school.'

'I pass this way often. I only stop to rest. There's no harm in that.'

The woman was unconvinced. She made a shooing movement towards Nelly. 'Be on your way,' she said. 'Don't let me see you here again.'

She went back inside, slamming the door.

Nelly's heart was pounding. The encounter had unsettled her, but she had no intention of leaving without at least attempting to glimpse her daughter. She followed the wall around the side of the building. Soon, it gave way to the railings that enclosed the garden. There were no street lamps, and she was hidden from the view of the school in the lee of the lime trees planted in the pavement.

When Nelly's eyes became accustomed to the dark, she spotted, through the metal verticals of the railings, a small figure in the far corner of the garden, leaning over the rabbit hutches.

It took her a while to be certain, but when she was, her heart gave a leap of joy. The child was Harriet.

13

Nelly could not call out to her daughter. She was not supposed to know Harriet's name.

All she could do was watch and wait, and hope that Harriet might catch sight of her.

And she did. At last Harriet turned. She waved, and Nelly waved back. Harriet hitched up her skirt so she could climb over the fence that kept the rabbits contained, and then she ran across the blustery garden to Nelly. They stood looking at one another from either side of the railings. Harriet was wearing black stockings, and a grey striped pinafore dress, her hair tied back severely so that her neck was exposed. Even in the gloaming, it was plain to see that her face was paler than it should have been, dark circles beneath her eyes, and she had grown thinner since Nelly last saw her.

'Hello,' said Harriet.

'Hello. Why are you out here all alone? Why aren't you wearing a coat?'

'I was sent out while the others eat supper.'

'As a punishment?'

'Yes.'

'What did you do?'

'I laughed in the hallway when I was supposed to be silent.'

For that, she'd been sent out into the cold, at dusk, on this windy evening, alone?

'Miss Salmon says I am wicked,' Harriet said in a matter-of-fact voice, as if that explained everything.

'Who is Miss Salmon?'

'The headmistress.'

'Ignore her. She is jealous of you. She knows the breath you exhale is more valuable than anything she'll ever say, or do, or be. Don't listen to her. Don't let her words take root in your heart.'

'How do you know what she's like?'

'I've met people like her before.'

Harriet toed a pebble. Then she wiped her nose on her sleeve. Her clothes were insubstantial and there was a significant chill in the air; she must be cold. Dear God, what if she became ill? Hundreds of people had died of influenza last year. And the spectres of tuberculosis and scarlet fever were still haunting the city; disease and its repercussions were never far away.

Nelly dug the fingers of one hand into the palm of the other to stop herself from panicking.

'Were you talking to the rabbits?' she asked gently, hoping both to calm herself and to raise Harriet's spirits a little by changing the subject.

'Yes.'

'You sound sad.'

'They're going to kill them,' Harriet said.

'They're going to kill the rabbits? Why? And who would do such a cruel thing?'

'The caretaker and the cook. They said they are not worth the trouble for the little meat they get off them, so they're going to kill them and serve them up as stew and keep pigs instead.'

Harriet's distress was so intense that Nelly could feel her daughter's suffering vicariously. She was frustrated by her own impotence; what was the point of a mother if not to protect her child? She would do anything, *anything at all*, to make Harriet happy but she could not think how she might save the beloved rabbits.

She resorted to a different tack.

'Sweetheart, you won't be here forever,' Nelly said gently. 'Your life will become better.'

'How do you know?' Harriet asked. 'You don't even know me.'

She took a step back, away from the railings, becoming less substantial as she faded into the gloom of the night garden, the reform school building towering above her.

'I'm going to let the rabbits out,' she said. 'That's what I'm going to do.'

Harriet turned from Nelly, and ran back towards the hutches, her hair flying behind her, the small heels of her boots kicking up clumps of grass.

She went to the hutches and the next thing Nelly saw was the blurred shapes of rabbits leaping from their wooden prisons and lolloping off into the darkness.

Nelly could not have said which emotion was uppermost in her heart: pride at Harriet's determination and courage, or fear for the consequences her brilliant, brave daughter was certain to suffer as a result of her rebellion.

Her hands gripped the cold railings.

She stood there, in the gathering darkness, paralysed by her own impotence, until Harriet was called back into the school.

14

On the way back that evening, Nelly crossed through Bristol's docks.

She knew the risk she was running, but she did it anyway. The docks were the busiest part of the city, where local labourers, often poorly paid and overworked, converged with sailors from all over the world. It was vibrant and exciting, the hub of Bristol. It was also where the most violent fights, robberies and assaults took place. And on top of those there were the suicides, the drownings and the accidents that happened amongst the shipbuilders' yards, the warehouses and the ships themselves.

Nelly didn't know what, exactly, she was looking for, but she wanted to see what Eliza Morgan had seen in the moments before she went into the water. She wanted to feel how Eliza had felt.

Bristol's docks were long and dark; the harbourside cluttered with barrows and carts. People moved like shadows amongst the cranes. There were myriad places where assailants might make themselves invisible.

The boats in the harbour appeared still, yet the clinking,

ticking and knocking sounds emanating from the ropes and masts and the sails made a noise like an orchestral percussion section. The timbers of the great wooden vessels creaked and groaned; small waves and eddies slapped the sides of the hulls. Gulls perched on the uppermost yard spars of the masts, heads tucked under their wings.

Lamps burned, illuminating patches of the decks. Watchmen sat around their braziers and smoked, and in the shadows round the edges of the warehouses and the ferry slipways, men and women laughed and coughed and spat and swore. Destitute people shuffled through the cut-throughs and alleyways, searching for a safe spot to bed down for the night. The air was damp and cold, the harbour water black as night, thick as oil.

Nelly went to the place closest to where Eliza's body had been found. The steam packet had left now, and no other vessel had taken its mooring. There was no barrier between the cobbled landing stages around the harbourside and the water. It would be all too easy to slip and fall, or to trip over one of the cast-iron bollards, or to get one's boot caught in a rope, or to be knocked into the water, especially after a few glasses of port, but only if one was close to the edge. And Nelly did not believe Eliza would have been; not if she had the choice.

Two plump women wearing tightly corseted dresses and worn velvet bonnets with floppy, false flowers sewn into the bands were standing close together, huddling beneath their shawls and sharing a bottle of brandy, taking turns to drink from its mouth. Nelly approached them. They eyed her, not in an unfriendly way, but amused. They assumed, thought Nelly, that she was some kind of do-gooder. Probably, people tried to do-good to them most evenings.

'Good evening,' she said.

'Evening.'

Nelly smiled as confidently as she could.

'May I ask if you ladies were here last night?'

'On and off, we were here,' one of the women answered. 'Why d'you want to know?'

'I'm hoping to find someone who might have seen an acquaintance of mine. Her name was Eliza Morgan. She was a woman of about the same size and build as I am, with ginger hair. She was wearing a brown dress.'

'The one that was fished out the water this morning?'

'Yes. That's her. Did you see her?'

The two women exchanged glances.

'We didn't see her, my love, no. But there were some kids playing on the dockside just before dark who were throwing stones at something drowned, by the packet steamer.'

'Nobody went to investigate?' Nelly asked.

'The watchman was standing at the water's edge. He chased the lads off,' said the younger woman. 'And whoever or whatever it was in the water was beyond mortal help.' She looked at Nelly apologetically. 'If we'd've known it was a friend of yours...' She tailed off.

Nelly surmised that nobody had wanted to get involved.

'I don't suppose you heard anything about an argument, or a scuffle, at the dockside earlier in the evening?' she asked.

'There's always a great deal of comings and goings round here. People coming on and off the ships. Dockers going home.'

'But someone would have noticed a woman falling into the water, wouldn't they?' Nelly persisted. 'She'd have screamed and splashed...'

A group of men had come out of one of the pubs and was walking towards them.

'I'm no expert on drowning, miss,' said the older woman, 'but if you fall in the docks, the last thing you wants is a mouthful of that vile water. You keeps your mouth shut. Though the second your skirts are wet, they'll drag you down like an anchor anyway.' She shook her head sadly, one eye on the approaching men. 'If that woman hadn't got stuck on the packet's propellor,' she added in a low voice, 'her body wouldn't ever have seen the light of day again.'

The thought of Eliza slowly falling through the filth to the mud on the harbour floor was enough to make Nelly feel nauseous.

She tried to shake the image away.

'One last thing,' she said, 'you mentioned a watchman who was standing close to where Eliza drowned... Might he have seen something?'

'He might have.'

'Might have done something, and all.'

'What do you mean by that?'

The woman who had spoken shrugged.

The men were only yards away.

'What's his name?'

'He doesn't have a name. He's just "the watchman".'

'How do I find him?'

'You don't find him, sweetheart, he finds you. Officially he works for Mr Scarrat but he'll take money from whoever'll pay him. He'll turn his hand to anything.'

Nelly sensed something malevolent in the words: something the woman was not saying. A chill ran through her.

She wanted to ask more, but there was no time.

The woman turned from Nelly and smiled at the men, who were standing close by now, looking the women up and down. 'Good evening, my dears,' she said. 'How are you tonight? Is there anything round here that you fancy?'

Nelly recognised that was her cue to leave.

15

THURSDAY, 27 OCTOBER

At ten o'clock the next morning there was an editorial meeting to plan the *Courier*'s Clifton Bridge opening supplement. All the reporters, including Nelly, went into George Boldwood's office and took their seats around the table, which was circular, like King Arthur's.

Nelly was tired. The previous night, her dreams had been disturbed by flashbacks to Harriet, small and unhappy, standing in the garden of that dreadful school, in the darkening of the evening, without a coat and no supper in her belly. She hadn't looked well.

Nelly had overslept and had to rush to work and as soon as she reached the bottom of the Christmas Steps, she found herself looking at every man who looked at her, wondering if he was the watchman. It was as if she was playing some sinister game, where she was the prey, and she had no idea who was the predator.

Now, in Mr Boldwood's office, Nelly turned the locket that contained her daughter's hair and the dried daisy – such pathetic treasures – between her fingers. She tried to concentrate, but her thoughts veered between the watchman and the fact that she could do nothing for Harriet but love her from a distance, and that, right now, was as futile as a single raindrop falling into the sea.

* * *

After lunch, Nelly made an entry in the communal diary saying that she had to go out to speak to the drapery buyer of one of Bristol's new department stores. This was a fabrication, but she could not tell the truth.

Once outside the *Courier* building, Nelly noticed a tall man, with a large moustache, deeply set eyes and white hair, standing on the corner, apparently looking at his pocket watch. When she started to walk, the man put the watch away and followed in her footsteps. She made a diversion towards the docks, checking every now and then to see if the man was still behind her, and he was.

Nelly quickened her pace. He quickened his.

She felt the first stirrings of panic.

To shake him off, Nelly went to the harbourside, waited until the last call for passengers, then trotted down the ramp and climbed aboard the ferry. From her perch on the planked seat, she could look back to where she'd just been.

It took a while for her eyes to find the man with the moustache, but when she at last identified him, she saw that he was amongst a group outside one of the sugar warehouses, oblivious to Nelly.

She exhaled and let the tension ease from her shoulders. He had simply been following the same route as she. There'd been no malice in his actions.

The ferryman rowed his small wooden vessel between ships

that were monstrous in comparison, their huge bulks blocking out the sky. The spoons of his oars dipped in and out of the murky water. The smell, this close, was hideous. Nelly held a handkerchief to her nose.

The ferryman's dog, a brown and white terrier, stood at the prow, panting and wagging its tail. It had been crossing the harbour for as long as Nelly had been in Bristol.

A great noise emanated from the shipyard where one of the new generation of steamers was being constructed: a clamouring of hammers, the glow and spit of hot metal. How quickly technology changed. How hard it was to keep up with it all.

* * *

When the little boat reached the slipway on the other side of the harbour, the ferryman took Nelly's hand and helped her onto dry land. She thanked him, scrambled up the slope, dusted herself down and headed for Park Street.

She found the tailor's premises easily enough, about a third of the way up the hill, close to the turning to St George's church. It was a small shop with a sign saying 'Lilley's, Tailors for Discerning Gentlemen' hanging from a bracket to the side, and blinds over the window to protect the valuable cloths from the sunlight.

Nelly opened the door and stepped inside. The interior was dark, and cluttered. Racks held skeins of linen and wool in different weaves, weights and colours. A wooden table was marked out in feet and inches, with a large pair of scissors lying on its surface, a measuring tape, and an enormous box of pins. As Nelly closed the door behind her, a bell rang and a man came out from behind a black curtain. Beyond was a workroom with a large window.

'Good afternoon, madam. How may I be of service to you?' the man asked. He was of middle-age, with an unremarkable face and a head full of milk-coloured curls, like a sheep's fleece.

'Good afternoon,' Nelly replied. 'Might I enquire if you are the proprietor, Mr Lilley?'

'I am he.'

Nelly spoke solemnly. 'I don't know if you are aware, Mr Lilley, and I'm sorry to be the bearer of bad news if you are not, but there has been a dreadful incident concerning a woman of your acquaintance.'

'Eliza Morgan? Yes, I know, she drowned. The police came to tell me.' He clasped his hands and shook his head sorrowfully. 'Utterly tragic.'

'Had you known Miss Morgan for a long time?'

'At least ten years. She was a respectable woman and an excellent seamstress.' He pursed his lips. 'Unfortunately, she'd become a bit too fond of the gin lately and was less reliable than she used to be. The last time I saw her we had words.'

He dragged his fingers through his woolly hair, then looked at Nelly with renewed interest.

'What does Miss Morgan's demise have to do with you?'

'I was with her shortly before her death.'

The tailor's eyes narrowed.

'In that case, do you recall, by any chance, whether she had a gentleman's coat with her? She was supposed to return it to me.'

'I believe she did have it, in a wicker basket.'

'Where might that basket be now?'

'Lying on the mud on the bottom of the harbour, I would imagine.'

The tailor flinched. 'Oh my! That beautiful coat!' His face crumpled in distress. 'The gentleman who owns it is my most prestigious client! It will inconvenience him dreadfully that it is lost.'

'I'm sure he will be sympathetic when he is made aware of the circumstances.'

'I would never dream of troubling him with my problems. There's nothing for it: I'll have to make another to the exact same pattern.'

Nelly was perturbed that the tailor seemed more troubled by the loss of the coat than that of the seamstress with whom he'd been acquainted for a decade. She waited for him to compose himself, then she asked, 'Did Eliza Morgan have any family who should be informed of her passing?'

'Family? Nobody that I know of. She did have a sister but she passed some years ago.'

'Could you tell me where Eliza once lived, please, Mr Lilley?'

One of the advantages of being a small, unremarkable woman was that, as long as she spoke politely, people usually went out of their way to assist Nelly. Nobody felt threatened by her. The tailor did not think to question why she might want to know Eliza's address.

He moved to the desk, where a ledger lay open, details of jobs being undertaken neatly listed on a page made of the same paper on which Eliza had written her original note, and turned to the front of the book.

'Eliza Morgan,' he said quietly, running his finger along a list of seamstresses. 'She lived in a lodging house on Benbow Street. Here we are. Number 35, not far from the Trooper inn.'

'Thank you,' said Nelly. 'That's most helpful.'

Now she braced herself to ask for the information she *really* needed to know.

'When I spoke with Miss Morgan the other day,' she said as

casually as she could, 'she mentioned you had a client whose wife and infant had died in childbed.'

The tailor looked up sharply.

Nelly continued. 'Indeed, from what she said that day, I believe it may be the same client whose coat is now lost. Eliza didn't give me their names so perhaps—'

'Miss Morgan had no right to discuss the private lives of my customers.'

'I assure you, she was most discreet. But she was obviously concerned about the circumstances of the deaths and I wondered if you—'

'No,' he said. 'No, madam! This is precisely why Eliza and I argued. I won't say a word about the people on whom my livelihood depends, and neither will the people in my employ. My clients trust me. Everything I know about them, and their lives, is confidential. Without that trust, I do not have a business!'

He peered at Nelly, scrutinising her properly for the first time. 'Who are you anyway?'

'My name is Nelly Brooks.' Deep breath. 'I am a reporter with the Bristol *Courier*.'

'A reporter? But you are a woman!'

'You're most observant.'

Mr Lilley stared at her for a moment. Then he raised his arm and pointed to the door.

'You had no right to come here! No right to ask about my clients! Get out of my shop! Get out now! And don't come back again. Ever!'

16

Nelly Brooks was, by nature, someone who preferred people to think well of her. She was adept at hiding her feelings; at pretending criticism did not hurt. During the entire ten years in the asylum, she had never once admitted that she cared about her parents regarding her in such a bad light – but she had cared, and deeply.

She was sorry she had upset Mr Lilley, although, if she was honest with herself, she had known that she would.

But more than wishing she hadn't riled him, Nelly was experiencing a new sensation: a buzz of excitement.

She was elated because Mr Lilley had effectively confirmed the most important elements of Eliza's story. He had not been surprised when Nelly mentioned the deaths of the mother and child, nor had he denied the fact of them. And if that was true, if the young wife and her baby had existed, and had died, it meant Nelly had no good reason to doubt the rest of Eliza's story.

Also, the tailor had used the phrase 'my most prestigious client' in relation to the dead woman's husband. This man, whoever he was, must be someone from the highest echelons of Bristol society.

Identifying the man was the key to unlocking the mystery. And if he was as important as both Eliza and Mr Lilley had said, and if it turned out that the deaths of his wife and child were not natural, then might this not be the biggest story of the year? The *decade*, even?

And it was *her story*!

Nelly shrugged off any awkwardness she'd felt about distressing the tailor. This was it. This was her big opportunity. If she was a sighthound chasing a deer, to use Will's analogy, then she was gaining ground. But she had to stay calm. She had to plan her next move carefully.

The logical step, surely, was to go to Benbow Street, where Eliza had lodged, to locate the diary that Eliza had mentioned, the one the young wife had given to Eliza to keep safe. Nelly was desperate to find the diary and read it. She hoped it might answer all her outstanding questions, but right now she needed to get back to the office, before her extended absence attracted attention.

* * *

She was too late. When she returned to the *Courier*, the editor's secretary was waiting for her. He had the communal diary in his hands.

'Miss Brooks!' he exclaimed. 'May I have a word?'

'Of course,' said Nelly, hoping she did not look as flushed as she felt, after hurrying back through the city. She pushed back the hair that had come loose, fanned her face with her hand, and followed Mr Bagnet into his office. She sat on the chair indicated on the other side of the desk. Her mouth was dry.

Mr Bagnet spoke.

'It has come to my attention that you've just returned from a meeting with... I can't read the name, but you wrote that they are a representative of the Whitman department store, and that the meeting was in connection with a potential promotional feature.'

'Yes,' said Nelly, 'that's right.'

'Well, it's very odd, because a gentleman from Whitman's was here, today, speaking with our advertising fellow. And when I asked him, he said he was not aware that any reporter had arranged a meeting at his department store.'

Nelly could not tell a direct lie, nor could she think of an indirect one.

She opened her mouth, then thought better of it.

Mr Bagnet stared at her, his finger on the diary entry.

The silence became unbearable.

'I'm sorry,' Nelly said. 'I was out on *Courier* business, but I was not at Whitman's.'

'No,' said Mr Bagnet. 'Obviously you were not.' He closed the diary. 'I haven't said anything to Mr Boldwood, but if anything like this happens again, then I'll have no option but to raise the matter with him. He would be most disappointed to hear of your deception.'

'Yes,' said Nelly. 'I know that he would.'

'We are a team, at the *Courier*, Miss Brooks. Trust is the glue that hold us together. Do not abuse that trust.'

'No,' Nelly said. 'I won't.'

She returned to her cubbyhole; sorry for lying about where she'd been, although strong in her conviction that what she was doing mattered more than Mr Bagnet's approval. She hoped that, when she'd written her trailblazing story and the reason for her subterfuge was revealed, Mr Bagnet would understand and forgive her. In the meantime, she knew she must tread more carefully.

She spent what was left of that working day writing a light-hearted feature about the enduring fashion for crinolines, as a self-inflicted punishment for her deceitfulness.

The hooped skirts that were being introduced to replace the heavy petticoats that had been standard up to this point made the dresses easier to wear, but their width and bulk meant women were constantly knocking things off tables and shelves. Nelly thought they were ridiculous.

Sitting on a low chair in a crinoline was awkward, for the hoops had a habit of springing up, hiding one's face and exposing one's legs and undergarments. Nelly's landlady's daughter, Eveline, claimed to have seen a woman blown off her feet when a gust of wind caught in her skirt on the Downs. Imagine what might have happened had this poor soul been standing on the new Clifton bridge! She could have been lifted into the air and carried away like a dandelion seed! Nelly tapped the end of the pencil against her teeth and imagined women floating over Bristol, the sun shining through their multi-coloured skirts as they looked down over the city, never to be seen again.

A crinoline has become the essential item for ladies of discernment,

she wrote in conclusion, then added boldly,

although I, for one, look forward to the day when we women exchange our petticoats for trousers like our brothers. We shall at last be able to stride, where now we tiptoe!

Mr Boldwood would not like the last paragraph.

Nelly raised her pencil to cross it out, then changed her mind. If challenged, she was quite prepared to defend her position.

* * *

Nelly felt obliged to stay at work until after George Boldwood had left that evening – she could not bring herself to walk past his office and out of the door while he was still incumbent at his desk. The moment he had gone, she gathered her things together and followed. Everyone else had already left, apart from Will and Duncan. The two were together in Will's cubbyhole, talking quietly, but intently.

Will looked up as Nelly walked past.

'Are you going home, Nelly?' he asked. 'Would you like me to walk with you?'

'No, thank you,' Nelly answered.

She sensed, rather than saw, Will's disappointment and she guessed that Duncan had put the younger man up to the offer. Duncan persisted in trying to persuade Will and Nelly into some kind of contrived attachment that she definitely did not want. She suspected Will didn't either.

She felt heat in her cheeks: she did not like being the subject of their speculation. Much as she liked Will, she had made it perfectly clear that she had no interest in a romance with him, nor anyone else; she would never make that mistake again.

This would not happen to me, if I were a man, she thought. *If I were a man, they would leave me alone.*

She pulled the edges of her jacket closer together and hurried to the door that led to the staircase.

17

Back at 12 Orchard Hill, hungry and tired, Nelly went into the dining room and helped herself to the supper dishes of pie and potatoes left out by Sarah. She stoked the fire, and then pulled her chair closer to it. Outside, beyond the window, darkness had already fallen. The maid, Ida, had left the curtains open – the sunset had been pretty this evening and she must have wanted to hold onto the day for as long as she could. The lamplight made flickering shadows and the air, beyond the warmth cast by the fire, was chilly. Nelly felt a longing for the light evenings of summer, already out of reach. It would be months before the year turned its face back towards the sun and the prospect of the long winter ahead weighed heavy on her shoulders.

Nelly was warm and quiet. She did not mind being alone. Society frowned on single women living without husbands or families, for feminine solitude was deemed to be outside the natural order. Nelly genuinely didn't care what society thought. Society was a hypocrite and a fool and she hadn't cared about its opinion for years.

If only, she thought, there were some way of having Harriet

here at Orchard Hill, with her. There was no physical impediment to Nelly's daughter moving in. There was room for a second bed in Nelly's room, or they could share the existing one. The dining room table could accommodate a fourth lodger; Mrs Augur and Eveline would, no doubt, appreciate the extra rent. Nelly could picture the girl sitting beside her, swinging her legs while she ate, chatting about her day – for if Harriet were here, she could go to the little school at the top of the hill. The teacher was a kind woman, who laughed easily. Nelly knew that Harriet would be happy there.

No sooner had the fantasy settled in her thoughts, then all the reasons why it was impossible brought it crashing down. The reasons were all societal: rules and regulations made up in the main by men, but women were complicit also, that made no sense to Nelly; their existence only served to make life complicated for some, almost impossible for others.

Nelly had found these rules tiresome and difficult to navigate from an early age.

'What's wrong with you, Helen?' had been Nelly's mother's favourite question when Nelly was a child. 'Why can't you be normal?' What she meant by 'normal' was 'feminine', 'compliant', 'obedient'.

Ever since she was four or five, old enough to remember, Nelly had realised that her experience of the world was not what it should have been.

She did not want to sit in the nursery throwing pretend tea parties for dolls. She wanted to be outdoors, tramping down the long, narrow garden behind her parents' house, pretending she was a pirate or an explorer, or that she had found a secret colony of tiny people living at the back of the shed, in the wilderness of brambles and blackthorn bushes that separated the ends of the gardens from the little stream that ran between them.

The Emerald Shawl

Once, Nelly found a starling with a broken wing amongst her father's delphiniums and brought it into the house, hiding it in a box in the spare bedroom where it would be safe and bringing it food and drink. The bird, unfortunately, was discovered by her mother, who told the maid to dispose of it. Nelly pleaded and begged for the starling's life to be spared. The maid claimed she had set it free, but Nelly knew that was not true.

Mrs Brooks made a great fuss about the starling. For weeks after, she said the finding of the 'verminous creature' had given her nightmares. She insisted that it had infested the house with fleas, and had the paid help take everything out of that bedroom, even the rug, so that it might be hung over the washing line and beaten until all the flea eggs were dislodged.

'This is all your doing,' Mrs Brooks said to Nelly as the maid and the charwoman grumbled about the extra work.

Nelly, who had loved the starling with all her heart, said nothing.

She did not cry.

She dreamed of having a home of her own that she might fill with animals she had rescued. She did not understand, as a child, how difficult it was for a female to be truly independent. But when she did understand, she was determined to be one of those who successfully took care of herself.

She had a friend. A quiet boy and a kindred spirit. He did not, like Nelly and her family, live in one of the big houses on Culverdale Avenue, Colchester, but in one of the tied cottages on the nearby Blackwood Estate. His father was the gamekeeper; his mother had died of tuberculosis. He was the youngest of four brothers. His name was Sidney Hayden.

Harriet had Sidney's eyes.

Nelly sighed. She heard the first-floor lodgers, the misses Sylvester and Norton, moving about upstairs; heard their voices, and the clink of glass that meant they were sharing an evening drink together. It was good to hear their laughter.

The fire in the grate gave a sudden roar, the flames drawn by a gust of wind outside. Nelly put her knife and fork on her plate, and stood to draw the curtains, conscious of how she would appear to anyone looking in from outside. The reflection of her own face in the window pane startled her.

She sat down again. Flossy leapt onto her lap and began to claw at her skirt, purring deep within her throat.

Nelly thought of the tailor, Mr Lilley, still in his shop, working all night to recreate the coat that had been lost with Eliza. She imagined him straining his eyes to see the tiny stitches by lamplight like a character in a children's book.

She thought of Eliza Morgan's empty bedroom, and the diary that contained all the secrets hidden somewhere in that room.

Then she thought of Harriet, all alone in her narrow bed in the dormitory of the reform school, Harriet who did not know, and might well never know, that the lady who came to stand at the railings to watch her, the one to whom she had once given a single daisy, was her own mother. Nelly's heart ached with sadness and longing and hopelessness.

Even now, twelve years after Harriet's birth, Nelly could not think what she might have done differently, or how her own story could have led to a different outcome. She could not see the path she should have taken – nor, frustratingly, the one she should take next.

18

Nelly yawned. She was ready to go up to her room. She put Flossy on the floor and reached for the fireguard. As she did so, she heard the front door open and close and then voices in the hallway. A few moments later, the door to the dining room opened, and the landlady, Mrs Augur, and her daughter, Eveline, came in, flush-cheeked and bright-eyed, bringing with them a rush of cold air. Both were short women, but well-built; similar in appearance, each with a pleasant, round face, a creamy complexion and small, pretty features.

It lifted Nelly's heart to see them; they were such good friends to one another. They represented everything Nelly would have wished for herself and Harriet; the closeness Nelly and her own mother did not – and never would – have.

'Good evening, good evening,' they said to Nelly as they peeled off their gloves, and they continued to talk over one another as they always did, with ineffable good humour and affection.

'Brrr,' said Eveline with an exaggerated shiver. 'It's proper cold out there!'

'Are you comfortable, Nelly?' Mrs Augur asked. 'Shall I ask Ida to put more coal on the fire?'

'I'm perfectly warm,' Nelly said. 'I've been toasting myself. But thank you for your consideration.'

Eveline put her gloves on the end of the table, and untied her bonnet, blowing a pale wisp of hair from her eyes. She was full of energy, almost dancing around the table as she lifted the lids to the dishes and peered inside.

'Oh my goodness, Nelly, we've had an *incredible* evening!' she cried.

'Wonderful!' said Mrs Augur. 'The things we've seen and heard!'

'Really, Nelly, you wouldn't believe it!'

'This chicken pie looks delicious! Take some potatoes, Eveline.'

'Where have you been?' Nelly asked.

'At a spiritualist meeting.'

'We'd heard the medium was excellent. And oh, she was, wasn't she?'

'Well, it was our first time, so we have nobody with whom to compare her...'

'But I cannot imagine anyone else would have been so good! I was not convinced before that there was life after death, but now I am a convert! Pass me the buttered leeks, would you, Mother dear?'

'It was uplifting,' said Mrs Augur. 'That's what it was. I'm certain every single person in that hall left feeling better about themselves and the world than they did when they arrived.'

'Really, Nelly, you should come with us next time. You could write about it in the *Courier*. I am certain your lady readers would be interested!'

'They absolutely would!' Mrs Augur sprinkled salt onto her

vegetables. 'The gentlemen readers too. The stories we heard, Miss Brooks, would make your hair curl!'

'I don't think my editor would approve,' Nelly said. 'He's a traditionalist churchman.'

'Does he have the final say over everything you write?'

'Everything that is printed.'

'Well! What does he know?'

Eveline sat down and began to eat. 'Mmm! Delicious! Come anyway,' she said. 'You'd enjoy it. And you'd like hearing from the living people, and the dead.'

'What happens there?' Nelly asked.

'The medium asks the audience if any of them has specific souls who have passed who they wish to contact, and then she summons those spirits. Sometimes they come, sometimes they do not. But they came tonight, didn't they, Mother?'

'They did!' Mrs Augur began to eat. 'I thought the mystery woman was the most interesting,' she continued. 'Be a darling and pass me the wine, Eveline.'

'Ooh yes! You'd have liked this one, Nelly.' Eveline widened her eyes dramatically and waved her fork at Nelly. 'It was the spirit of a woman who said her death had been passed off as an accident, when really it was murder.'

Nelly felt a jolt in her body.

'Who was this woman?'

'Her voice wasn't clear enough for the medium to get her name, but she was most distressed. She said she was trapped in the dark and couldn't be freed until the wrong that had been done to her had been righted.'

Nelly felt a flicker of anxiety.

'Did she say how she died; this trapped woman?'

'She didn't.'

Nelly considered herself a sceptic when it came to matters

such as this, but her mind was open to being proved wrong and Eveline's description of the poor soul in purgatory fitted Eliza; the woman for whose death she felt an uncomfortable responsibility.

'Perhaps I will join you next time,' she said hesitantly.

'*See!*' Eveline gloated. 'I knew she'd be interested, didn't I, Mother? I knew it! You can no more resist a mystery, Nelly Brooks, than I can refuse a second helping of dinner!'

19

FRIDAY, 28 OCTOBER

The weather had taken a turn for the worse. Rain was falling in stair rods. Nelly Brooks held tight to her umbrella as she negotiated the Christmas Steps, treading gingerly in the river of slime and filth that was washing downhill, trying not to slip.

She anticipated disaster, but she did not fall, although the hem of her skirt was dirty and sodden by the time she reached the foot of the Steps.

Few people were about the docks as she walked alongside the water; those queuing outside the hot-food stalls huddling beneath whatever shelter from the rain they could find. She looked about her, but saw nobody who might be the watchman. She wished she could forget about him, but he seemed to be almost permanently on her mind.

Nelly hurried to the *Courier* offices, waited until Mr Snitch had written her name in the ledger, then went upstairs, where she hung up her wet outer garments. The interior of the building was not cold, thanks to the preponderance of new stoves in the corners of the rooms, and the coats of the reporters already present were beginning to steam in the warmth.

On the way to her desk, Nelly popped her head round the door to Maud Mackenzie's cubbyhole. Maud had her spectacles perched on her nose and was leaning over a board designing an advertisement for a beautifier.

'Good morning, Maud.'

'Morning, my dear.' Maud pushed her glasses down her nose and looked at Nelly over the rims. 'You look awfully tired, Nelly. Is everything all right?'

Maud was the only person at the *Courier* who knew about Nelly's history: about Harriet, and the asylum, and consequently, she was always on alert for signs of mental fragility. She was motivated purely by kindness. Maud had acted as a surrogate mother, firstly to the young Will Delane, and now to Sam, the errand boy, who lodged with her. Caring was in her nature, but Nelly wished Maud did not know so much about her. She found her concern oppressive.

'Nothing is wrong,' she said cheerfully, and she continued to her own cubbyhole, where she laid her notebook and pencils on her desk, and lit the lamp.

She needed to go to Benbow Street, to find Eliza Morgan's lodgings, but she did not know how she might justify a further extended absence from the office.

She had barely settled when Sam rapped his knuckles on the partition.

'Pardon me, Miss Brooks, but there is a couple down in the reception that wants to speak with you.'

He was thirteen years old, a small boy with a thin face, close-together eyes and ears that stuck out on either side of his head, like handles. In stature, he was no larger than Harriet, and his desire to please invoked protective feelings in Nelly. The buttons on his jacket were not fastened in the correct holes, and it took a great strength of will for Nelly not to fix them for him.

'Do you know who they are, Sam?'

'Name of Skinner. Mr and Mrs.'

'Are you sure they didn't ask for Mr Delane?'

'They asked for you. And there's a couple of nippers with them an' all.'

'Children,' Nelly corrected gently. 'Very well, I'll—'

She was interrupted by the ringing of a handbell calling the editorial staff to the morning conference. She turned to Sam. 'Sam, would you convey my apologies to Mr Bagnet? Tell him I've gone to see the people downstairs.'

'Yes, Miss Brooks,' said Sam, saluting like a little soldier.

Nelly took a notebook and pen, and her lunch from her satchel, and then went downstairs.

* * *

The Skinners looked barely different from the last time Nelly had seen them, except that now their clothes were soaking wet and small puddles had formed around their boots. They had a girl of about nine years old with them as well as little Archie, the older child having evidently been brought along to keep the younger occupied while the Skinners talked. She was holding the infant on her hip and he was examining strands of her damp hair and shivering profusely.

Nelly could tell at once, from their demeanour, that Gerty Skinner had not come home.

'I hope we're not being too much of a bother,' said Mrs Skinner, when they had all shaken hands, 'only you was so nice to us last time we was here... You listened.'

'My colleague, Mr Delane, listened too,' Nelly said. 'He published an appeal for information as to Gerty's whereabouts in yesterday's newspaper.'

'We know, and we're grateful, but events have overtaken us,' said Mr Skinner.

'Has there been news of Gerty?'

'In a manner of speaking.'

'We went back to the dead-house,' said Mrs Skinner. 'We implored them to listen to us. We assured them, didn't we, Albert, that the girl with the scar on her chin was our Gerty.'

'That's right,' said Mr Skinner.

'And the dead-house people was most sympathetic. They told us that them as came and took the body was two respectable ladies.'

'The crucial fact is,' said Mr Skinner, 'the ladies never looked at the poor, dead soul closely!'

'They was in a state,' said Mrs Skinner, 'as anyone in that situation would be. The fellow at the dead-house said he pulled back the shroud as was covering the face of the corpse and they glanced at it...' she acted out the scene, tipping her face towards an imaginary corpse for the briefest instant, then looking away. '"That's her," they said, "that's our sister!", but they never gave her a proper look, did they, Albert?'

'We're sure it was a mistake. No malice intended.'

'They probably still haven't realised they've got the wrong girl.'

Mrs Skinner handed a piece of paper to Nelly. 'This is the address of the two ladies as took the body. There's no way we can get there. But we thought maybe, if it's not too much trouble, Miss Brooks, you could.'

Nelly looked at the scrap of paper. The address had been written in large, clear letters, but Mrs Skinner had been holding it upside down. 132 Myrtle Gardens, Keynsham. The names of those who had collected the body were Misses Anne and Martha Smith.

The Emerald Shawl

Keynsham was a town between Bristol and Bath. It was no more than six miles away by road, but to the Skinners, it might as well have been on the other side of the world.

'It's most unorthodox,' said Nelly, 'for the mortuary staff to disclose the details of a bereaved family in this way. I cannot comprehend why they would have done so.'

'You didn't tell her *why* they helped us,' Mr Skinner said to his wife.

'You're right, Albert, I didn't,' said Mrs Skinner. She turned to Nelly. 'It's because we showed them the photograph of Gerty, and they recognised her.'

'You have a photograph of your daughter?'

'Yes. Like I said. Where's the photograph, Albert?'

Mr Skinner delved into his pocket, and took out a damp envelope.

'It's here.'

20

Back upstairs, Nelly could hear the murmur of her colleagues' voices behind the closed door of George Boldwood's office and the occasional burst of laughter. The editorial conference hadn't yet finished.

She took the photograph the Skinners had given her to her desk, pulled the lamp closer, and studied the image, printed onto a card of the kind used to promote Bristol's booming tobacco industry.

Gerty was one of five attractive young women posing inside the factory, around a huge pile of raw tobacco. Like the others, she was wearing a long apron over her dress. She resembled her mother, although she stood taller and straighter. Her dark hair was parted neatly down the middle and pulled back on either side. Her eyes were bright, and she looked as if she was suppressing a smile.

In her uniform, in the factory, Gerty did not look like a poor girl from one of the city's worst slums: she looked healthy and confident and strong. That, thought Nelly, was what good employment could do for a person: it gave one dignity. Gerty must have been chosen from dozens of other women for that picture. Her good looks would have had something to do with it, but she must have stood out from the crowd in other ways too.

Nelly picked up the magnifying class she kept at the side of her desk to help her read tiny typefaces. She studied Gerty's face close up and in detail. She could just make out the scar, an inverted crescent moon, beneath her lower lip.

Her parents had mentioned that Gerty sometimes 'went on drinking sprees', and she had an illegitimate child. Her life could not have been easy, yet she had managed to keep her job, and, with the support of her family, her son.

No wonder the Skinners were so proud of their daughter.

Nelly exhaled slowly.

'You did better than me, Gerty,' she said quietly.

She understood the Skinners' desperation to find their girl. She knew why they needed to know where she was, and why they must have her back.

* * *

The *Courier* had its own pair of horses, which took it in turns to pull the company's hansom cab around Bristol, delivering reporters to meetings and interviews.

The cab was managed by a fearsome-looking man called Cuddy, who was renowned for his distrust and dislike of the editorial staff. Fortunately for Nelly, he did not despise her in the same way as he did the others, regarding her as a breath of fresh air in a swamp full of liars, cynics and manipulators. She was touched by his conviction that she was morally superior to the rest, although at an intellectual level she understood that this idolisation was another form of diminishing the true nature of women. This did not stop her exploiting Cuddy's favouritism for her own benefit, which was so cynical, dishonest and manipulative that Nelly felt obliged to point it out to him each time she did it. Ironically, Cuddy regarded her confessions as another example of her purity of spirit.

When she went to find him in the stables at the back of the building, he was leaning against the wall, arms crossed, chatting with the farrier, who was attending to the hooves of the smaller of the horses, both smart bay geldings. The larger had already been re-shod.

'Good afternoon, Miss Brooks,' Cuddy said, taking off his hat and bowing as she approached, showing off for the benefit of the farrier. 'What can I do you for today?'

He stuck his thumbs in his braces and rocked on the heels of his boots.

Nelly told him the gist of why she wanted to go to Keynsham – it was a story she was working on; it could not wait, she needed to visit the address she'd been given at the earliest opportunity.

Cuddy went into the feed-room, which also served as his office-cum-kingdom. Nelly followed him. The room was dark and warm and smelled of oats. There was a large leather chair, its stuffing seeping out through various cracks, but it was covered with a knitted blanket and beside it was the stove with a blackened kettle on top.

Cuddy consulted his calendar, making 'hmm' and 'hahhh' noises. Then he turned to Nelly. 'I could take you to Keynsham tomorrow morning.'

'Saturday... That would be perfect, Mr Cuddy, thank you.'

'Meet me here at eight o'clock. No later, or I shan't be back in time to take Mr Coulson and his fiancée to the races at Bath.'

Duncan Coulson was engaged to the second of George Boldwood's four daughters. When Cuddy was not otherwise employed, the Boldwood family had special dispensation to make use of his services. Duncan 'The Bristolian' being the *Courier's* best-known employee, nobody objected to him booking Cuddy for outings of this manner.

'I'll be here at eight!' said Nelly. She hesitated. 'Will it be a problem if Will Delane comes with me?'

'For you, Miss Brooks, nothing is a problem.'

The farrier held the foot of the smaller horse between his knee and hammered a shoe onto the hoof. The smell of burning was everywhere.

21

Nelly left a note on Will's desk, explaining what had happened, and telling him to meet her at 8 a.m. tomorrow, if he was of a mind to go to Keynsham with her.

Then she went back to her cubbyhole and she sat for a moment, clearing her head of Gerty Skinner, because there was nothing at all she could do about Gerty for now. She needed, instead, to concentrate on the matter of the murdered wife and child.

She could not get to Benbow Street today; she had no valid reason – in Mr Bagnet's eyes – to go; she could not tell the truth without having the story taken from her and she dared not invent another false mission. Was there any other way to further the investigation?

There were still no death notices in the *Courier* matching the woman that Eliza Morgan had described. Nelly wracked her brains to think of another means of identifying her. Eliza had said – hadn't she? – that she first met the young wife two years earlier, in the summer, to fit her wedding dress. There must, surely, have been something in the newspaper to commemorate the marriage of an important and prestigious man to his lovely, much younger bride?

Nelly returned to the archive room to search through the papers starting from May 1862 and working forward. She was looking for a wedding of someone of high status within Bristol.

She had been searching for some time when Duncan Coulson put his head around the door.

'Good morning, Nelly,' he said. 'What are you doing in the archive?'

'Looking for something,' she replied.

'Well, knock me down with a feather,' said Duncan, raising an eyebrow. 'Will it disturb you if I come in?'

'Not at all,' said Nelly.

She liked Duncan, but not as much as she liked Will, with whom she shared a bond, both being outliers in the *Courier*. They were younger than the other staff, untrained, and unlikely candidates to be reporters. They each had something to prove and as such they were natural friends and allies. Duncan was older, better connected, and had been engaged to George Boldwood's second daughter for almost a year. Sooner or later, he was expected to move to a role with one of the national newspapers in London.

Now, Duncan picked up the gloves that he kept for the purpose of scouring the cuttings, gloves that kept his fingers and his clothes clean, and crossed to the drawers where the envelopes were filed. He was famous for his pernicketiness. Nelly looked at her own inky fingers and sighed.

She looked down at the latest newspaper she'd picked up. It was dated 13 August 1862.

She turned to the list of marriages.

> CLITHEROE – Chapman. On Friday, 1 August 1862 at Stroud, Gloucestershire, by special licence, Thomas Clitheroe, playwright, to Minnie, daughter of Francis Willing Chapman, theatre manager.

A playwright. That might be considered an important job.

'Have you ever heard of someone called Thomas Clitheroe?' she asked Duncan.

'The fellow who writes for the Bristol Theatre? Yes.'

'Would you describe him as prestigious?'

'Prodigious maybe. He's quite a character.'

'How old is he?'

'Thirty-ish. Why?'

'Oh, it's of no importance.'

The next entry was:

> SLATER – Ray. On Saturday, 2 August 1862 at Nailsea, Somerset, Harry Wilson Slater, glassmaker, to Eileen Ray, teacher.

> PERRETTE – Tait…

'No, no, no,' Nelly murmured. She worked her way through the August announcements and moved on to September. Duncan found his cuttings and went away. Nelly wondered if she was on a wild goose chase.

There had been no funeral notice. Perhaps there had been no marriage notice either. Perhaps Eliza had been wrong about the date or had misremembered the marriage.

Or perhaps Nelly had missed it, somehow.

She reached the end of the list for that week, replaced the paper, and turned to the one beneath it.

And there it was, at the top of that week's announcements, in black and white.

MARRIAGE OF A MEMBER OF PARLIAMENT
Tuesday, September 9, 1862.

Sir Edward Ryburn Fairfield, member for Bristol North, was married at St Simon's church, Filton, to Priscilla May, only surviving daughter of the late Mr Henry Statton, parliamentary clerk, of Almondsbury. Owing to the recent death of Mr Statton, the wedding was a very quiet one. Afterwards, the couple returned to the Fairfield family home, Mordaunt Hall.

This had to be what she'd been searching for, didn't it? There was no man more wealthy, more influential, or better connected than Sir Edward Fairfield, certainly not in Bristol. And Mr Statton, presumably, had been the MP's clerk. The two men would have worked closely together. There would have been ample opportunities for Sir Edward to become acquainted with Mr Statton's daughter.

Nelly had met Sir Edward Fairfield briefly, the previous year. He was one of the *Courier*'s major shareholders, and had come to the offices for a tour before he departed for a trip to India. The whole building, including the print room, had been cleaned from top to bottom, and Mr Bagnet had carried out an inspection of the reporters' cubbyholes to make sure they were tidy and free of clutter. It was like being back at the orphanage, Will had said, where there had been regular dormitory inspections.

The staff – boots polished, hair combed and oiled, moustaches (where applicable) waxed – had stood in a line, waiting to shake Sir Edward's hand. Nelly had been nervous. She had never met an MP before, although she'd seen several, at a distance, when she was locked up in the asylum and they came for inspections. Nelly always suspected the honourable gentlemen were particularly interested in dishonourable women.

Because of her experience at Holywell, Nelly had been anxious when Sir Edward had reached her, at the end of the line of editorial staff. Rationally, she'd known he wasn't going to make a personal joke about her appearance, or comment pityingly on her ruined life as the politicians who visited the asylum had, but her body had gone into defensive mode – as if he might.

Inwardly she'd panicked, but outwardly she'd remained composed as Mr Boldwood introduced her as, 'The *Courier*'s first female writer.'

'Nelly has an unusual talent,' the editor had said. 'She submitted some unsolicited work and I recognised her ability at once. It would have been a sacrilege not to employ her.'

'Then it is I who am honoured to meet you, Miss Brooks,' the MP had said, which was, superficially, a nice thing to say, but Nelly had sensed that Sir Edward was the kind of man who said the things to people that people wanted to hear. She'd had the impression that he was aware of her presence, but it was as if he were looking at her through a window: he did not connect. When he'd taken Nelly's hand, his had been cool and powdery.

Now, more than twelve months later, Nelly closed her eyes and tried to remember the details about Sir Edward. He had been immaculately dressed, she'd noticed that, although in an old-fashioned style. His hair was grey, and when he removed his hat, the top of his head was bald, and waxy, reminiscent in colour and texture of the boiled tongue Nelly's father used to like to eat at teatime. He was thin, his hands were veined and bony, and he had a wattle beneath his chin. When he spoke, it was slowly as if he was picking his words deliberately. She had not formed an

The Emerald Shawl

opinion about the man, neither liking nor disliking him. But he had seemed old to Nelly; older than a father, more like a grandfather.

It made her feel uncomfortable to imagine his dry hands, with a fur of dark grey hairs covering the knuckles and the backs of the fingers, touching a young woman's skin.

'Stop it!' Nelly said to herself.

She took the newspaper that contained the announcement, folded it, and tucked it under her notebook.

She went back to her desk, and sat for a few minutes trying to join the dots of what she knew to make a full picture.

The information in the short article about Sir Edward's wedding fitted with everything Eliza Morgan had told her.

The wedding had been small, no fuss, because the young bride's father had recently died. Mr Statton had been a parliamentary clerk, so, although of a different class, would have moved in the same professional circles as Sir Edward. After his death, his daughter, alone in the world, grieving, and vulnerable, might well have been grateful for, and flattered by, the attentions of a wealthy, older man.

If Nelly was right, and this was the man about whom Eliza had spoken, then the story was big; far bigger than Nelly had even imagined. It was the kind of story that could turn into a national scandal. Good grief, if Sir Edward had murdered his wife and child, might it even bring down the government?

It was the story of a lifetime. It could be the making of Nelly. If she pulled this off, she would be famous. She would have status. She might even be in a strong enough position to employ the services of a lawyer to help her win back Harriet.

It could be the story she'd dreamed of.

Her heart was pounding. She tried to contain her excitement.

She reminded herself that she might be following the wrong lead. She shouldn't let her hopes rise too high.

She still didn't know whether or not the story was true.

But what if it was?

22

Back at her desk, Nelly copied out the wedding notice of Edward Fairfield and Priscilla Statton by hand into her notebook.

Will came to find her, holding the note she'd left on his desk.

'Having an address for the people who took Gerty's body is a turn-up for the books,' he said.

'Isn't it just?'

'Do you have the photograph of Gerty?'

She showed him. He held it up to the light. 'Which one is she?'

'The second from the left.'

Will whistled softly. 'Poor creature,' he said.

'Are you coming to Keynsham with me tomorrow morning, Will?'

'Of course I am. Wild horses wouldn't stop me.' He tapped the photograph. 'I'll have this cleaned up and a larger copy made. Whatever happens next, we'll have the reproduction framed before we return it to Mr and Mrs Skinner.'

'That's a good plan,' said Nelly.

'Then leave it with me.'

* * *

It was traditional on Fridays for those *Courier* editorial staff who were available, to go for lunch together at Pierre's restaurant just down the road from the offices. This was a chance for the reporters to catch up and exchange information in an informal setting. George Boldwood presided over the table like a benevolent uncle, anxious that everyone was enjoying themselves. From time to time his second daughter, Julie, the one who was engaged to Duncan, came too and she sat beside Duncan, hooting with laughter at his irreverence and sarcasm; he basking in her adoration.

The restaurant was dark and bohemian in its décor, its walls decorated with posters of actors and actresses, artists, poets and writers. There were candles in bottlenecks and jars of flowers, or, at this time of year, twigs bearing berries, on every table. Monsieur Pierre and his sons and daughters-in-law did the cooking and waiting, while Madame, a dark-haired, large-bodied beauty, took charge of the front of house. Madame Pierre and Mr Boldwood adored each other, and had an ongoing flirtation that was so charming, joyful and innocent, neither their spouses nor their children were offended by it.

The *Courier* staff always took the same table on the first floor, next to the long window that overlooked the street. The building was old, the floorboards bowed and warped; the atmosphere was convivial. Wine and beer flowed. The mood amongst most of the reporters was celebratory, marking the end of another week.

The Friday lunches were not such a treat for Nelly, who usually found herself squashed into a small space. Even when Will saved a spot for her, and despite her skirts, she didn't take up as much room as the men. No matter how she tried to stick out her elbows and make herself present at the table, she felt like an afterthought, and one of her colleagues always seemed to have taken her knife, or used her wine glass.

She knew the older ones resented her joining them at the restaurant, even those who accepted her in the office. Because of her, Mr Boldwood expected them to moderate their language and the topics of their conversation. Some refused to do this, even when Julie or Mrs Boldwood were present. They continued to make crude jokes and tell disparaging stories about women as a kind of defiance: why should they change the way they'd always done things? Why should they take the sensibilities of others into account? They were here first.

That afternoon, as the *Courier* staff ate a hearty and delicious meal, the chatter around the table was mainly about the imminent opening of the new Clifton Suspension Bridge. Some believed the bridge would last for a hundred years or more; others said it looked flimsy, was clearly dangerous, and would soon be taken down. There was a rumour that the Prince of Wales might come to the opening, to cut the ribbon. Everyone, even those whose hearts were republican, were excited about this prospect.

'Did Sir Edward mention the prince at the planning meeting?' Will asked Duncan.

Nelly's ears pricked up at the mention of the MP.

Duncan nodded. 'He told me he doubted the prince would be present, and even if he was, he would not be staying with Sir Edward at Mordaunt Hall.'

'Why not?' asked George Boldwood. 'Fairfield and the prince are great shooting pals. He brags about their friendship all the time.'

Duncan shrugged. 'Perhaps they've had a disagreement.'

'How peculiar,' said Mr Boldwood.

The waitress interrupted the conversation, bringing a tray of pudding bowls. She put one before each diner, and by the time she had done this, the conversation had moved on.

Keen to bring it back to Sir Edward, Nelly turned to Duncan, who was sitting on her right.

'Does the Prince of Wales usually stay at Mordaunt Hall when he's visiting Bristol?' she asked.

'Always,' replied Duncan. 'The royals relish their privacy. They tend not to use hotels. Plus it's easier to accommodate an entourage in a stately home.'

'Have you ever been there?'

'To Mordaunt Hall? Several times. Sir Edward hosts annual dinners there for his political sponsors, to which I have, on occasion, been invited.'

'Is it very grand?'

'It's ostentatious, impractical and cold. Full of ghosts, I shouldn't wonder. Henry VIII and Anne Boleyn stayed there once, I'll have you know, and it has barely been modernised since.'

'My goodness,' said Nelly. She waited a moment, then asked, 'Did you ever meet either of Sir Edward's wives?'

Duncan took a spoonful of dessert.

'My goodness, Nelly, you're full of questions today.'

'I'm a reporter,' said Nelly. 'It's my duty to inquire.'

'I cannot argue with that. To answer, I knew Sir Edward's first wife, Maria, quite well. She was an anxious woman, dreadfully cowed. Not unattractive but twitchy. She used to accompany Sir Edward to civic functions and suchlike. She died a while back.'

'I heard she had a weak heart.'

'That was the party line.'

'What do you mean by that?'

'There were rumours that she'd...'

'What?'

'It's not a topic suitable for the lunch table.'

Nelly lowered her voice to a whisper. 'You're implying she took her own life?'

'I'm not implying anything. The fact is, Fairfield wanted an heir and Maria hadn't provided one.'

'Why was that her fault?'

Duncan shrugged. 'She'd managed to produce children with her first husband.'

'Then perhaps Sir Edward was the problem.'

'Nelly, please!' Duncan made a face as if he had a sour taste in his mouth and shook his head. Then he added, quietly, 'No matter what the root of the Fairfields' inability to produce offspring, Maria bore the brunt of her husband's frustration.'

He ate some more pudding. 'I visited Mordaunt Hall after Maria's death. Her daughter, Sir Edward's stepdaughter, was looking after the household. Madeleine, she was called. Madeleine Avery. I got the impression she was most awfully put upon by Sir Edward.' He paused. 'It was she who first intimated to me that there may be more to her mother's death than met the eye.'

There she was, the 'mousy' stepdaughter Eliza had mentioned.

'What did she intimate, exactly?'

'That her stepfather's mistreatment had contributed to her mother's demise.'

'Mistreatment?'

'She said she'd seen him beat her mother.'

Nelly put down her spoon. 'Dear God, that's terrible.'

'Sir Edward is an old-fashioned aristocrat. Producing a son was important to him.'

'That's no excuse!'

'I'm not excusing Fairfield's behaviour. I'm explaining it.'

'Did you take what Madeleine Avery told you any further?'

'There was nothing to take further, Nelly, and nobody to take it to. All I had was a hint of an accusation dropped by a young woman mired in grief, who clearly hated her stepfather. It was hardly a reliable basis for a story. One cannot conduct an investigation on hearsay.'

Nelly did not give herself time to dwell on this statement.

'What about the second wife? Priscilla?' she asked.

'What about her?'

'Did you meet her?'

'No. The second wedding was a low-key affair; no gentlemen of the press were invited, not even Mr Boldwood.' He frowned as he considered Nelly's question. 'Now that you mention it, I don't recall ever seeing the second wife anywhere. She was a good deal younger than him. A looker by all accounts. Perhaps Sir Edward was worried she'd bolt with some handsome chap closer to her age, and kept her locked up in Mordaunt Hall away from temptation.'

He took a drink of wine.

'Were you aware that Priscilla Fairfield died a few days ago?' Nelly asked.

'I was aware, yes.'

'Do you know how she died?'

'In childbed. The infant too. One of the *Courier*'s directors told Mr Boldwood privately, and asked him to make sure Fairfield's privacy was respected. Nothing was to be printed in the paper.'

Nelly frowned. 'Don't you think it's peculiar, Duncan, that nobody knew Priscilla, nobody ever saw her with her husband and now nothing's being said about her death?'

'People born into money live by a different set of rules from the rest of us.'

'And we're supposed to accept that?'

Duncan was becoming irritated now. 'It's how it always has been, and always will be,' he said. 'Best not to dwell on it.'

That didn't satisfy Nelly.

If it hadn't been for Eliza Morgan, she would never have heard of Priscilla Fairfield. If it weren't for Eliza, the MP's second wife might as well never have existed at all.

23

After the meal, the *Courier* staff dispersed. George Boldwood was taking his wife and daughters to the theatre that evening and wanted to be home in good time. Will had an interview to conduct, Duncan had to finish writing his story, and the older reporters tended not to work Friday afternoons, preferring to go home to sleep off their dinners, or head to a pub, to continue drinking. Jeremiah Bagnet had taken the afternoon off.

This was an ideal opportunity for Nelly to go to Benbow Street, to see if she might talk her way into Eliza's lodgings to search for Priscilla Fairfield's diary.

The rain had eased off, but Nelly took an umbrella with her, carrying it open with the stalk balanced on her shoulder where it afforded her some protection from the wind. She kept stopping, to check that she was not being followed. The streets were busy and it was difficult to be sure, but she didn't catch anyone watching her. If she *was* being followed, she thought, her pursuer would have had a dull time of it so far.

When she knew she was close, she asked at a grocer's shop and was directed to Benbow Street, a shabby road with terraces of small houses. Each had a door and window on the ground floor with two windows, side by side, above.

The street was not well kempt. Washing lines had been strung between the houses, and the smell of sewage was strong enough for Nelly to be quite sure there were not sufficient privies in place for the number of residents.

Nelly soon identified number 35. In a street of scruffy houses, 35 was the worst, and something about its aspect, and the gathering clouds glowering overhead, together with the gull cawing on the chimney pot and a crack in the glass of the narrow window above the door, made Nelly feel apprehensive. She did not have a plan, as such. She hesitated on the other side of the road, trying to avoid being splashed by dirty water in the puddle that was being disturbed by a rough group of small boys.

'You've come all this way,' she told herself. 'You might as well knock on the door.'

This was how it felt to be a real reporter. She had to be strong. She did not have to tell any lies, but she did have to go beyond the usual behaviours with which she felt comfortable.

She reminded herself of what evidence she might find in Priscilla's diary, took a deep breath and stepped forward. She opened the small, wrought-iron gate set into the brick wall, but with a broken latch, and went to the front door. There was no knocker, so she rapped with her knuckles.

A dog yapped inside the building, and a few moments later the door opened with a squeak. A short woman with a pasty face and wispy grey hair stood before Nelly, wiping her hands on the skirt of her dirty apron. The smell of boiling offal assaulted Nelly. She recalled the slops put before her in the asylum, the stink of the slimy grey gruel with fragments of grain and gristle that was served to the inmates, day after day. She had to fight to stop herself from retching.

'Good afternoon,' said Nelly, as the dog, small and hairy, jumped at her skirts. 'I've come about—'

'The room? Of course, you have. You saw the notice in the coffee-shop window, single ladies only to apply? You've come to the right house, my love. Leave the umbrella there, it's bad luck to bring it inside, and come on in, this way, that's it, don't mind Sparky, he's a good boy really, he only wants to say "hello".'

Sparky fastened his front legs around a clump of the fabric of Nelly's outer skirt and began to hump it, an expression of grim determination on his whiskery face. Nelly scowled at the dog, who ignored her.

The woman ushered Nelly into an extremely narrow hallway. 'Up the stairs,' she said. 'It's the small room at the front. It's available right away. Poor woman who used to rent it won't be coming back. You pay me a deposit, and it's yours.'

Nelly opened her mouth to explain that she was from the *Courier*, and wished only to look inside Eliza's room, not to rent it, but the opportunity with which she was presented was too good to discard. What harm would there be in the landlady assuming she was a potential tenant?

'Thank you,' she said. 'I won't be long.'

'Take your time. Only not too long. There's people queuing up for this room. It's in great demand. What else do I need to tell you? There's a privy out the back we share with the neighbours, and you can help yourself to a bucket of fresh water from the standpipe every day. There's not many places as'll offer you that. Not for what I'm charging. For a few pence extra, I'll make you a dinner each evening. Payment is weekly, in advance. That's my terms. I can't say fairer than that.'

'No.'

'Stop that, Sparky. He likes you! He doesn't do that to everyone, you know!'

She picked up the little dog, and Nelly started up the stairs. The banister was rickety and the paint was peeling from the wall on the other side.

There were three doors upstairs, two were closed, the other, the front one, was ajar. There was no carpet, and the floorboards were dirty. Plaster had fallen from the ceiling, revealing the bare laths and the darkness of the attic above.

Nelly shuddered at the thought of the mice, and perhaps rats, who almost certainly lived up there.

She pushed the door before her, and it swung open. She stepped into Eliza Morgan's old room.

The first thing she noticed was the draught. The window frames were ill fitting, and cold air whistled in through the cracked pane. The puddle on the sill indicated that rainwater had found ingress too.

The next feature of the room that caught Nelly's eye was the black mould blooming on the cornicing, the walls and the ceiling. Eliza had clearly made an attempt to clean it, but had not been able to reach beyond a certain point, so there was a disconnect between the upper and lower portions of the walls.

A chair had been pulled up to the small table placed by the window, so that Eliza could make the most of the light while she was sewing. This was evidenced by a sewing basket tipped on its side on the scratched tabletop. The needles, threads and thimbles that the basket had once contained were now spilled on the table and over the floor beneath. The basket was empty.

So were the gin bottles lined up beneath the window. Blankets, a stained pillow and sheets were heaped at the foot end of the mattress.

There was a tiny fireplace, the ashes from its last fire still in the grate.

A matchbox sat on the narrow mantelpiece, beside a comb

and a pot of skin cream. Tucked behind it was a leaflet promoting the spiritualist church in Stokes Croft. Inside was a list of dates when meetings were due to take place led by the 'world-famous medium, Eldora Chauncey'. Nelly checked and the previous day's seance, the one attended by Eveline and Mrs Augur, was listed.

It made Nelly feel sad that Eliza had lived alone in this mean little room, but she didn't have time for reflection: she must concentrate on finding Priscilla's diary. The room being so small, there were few places where it might be hidden.

Nelly looked beneath the bed and found boxes containing clothes and lengths of fabric, crumpled as if they'd been shaken out and then stuffed back in. She emptied the boxes, but found no diary.

She felt beneath the mattress, reaching as far as she could between it and the bed-frame, but her fingers found nothing. She looked beneath the bedding; behind the curtain, to no avail. There was nowhere else in the room to hide anything – unless one of the floorboards was loose. But it was too late to check, for now there were footsteps on the stairs and the pattering of little paws.

Sparky burst into the room. Nelly greeted him, trying to keep him away from her skirt.

The landlady arrived right behind him. 'What do you think?' she asked.

'Are these the belongings of the woman who used to live here?' Nelly asked, indicating the sewing basket and the boxes stored beneath the bed.

'Everything she owned, except the clothes on her back when she died,' said the landlady. 'She didn't die here,' she added hastily, 'so you needn't worry about that. Fell into the docks, she did, poor thing.'

'When did you find out?' Nelly asked.

'A couple of days back. Tuesday evening, I think it was. Late.'

Eliza Morgan's body had still been in the docks on Tuesday evening. Nelly was about to point out that the landlady must be mistaken, but she was still talking.

'I was snoozing in my chair with Sparky when Mr Scarrat, my landlord, tipped up. Said he needed to search my tenant's room. I said to him: "Couldn't this have waited until the morning?" and he said that it couldn't. I said: "What's the rush?" and he said Eliza Morgan had drowned, God bless her soul, and that she had something up here in her room that didn't belong to her.'

'Are you sure this was Tuesday?' Nelly asked, while she tried to remember where she'd heard the name 'Scarrat' before.

'It must've been because the police came the next day and I know that was Wednesday because that's the day I goes charring.'

If this woman's landlord had known Eliza was drowned on Tuesday, either he, or someone close to him, must have witnessed her fall into the docks, or been directly responsible for her death.

Hadn't the women at the docks mentioned Scarrat?

Hadn't they said the watchman was employed by him?

For the first time, Nelly felt real fear. Until now, she had not known for certain that harm had been deliberately done to Eliza. Now, she knew that it must have been.

And if Eliza *was* being followed, as she was convinced she was, by someone who went on to kill her, that person must know that she had been in the Llandoger Trow, talking to Nelly.

The hairs on the back of Nelly's neck stood on end.

'Did your landlord take anything from the room?' she asked. Her voice, for the first time, sounded a little shaky.

'Bits and bobs. It wasn't like there was anything worth more than a few pennies. Gin was Miss Morgan's poison. She spent all her spare money in The Trooper. Only thing she valued was the green velvet shawl, given to her by a grateful customer. She loved that shawl. Wore it everywhere. It meant the world to her. She must have had it with her when she fell in the docks, for Mr Scarrat didn't take it and it's not in the room now.'

The shawl was folded in the drawer of Nelly's desk. When Eliza had rushed from the pub that afternoon, she'd been so consumed with fear that she forgot her most precious possession.

Nelly must have been blind not to realise the terror Eliza had been experiencing.

The landlady was looking at Nelly as if expecting her to say something.

'It must have been terribly distressing for you, discovering your tenant had died in such an awful manner,' Nelly said.

'Oh, it was! Miss Morgan owed me a week's rent. I'm not going to get that now, am I? And I still have to pay *my* rent. I'm too soft-hearted, that's my trouble.'

24

The landlady was still speaking as Nelly followed her down the stairs.

'I'm sorry,' Nelly said. 'I missed what you said.'

'I said, I hope you're not a drinker, Miss—?'

'No,' Nelly said.

She stepped out through the door, desperate now to be away from the house.

'That's settled, then,' said the landlady. 'I'll have the room emptied tomorrow, when my neighbour brings his donkey cart. When will you move in?'

'I'm most grateful for your trouble,' Nelly said, 'but the room isn't what I'm looking for.'

'You won't find anything better for the money in Bristol!'

'Nonetheless it's not for me.'

'Your loss!' the landlady called. Nelly heard her mutter, 'Timewaster!' before she slammed the door.

Nelly shuddered, and took a moment to steady herself.

She knew now that Eliza was right when she said she was being followed, and that her terror had been entirely justified.

This was precisely the kind of street where one might reasonably expect to find footpad robbers, or even the new breed of urban thugs, the garroters. These terrifying criminals strangled their victims from behind before snatching their purses.

If whoever had killed Eliza was watching Nelly, this would be an ideal location to attack her.

But it was still light, and plenty of people were about. Nelly must not allow herself to be cowed. She straightened her back, and turned towards the pub at the far end of the street.

A dirty, painted sign of a soldier in a red jacket with a musket propped against his shoulder hung lopsided outside The Trooper, beside a door so small that Nelly had to stoop to step over the threshold.

Inside, the pub was dark as dusk and the clientele – all men – were wreathed in pipe smoke. A thin lurcher wound its way around the tables, hunting for scraps. As Nelly walked towards the bar, one of the men hawked, and spat on the floor, close to her skirt. His drinking partners cackled with laughter.

'Mind your manners, you dirty sod,' the woman standing behind the bar called. She was small and stout with dyed red hair piled onto the top of her head, a swollen and bruised left eye and a split lip. A large, grizzled man standing close to the bar nursing a pewter jug of ale glowered at the spitter, who raised a hand in apology.

Nelly put her bag on a bar stool, not wanting it to touch the floor, and her umbrella beside it. She felt self-conscious and prim.

The barmaid leaned towards Nelly. 'What can I get for you, miss?'

Several teeth were missing from the front of her mouth, which gave her smile a piratical quality.

The Emerald Shawl

Nelly took a coin from her pocket and put it on the bar. 'I'm looking for information,' she said quietly, pushing the coin towards the woman. The woman glanced at the grizzled man, then at a different man, hunched over a table in a dark corner. He was wearing a cap, and playing Solitaire, turning cards from the deck slowly and deliberately. The knuckles of his right hand were scabbed.

The barmaid slipped the coin into her pocket.

'What is it you want to know?' she asked.

'I'm an acquaintance of Eliza Morgan. I understand she was a regular here.'

The grizzled man put his mug down on the bar, slopping some beer. Nelly wondered if his fists were responsible for the barmaid's bruises.

'Eliza came in here most days,' the barmaid said, 'God rest her soul.'

The air shifted. Nelly sensed the men were listening now, straining for her next words.

'You heard what became of her?' Nelly asked.

'I have and it's a crying shame. She hated water. Makes you wonder, don't it? Do you think she *knew* she was going to die that way?'

Nelly had herself observed how often in life people were brought down by whatever it was they most feared. Perhaps they were subliminally drawn towards the hazards that haunted their nightmares: or perhaps, at some elemental level, all people were conscious of their own fates.

'What was your opinion of Eliza?' Nelly asked the barmaid.

'I liked her. She could be loud when she'd been on the sauce, but she was kindness itself.' She leaned across the bar, closer to Nelly, and added, 'Couldn't handle the gin though. I had to help her back to her lodgings and up them bloody stairs to her room more times than I can remember. It was a bloody miracle she never fell down and broke her neck.'

'But she still managed to sew.'

'Drunk or sober, when Eliza had a needle in her hand, she could sew anything, neat as a pin. She had a real skill. Not like me. I can't put a button on straight.'

The card player began to gather up the cards. The barmaid smiled at the grizzled man, who was tamping tobacco into his pipe. It was a fake smile, thought Nelly. A smile of appeasement. She was certain as she could be that he was violent towards her and that she would do whatever it took to avoid inflaming his temper.

'Who is that man?' she asked.

'My husband. Handsome bugger, isn't he?'

He was not.

'Have a drink,' the barmaid said to Nelly, 'or folk'll be wondering what you're doing here.'

'Does your husband work here too?'

'He works down the docks. Most of the men do.'

The barmaid poured a glass of ale. Nelly took it. The glass was smeared but she drank anyway.

'Did Eliza have any friends that you know of?' Nelly asked next.

'She was mostly alone, but there was one woman. They went to seances together. Not my cup of tea, but each to their own, eh?'

'Do you know who this woman was?'

'She had a funny name. Oh, what was it?'

She picked up a rag and began to wipe the bar, clearing the beer her husband had spilled. The card player was shuffling his deck.

'What was Eliza's friend called?' the barmaid asked her husband. 'That foreign woman?'

'Lucy,' the man answered.

'No, it wasn't.' The barmaid shook her head. 'It wasn't Lucy,' she said to Nelly. 'It'll come to me in a minute.'

Nelly spoke again, very quietly. 'Did Eliza ever mention a certain, upper-class young woman to you? Someone for whom she'd altered a wedding dress, and done some other work?'

At this, there was a marked change in the barmaid's demeanour. She tensed and her breathing became ragged.

Her husband moved to the fireplace, where he could toss his spent matches into the flames, but also where he could better hear anything Nelly said.

The card player began dealing out his cards again, but slowly. He hadn't turned round once.

Something was in the air.

The atmosphere had become sinister.

'You mean Edward Fairfield's wife?' the barmaid asked in a bare whisper.

Nelly nodded.

'Eliza spoke of her, yes.'

With a flick of her eyes, the barmaid indicated a slight man in middle age drinking alone, reading a copy of the *Courier*. 'That man over there is Obadiah Scarrat.'

Nelly's heart jumped. She felt a rush of panic. Despite this, she could not help but turn to look at this man, whose name she kept hearing. His face had a rodent quality: sharp-nosed, weak-chinned and beady-eyed. His lips were childlike, and wet.

This must be the man who had searched Eliza's room and removed Priscilla's diary.

The man for whom the watchman worked.

The man who had known Eliza was dead before her body was found.

She felt a dreadful chill in her blood.

'He owns most of the property round here,' the barmaid continued, her lips barely moving, 'including the house where Eliza lived. Not to mention slum buildings and doss houses around Squires Court in Bedminster.'

It could not be coincidence that Scarrat frequented the same pub as Eliza; that the man he employed had been there, on the dockside, when Eliza died; that he knew of her death.

'He's a pal of Edward Fairfield's,' the barmaid murmured, concentrating on her cleaning, 'and he's here most afternoons. Round about the same time as Eliza used to come in, if you get my drift. And Eliza wasn't one for keeping her mouth shut when she really should have.'

Nelly struggled to suppress her terror. She turned so that her back was to Scarrat before she asked her next question in the quietest of voices. 'So, Mr Scarrat might have heard Eliza talking about matters she shouldn't really have been discussing in public?'

The barmaid nodded.

'Like a diary she'd been given for safekeeping?'

'Like that, yes.'

And, thought Nelly, *if Scarrat heard Eliza talking about the contents of Priscilla Fairfield's diary, wasn't it likely that he'd report straight back to Sir Edward?*

The barmaid hooked a brown tooth over her bottom lip and sucked it for a moment. She glanced towards Mr Scarrat, who was staring at his news-sheet, then she looked at her husband, and finally at the man poring over his cards, before turning back to Nelly.

'I don't know who you are, miss,' she said, in a whisper, 'but you seem a nice woman. You want to be careful, with your questions. You want to be careful who you trust.'

'I will be careful. Thank you. You've been most helpful.' It didn't seem enough. Nelly felt in her pocket, but she had no money left.

'Aren't you going to finish your beer?' the barmaid asked.

'You have it.'

Nelly turned to pick up her bag, and as she did so she bumped into a man who had come up behind her. The stool tipped and the bag fell onto the floor. She looked up into the face of Mr Obadiah Scarrat.

She gave a gasp of shock.

He was standing too close to her, and she was cornered by the bar. She could not move away.

'Oh my,' he said, his breath warm and foul, 'how terrible clumsy of me! It's my destiny, I'm afraid, dearie, to knock things over and to break them. No, no, leave it to me. I shall retrieve your possessions.'

Nelly stared at Scarrat's red ears; the moles on the back of his neck, as he crouched down, making a meal of gathering her things.

When he stood up, he handed Nelly her bag and umbrella. The satchel strap was loose. Nelly slid it into the buckle.

'Thank you,' she said, trying not to let his fingers touch hers.

Scarrat tipped his hat. 'Always a pleasure to help a pretty lady.'

'Ushy!' the barmaid cried. 'Eliza's friend, the foreign woman. Her name was Ushy!'

Her words barely registered with Nelly. She left as fast as she could, her satchel tucked protectively under her arm.

25

Nelly didn't realise she was missing her notebook until much later that evening, when she was back at 12 Orchard Hill.

It had taken her some time to shake off her agitation following the visit to Benbow Street. She had tried to calm herself by reading in her room before dinner. After the meal, she spent a pleasant while talking with Mrs Augur and Eveline, before she went back upstairs to make her notes before bed. She took off her boots, put more coal on the fire, washed her hands and face and settled at the table – only to open her satchel and discover the notebook wasn't in it.

She was almost certain she'd put the notebook in the satchel before she left the office at lunchtime, but so many things had happened since, she couldn't be completely sure. Her original intention had been to return to the office after lunch at Pierre's, so perhaps it was still on her desk.

Although, now she thought of it, she could picture herself sliding it into the bag, on top of her gloves.

Damn, Nelly thought, pacing the length of her bedroom, backwards and forwards.

What if she had put it in her satchel and had lost it somewhere during the afternoon?

If it was at Pierre's, it would be safe. Monsieur Pierre would send one of his staff to drop it off at the *Courier*, if he hadn't already.

If it was in Eliza Morgan's old room, then Nelly was unlikely to get it back, but no harm would come of it. Even if the landlady could read, and could make sense of Nelly's handwriting, she was unlikely to have any idea of the significance of the words contained within the pages. She was the sort, thought Nelly, to tear out the unused paper for future use, and use the rest to light the fire.

The incident in The Trooper was a different matter. The satchel had tipped onto the floor when Scarrat had knocked into her.

It was possible that the notebook had fallen out then, and if it had, then Scarrat might have picked it up. Or maybe he'd deliberately removed it.

Nelly put her hand to her head.

All the *Courier*'s stationery was printed with the newspaper's title, symbol and the strapline: 'The Bristol Courier – keeping the city informed'. And Nelly had written her name and job title on the front, as was customary.

If Scarrat had the notebook, he would have read it. He would know exactly who Nelly was, that she had interviewed Eliza Morgan, and that she was interested in the marriage of Priscilla and Edward Fairfield. It wouldn't be a huge leap for him to establish why she was doing this.

If Scarrat knew the contents of Nelly's notebook, then Edward Fairfield would soon know them too.

The terror that Nelly had briefly experienced in the pub was back; this time with a vengeance.

* * *

After all she'd done during the day, Nelly should have slept like a baby that night, but she was worried about her notebook and she was worried about Harriet, as she always was.

She knew that even if those who had harmed Eliza hadn't known of Nelly's involvement in the story before, they would now. She knew they were prepared to kill. She knew she was vulnerable.

But as well as anxiety, there was a buzz in her veins. She could not remember the last time she felt so alive nor recall when she last felt so like herself – like the young girl who had boundless energy and enthusiasm and curiosity. The girl who couldn't bear to be repressed; the girl whose best friend was a gentle boy called Sidney Hayden. She had thought her time in the asylum had changed her fundamentally, the way an egg was changed when it was boiled in water – changed in a way that could not be reversed. But here she was, lying in bed, her mind racing in the way it used to race when she was fourteen and was planning to spend the next day with Sidney, in the forest, watching the birds.

At the beginning of the week, Nelly had been working on the women's page: recipes and knitting patterns and household tips. Now she had three investigations on the go, two of them involving potential murders, and one that was a case of either mistaken identity or body-snatching.

Round Nelly's thoughts went in circles. She felt as if she was missing something; something was there, in plain sight, but she was not seeing it.

Eventually her eyes grew heavy, and she did sleep. It wasn't Eliza Morgan who disturbed her dreams, nor Priscilla Fairfield, nor even fear of what might happen tomorrow, when Will and

Nelly went to Keynsham to find the women who had taken Gerty's body.

No, it was Harriet who tiptoed into Nelly's bedroom: the darling child, quite alone. Harriet, small, precious and utterly abandoned who haunted Nelly, who crept into the bed beside her as she slept and wrapped her cold little arms around Nelly's neck. Her hands were icy but her breath was warm.

She smelled of violets, and she whispered:

'Help me, Mama! Help me!'

26

SATURDAY, 29 OCTOBER

After her visit to Eliza Morgan's lodgings, Nelly appreciated anew the house where she lived, everything cleaned to a shine by cheerful Ida, and smelling of lemon and vinegar. She was grateful for the sturdy front door, that was kept securely locked. She delighted in the pile of clean laundry returned to her room, and for the collection of the soiled clothes she had worn during the week. She counted her blessings when it came to Sarah's talent with food and her unfailing ability to produce something warm and delicious at every mealtime. She adored sweet Flossy, enjoyed the company of Eveline and Mrs Augur, and was even glad of the two elderly misses who lived on the first floor; their chatter and laughter was always pleasant to hear. Really, Nelly knew, she was most fortunate.

If it hadn't been for her aunt Angel's intervention, she would still be in the ward at Holywell Asylum, eating gruel, wearing rags, longing for the days to end; dreading the endless nights.

She had everything she could ever want or need.

Except her daughter.

* * *

Nelly's concern for Harriet's well-being was made more pressing by the fact that the child had looked unwell when Nelly last saw her. The dream had not helped. Nelly was certain that the scent of violets lingered in her room; a harbinger of trouble, or even death. Perhaps Ida was using some new soap to clean; perhaps that accounted for the oversweet odour.

It was fortunate that Nelly was going to Keynsham that morning; the trip would distract her from her maternal concerns. She was glad that Will would be accompanying her so that she would not be alone with her thoughts. And also, she could not see how any danger could befall her while she was with Will and Cuddy, and away from Bristol, the city of secrets.

It was a cold morning, and Sarah had prepared a breakfast of warm milk and honey, porridge with apple sauce, and bread and jam. This Nelly ate at the kitchen table. Ida was busy completing all her chores as quickly as she could, for she had Saturday afternoons free to spend with her own family and wanted to be ready to go as soon as she could.

When she had finished eating, it being the kind of day when there would be no rain, Nelly put on her cloak and gloves and headed through a shiny, frost-covered city to the *Courier* building.

Neither Mr Boldwood nor Mr Bagnet worked on Saturdays as a rule, and there was no editorial conference, so Nelly was free to go about her business without interference.

First, she checked to see if the missing notebook was on her desk.

It was not.

She searched the rest of the office quickly, but there was no sign of it, so she took a new one from the store cupboard and put that in her satchel.

She knew the likeliest place for the notebook to have been lost was in The Trooper and had to assume Scarrat had it, as well as Eliza Morgan's diary, and that he would take both items to Sir Edward Fairfield.

The very thought made her fearful, for now her role would be obvious, and she would be in Fairfield's sights. At the same time, she was curious to see what would happen next. The move was his to make.

For now, she could do nothing about it. She must concentrate on the matter in hand: finding out what had become of Gerty Skinner's body.

At the back of the *Courier* building, Cuddy was waiting for her, with the larger of the horses harnessed, blowing clouds of warm air through his nostrils. Will was standing to one side, in his brown felt suit, looking a little awkward and clutching his briefcase.

'Do you have the photograph of Gerty?' Nelly asked, and Will nodded, yes.

Nelly said hello to the horse and stroked his cheek, before she climbed up into the cab; the compartment rocking wildly on its wheels as she did so, and Will followed.

Cuddy then took up his position as driver. 'Ready, back there?' he asked.

'We're ready!' Nelly answered.

Cuddy flicked the reins and they set off.

* * *

They travelled through the outskirts of Bristol at a steady pace, passed through a couple of coal-mining villages, and once they were out in the countryside, Cuddy stopped at a ford so that the horse could rest and have a drink. Nelly and Will climbed down out of the carriage to stretch their legs. Cuddy sat on a wall, smoked his clay pipe and chatted with a chap-book seller who was sitting on the bank by the remains of a small fire, while his wife washed their breakfast plates and pans in the stream, her hands and forearms mottled purple with cold.

Nelly enjoyed the feeling of the sun upon her face and the quietness of the immediate surroundings, although clangings and clankings from the industrial areas carried on the air and a train went by on the railway, puffing out clouds of steam. From this elevated distance, she could see the yellow-grey smog hanging over the city of Bristol, wreathing it like a scarf. By contrast, a perfect white mist shadowed the curves of the river. Here, amongst the hills and hedges, the frost was thicker; everywhere looked white, as if the snow had come. Nelly, wrapped in her cloak like a monk, felt a longing for the city. Everything she loved was in that place; everything that had ever caused her pain outside it.

But now it was tainted. Danger lay within and Nelly could no longer assume she was safe there.

The chap-book seller's wife laid the tin plates on the hedge to dry in the sun, and then she rubbed her hands with a scrap of towel to get the blood back into her fingers. They all stood together and passed the time.

The salesman and his wife had come from Birmingham. They'd been walking for six days, selling everything from songsheets to storybooks. The woman told Nelly they had slept under a hedge last night, huddled together with their blankets wrapped around them, trying to keep warm.

When they woke, the blanket was frosted.

'It sounds romantic,' the woman said, 'but it ain't. When the baby comes—'

'You're having a baby?'

'When it comes, I shall stay in the workhouse infirmary a while.'

'What's it like in there?' Nelly asked.

''Tain't so bad. At least it's warm and you get a bed and summat to eat.'

Cuddy tapped what tobacco was left from the bowl of his pipe and hitched at his braces.

'We'd best make a move,' he said. 'Where is it in Keynsham we want to be?'

'Myrtle Gardens,' said Nelly.

'Myrtle Gardens it is, then.'

* * *

Back in the carriage, Nelly's nerves began to get the better of her.

'What should we say to these women,' she asked Will, 'when the plain truth is, we have come to reclaim the body they believe is their sister's? It is an awful situation.'

'All we can do is be honest with them. Show them the photograph, be sympathetic to their predicament, but tell them Gerty must be returned to her family.'

'What if they refuse to listen to us?'

'Most people go through life trying to do the right thing,' said Will. 'It's clear that what happened here was a genuine mistake. Nobody is at fault; nobody is accusing anyone of anything. This can easily be put right.' He pushed his glasses up his nose. 'I'm not saying the next hour or so will be easy, but I'm sure everything will end up as it should. And the same logic applies here as it did earlier, with the Skinners. Because the body these two women have is not their sister's, it means she might still be alive and well.'

Nelly looked at Will's face. His hair was fair, his skin freckled, his eyes, behind the lenses of his glasses, a pale shade of green. He was a gentle man; Nelly had never seen him lose his temper, never heard him attack another with words. And he'd made a life for himself from nothing. He'd taken help, where it was offered, but repaid every kindness done to him a dozen-fold.

'I am glad we are friends,' she said to him now.

He pushed up his glasses and smiled. 'Likewise.' Then he asked, 'Is something the matter?'

'No. Why?'

'You saying what you said. It's unlike you.'

That was the trouble with people. You let them into your heart, even the smallest fraction, and they always wanted to push it further.

* * *

The town of Keynsham was mostly built on a hill overlooking the river. It boasted some fine houses and a historic church, as well as its own workhouse. Nelly sat forward in the cab, to get the best view of the place as they entered its streets. Cuddy kept the horse moving, and soon enough they found Myrtle Gardens, a fine road of terraced villas, recently constructed, each with two bay windows, one above the other, at its front.

Cuddy slowed the horse as they walked down the street. Each individual hoof made a clopping sound. They passed a hansom pulled by an elegant chestnut coming the other way, and Cuddy saluted the driver.

A servant woman was sprinkling salt on the frozen path outside one of the houses, children were sliding on an icy patch outside another, and pianoforte music issued from somewhere within a third. The gardens at the fronts of the villas were neat and tidy, some planted with shrubs and flowers that had died back now summer was over, others paved over. Curtains were swagged at windows, through which plants and vases and lamps could be seen. Nelly imagined that these homes would have all the modern conveniences: clean water on tap and gas lighting. It was a smart neighbourhood.

A little dog barked at the horse from behind a window, its front paws on the sill.

A small boy in a scarf and mittens chased a ball along the pavement.

They had reached the end of the street, where it joined with another, wider avenue at right angles to it.

Cuddy turned and leaned back towards Nelly.

'What number did you say?' he asked.

'One hundred and thirty-two.'

'I can't find it.'

'We'll get out,' said Will. 'It'll be easier for us to find the right number on foot.'

Nelly gathered her skirts, and her bag, and Cuddy helped her step down from the cab. Will jumped down after.

Cuddy kept the horse still while Nelly went to the last house on the right side of the street, Will to the last on the left.

'Ninety-four,' Nelly called.

'Ninety-three,' Will called back.

Nelly turned a circle, a feeling of dread growing inside her.

A nursemaid, holding the hand of a little girl, was walking towards them.

'Could you help us?' Nelly asked. 'We're trying to locate number 132 Myrtle Gardens.'

The nursemaid smiled kindly. 'I can't help you there, I'm afraid,' she said. 'This is the end of the road. There is no 132. It does not exist.'

27

Cuddy, Will and Nelly stopped to eat at a tavern, to give the horse a break. After that, it was a straight journey back to Bristol. On the outskirts of the city, they saw the peddler and his wife again, he stooped beneath a huge bundle, she with a lesser one, but still struggling. How in the world, thought Nelly, would she manage when she had a baby to carry too?

By the time they reached the city, the sun was sinking low in the sky, and it was too late for anything more to be done. The pubs were busy, people spilling out onto the streets, and every so often the smell of food cooking and the bitter, beautiful aroma of chocolate from the Fry's factory in Nelson Street mingled with the odours of the river and the tanneries.

'Shall we have dinner together?' Will asked Nelly as the carriage approached Old Market. 'My treat. I know a good restaurant where—'

'It's a kind offer, but no, thank you,' said Nelly. 'I want to get back to my room before it's dark.'

She tried not to dwell on the disappointment in his eyes prompted by her rejection. If only she were the sort of woman who could accept well-meant affection lightly; the kind for whom friendships came easily and without complications. But she was not, and never would be of that ilk.

She herself was feeling a combination of frustration, despondency, and curiosity. At the start of the day, she'd hoped the mystery of the disappearance of Gerty Skinner's body would have been resolved by the end of it; it was not.

The Skinners were going to be devastated when they discovered that their daughter's body had been stolen after all – it must have been taken deliberately, for if its removal had been accidental, why give a false address?

Will and Nelly had gone round in circles during the journey back to Bristol, trying to make sense of the situation. The most plausible explanation was that the two women who had fraudulently claimed Gerty's remains were body-snatchers. Neither Will nor Nelly had heard of female body-snatchers before, but, as Will pointed out, opportunities were opening up for women in many previously male-only preserves. The thieves, whoever they were, risked being hung if they were caught, so a great reward must be at stake.

The police would have to be involved, but theirs would be a hopeless task, for by now, Gerty Skinner's remains could be anywhere in the country.

Her body was probably already being dissected by medical students. How they would break that news to Gerty's parents, Nelly couldn't imagine.

She knew it would destroy them.

* * *

Back at the stable yard behind the print hall, Nelly and Will thanked Cuddy for his trouble and made a fuss of the hard-working horse. The animal shook his huge head as he was returned to his stable, fresh hay hanging at the door, his companion welcoming him back with a series of noisy whinnies.

Nelly and Will walked around to the front of the building in silence. They parted at the entrance, and said their goodbyes, brief and uncomfortable, and Will wandered alone into the darkening evening. As he turned a corner and disappeared, Nelly almost called after him; she was hungry and there was no good reason not to dine with him that evening, as he had suggested.

But she did not turn around, and she did not call his name.

They had discussed everything they needed to discuss in the back of the cab. They would not trouble Mr and Mrs Skinner tomorrow, it being a Sunday, but would visit them on Monday, to break the awful news. There was nothing else they needed to say to one another.

Nelly knew she was better off alone.

Always.

* * *

Walking back up to Orchard Hill that evening, with the darkness falling around her, Nelly felt uncommonly uneasy. Bristol was always busy on a Saturday night, but that evening the revellers and drinkers seemed rowdier than usual. Twice she was jostled by groups of young men; once she was almost pushed into the path of a carriage. Looking back over her shoulder, she saw a man in a black overcoat and flat cap watching her. The man had broad shoulders and a face that looked as if it had been hit with a shovel. His nose had been broken at some time, and healed lopsidedly. Nelly caught sight of him only briefly, but some visceral instinct told her he was the Solitaire man from The Trooper.

When she looked again, to check, the man had disappeared from view.

After that, she kept close to the shadowed sides of the buildings, where she would be less visible; the fact that she was alone less obvious.

Be careful, the barmaid in The Trooper had said.

Trust nobody, she'd said. Or words to that effect.

When, at last, Nelly opened the door to 12 Orchard Hill, she found Mrs Augur and Eveline in the hallway, putting on their capes and hats, with the energy of people who were looking forward to an interesting and enjoyable evening.

'There's a seance tonight,' Eveline said. 'Why don't you come with us?'

Nelly's instinct, as always, was to decline the invitation.

'I am tired,' she said. 'I've been out all day on a wild goose chase. And I'm hungry.'

'We'll have supper later,' Eveline said. 'Come with us, Nelly! I promise you'll find it enthralling!'

Nelly was already dressed for the outdoors. The alternative was another evening spent alone, in her room. With nothing to distract her, Nelly knew well that her imagination would drive her out of her mind with anxiety; the spectre of the watchman would loom disproportionately large. And Eveline was right: Nelly *was* curious to see what all the fuss was about. Thoughts of the spirit that might be Eliza trapped in the darkness had been playing on her mind for days.

'If you're sure I won't be intruding...' she said.

'You won't be!' cried Mrs Augur cheerfully. 'The more the merrier, eh, Eveline?'

'If a seance can be described as merry!'

With that, each of the Augurs slid a solid arm under one of Nelly's and the three of them set off out into the evening.

28

The seance was held in the spiritualist church at the Stokes Croft end of the Gloucester Road. A crowd was queuing outside when Nelly, Eveline and Mrs Augur arrived. There was such a buzz of excitement about the people – a mix of men and women, many of them wearing mourning clothes – that Nelly found herself invigorated. She heard snatches of conversations; people recalling the spirits of departed souls who had made themselves known at previous meetings, and discussing who they hoped would put in an appearance tonight. Some were clutching photographs, or items of clothing: a man's jacket; a pair of gloves; a doll.

Posters of the medium, Eldora Chauncey, had been plastered over the walls of the buildings at that end of the road. Her image depicted an older woman with a severe face and hair scraped back into an old-fashioned bonnet. The posters claimed that Mrs Chauncey was skilled at 'levitation, table-turning, and automatic writing'.

'What is automatic writing?' Nelly asked Eveline.

'You don't know? Why, Nelly, it's where the spirit directs the hand of the medium. It's quite thrilling to observe!'

'Mrs Chauncey is *very* good at it,' said the woman in front of them. 'Is this your first time here?' she asked Nelly.

'Yes.'

'Nelly is our lodger,' said Mrs Augur. 'She writes for the *Courier* as "Helen Brooks".'

'Do you intend to report on this evening's events?'

'Definitely not,' said Nelly.

They had reached the front of the queue. A woman with frizzy brown hair took their money.

'I couldn't help overhearing your conversation,' she said. She had a Northern European accent. 'You're Helen Brooks, from the *Courier*?'

'I am.'

'How good of you to join us. Please, go on in. I hope you enjoy the evening.'

'That's Ursula,' Mrs Augur said in a stage whisper as they passed into the church. 'Mrs Chauncey's assistant.'

Nelly and the Augurs hung up their outer garments in the cloakroom before proceeding into the main hall. Gas lamps illuminated the nave, and a raised stage on which were a table, covered with a dark green and gold fringed cloth, and two chairs, facing each other, side on to the audience. A candelabrum with four arms was in the centre of the table and other candles had been placed in a semicircle around it. Drapes tied back with gold ropes framed the stage. Nelly was dubious about the movement, but nobody could deny the possibility that spiritual awareness might exist after physical death; how could it be proven otherwise? And if it were so, then wasn't it reasonable to assume that Eliza might make herself known at this meeting? Indeed, that she might have been present at the previous one?

The Emerald Shawl

They took their seats. On each chair was a copy of the same leaflet Nelly had found in Eliza Morgan's room. This felt like a portent.

At the front of the hall, Ursula came to sit at the pianoforte, and began to play a mournful tune.

Nelly fingered the locket at her throat and thought of Harriet.

Once the audience was in, and settled, the lights were dimmed. The chattering stopped, and in its place were nervous whispers.

The music finished with a dramatic crescendo followed by a long, lingering chord and all the remaining lights went out at once. There was the odd, anxious giggle. Nelly felt an icy draught whisper by her neck. Eveline, beside her, grabbed her hand. For a moment everything was in complete blackness, then the candles on the table were illuminated as if by magic, and there, in the centre of the stage, wearing a black dress with white lace cuffs and collar, was a woman. Her skin was white as porcelain, her lips were blood red, and her eyes were shadowed, so that they seemed barely human.

'Good evening,' the woman said, holding out both arms, the palms of her hands turned upwards, 'and welcome to our seance. I am Eldora Chauncey, your spirit medium.'

Her voice was high-pitched, even birdlike, and although she appeared softly spoken, Nelly noticed that even those members of the audience seated at the back of the church heard her clearly.

'We are all here tonight for the same reason,' said Mrs Chauncey. 'You have lost someone you love, and you wish to find them again; to reconnect. Is that so?'

A murmur of assent rippled through the audience.

'Did you remember to bring an item that was important to the deceased?'

A good many people answered, 'I did.'

Nelly wished she had the green velvet shawl with her, for wouldn't that be irresistible to Eliza Morgan's spirit, if Eliza's spirit was present?

'You dear souls,' Mrs Chauncey said. 'Be assured, the ones you love are not lost, they have simply moved to a different place as if they had walked out of one room, and into another. All we have to do is open the connecting door, remove the barrier between our world and the next, and you shall be reunited.'

She spread her arms wide, and said, 'I am here to open that door!'

There was a smatter of applause, which Mrs Chauncey hushed.

'We are close to the night of All Hallows,' she continued, 'when the fabric between the two worlds is at its thinnest. I feel the spirits amongst us. Do you feel them too? Do you feel a drop in temperature? A vibration? Are you aware of an unfamiliar smell? All these are signs that the dead are present.'

A heartbeat's pause elapsed, then she asked, 'Who would like to begin?'

A forest of hands shot up. Mrs Chauncey's face moved slowly from left to right, acknowledging every one of them. 'I will strive to help as many of you as I can.' She pointed towards a woman in the second row. 'You, dear,' she said. 'We'll start with you. Come forward. Take my hand. Don't be afraid. Never be afraid of the dead. They mean you no harm.'

* * *

The next two hours passed quickly.

Each time a spirit voice spoke to Mrs Chauncey, Nelly found herself listening intently, *willing* it to be Eliza.

She knew at an intellectual level that the event was probably staged, but her response was entirely emotional. The theatrics were genuinely frightening; every now and then Eveline grabbed Nelly's arm crying, 'I can't look! Tell me when this part is over!'

The table flipped, and at one point the cloth took off of its own accord and flew into the vaulted ceiling of the church, causing the audience to gasp and scream. It disappeared into the dark recesses, and a substitute had to be found. Each time there was any kind of supernatural violence, Mrs Chauncey grasped the candelabrum, as if she were struggling to contain the forces she was summoning, to prevent it from tipping and setting the place on fire.

The highlight of the evening was when Mrs Chauncey levitated. Nelly was so immersed in the seance she was quite prepared to believe it was the hands of unseen spirits raising the medium, and not some trickery involving invisible wires. Her only disappointment was that none of the ethereal visitors who made themselves known that evening could possibly have been Eliza.

At last, Mrs Chauncey, hair all come loose now, the neck of her dress torn, and her eyes heavy with tiredness, said a prayer, thanked the audience and left the stage, leaning on her assistant.

The lights went up and the audience applauded for a good five minutes, before exploding into a barrage of excited chatter. Tea was served from a large pot on a trestle table at the back of the hall, and there were plates of cut white and brown bread with butter, and some little cakes.

Nelly helped herself to food while Eveline and Mrs Augur socialised, asking those who had been chosen to go onto the stage to describe the experience.

It was as she was pouring her second cup of tea that Nelly felt a tap on her shoulder. Turning, she saw Mrs Chauncey's assistant: Ursula.

'Good evening,' Ursula said. Her accent reminded Nelly of the German woman who used to teach pianoforte to her and her sisters.

'Eldora asked me to give something to you.'

She passed a scrap of paper to Nelly.

The message was brief.

Beware the Watchman.

29

Nelly read the message several times, staring at the paper to mask her shock. The other people present laughed and gossiped and clinked their cups into their saucers and she stood still, feeling as if the world were spinning too fast. If she was not careful, Nelly feared she might fall off and tumble helplessly into the void.

When she managed, at last, a coherent thought, it was that she must speak to Mrs Chauncey. Ursula had disappeared. The woman serving the refreshments told her to look in the dressing room. Nelly hurried through the hall and into a dark passageway at the side of the stage. At its end, a door was open to the outside. As she reached it, Nelly saw a carriage disappear into the darkness of the night.

'Who is in that carriage?' she asked the man bringing in the advertising boards.

'Mrs Chauncey and her sidekick,' he replied. 'You just missed 'em.'

* * *

When Nelly and the Augurs arrived back at the Kingsdown house, they went into the dining room, where Sarah had left a spread for them for supper. Nelly accepted a glass of cider, and she sat with the older woman, and the younger one, and they ate pickles and cold plates as they talked about what they had witnessed that evening, and also the ghost of the hanged woman, who was supposed to haunt that very house. As they were doing this, they heard a loud bump from one of the first-floor rooms above them, and of course it was only Miss Sylvester or Miss Norton dropping a book or something of that kind, but it made the three of them jump, and afterwards, although Eveline and Mrs Augur giggled about it, Nelly, with the piece of paper in her pocket, felt quite uncomfortable.

'We really ought to ask Mrs Chauncey to come here and make contact with our own restless spirit,' said Mrs Augur.

'No, Mother!' Eveline said in a strict tone of voice. 'That might lead to goodness knows what upset.'

Nelly agreed strongly with Eveline.

She did not enjoy going up the two flights of stairs to her room alone that evening. She had to remind herself sternly that everything she'd witnessed at the seance could be explained logically. Ghosts were not real. Mediums, like fortune tellers, and soothsayers, were skilled in reading people's expressions and the language of their hands and bodies. They worked out what it was they wanted to hear, and reflected their hearts' desires back to them. Believers, desperate for validation, were happy to accept what they were told.

Nelly knew that Eliza Morgan was dead. It was unlikely that Eliza had sent a message to Nelly from the spirit world. Nelly couldn't work out how Eldora Chauncey had known that Nelly knew Eliza, or how she knew about the watchman, but somehow, she had.

Unless the note really was from Eliza.

The piece of paper with Eliza's words purportedly written upon it stirred a visceral fear, deep within Nelly's soul. She sensed, now, that whatever malice had brought about Eliza's death was closer to her. She was more afraid than she had ever been before.

It felt as if forces she did not understand were lining up against her, like crows on a fence.

* * *

Nelly was cold in bed that night. She kept sensing movement in the room. Eventually, she realised the window had been left open a fraction.

She was reluctant to get out of bed to close the window – the childhood fear of a monster hiding beneath the bed niggling at her conscious mind, only it wasn't a monster, but the ghost of the drowned woman. She could picture Eliza's body, that halo of webbed hair around her pale face, those thin arms with the bony fingers, waiting to grab her ankle the minute she put a foot out from under the covers.

In the end, Nelly relit the lamp that she'd brought up from downstairs, and she put her leg over the side of the bed tentatively – it was fine, see! Nothing there – and she walked across the room and shut the window.

A tiny light flared below. Someone was standing on the corner, beside the privet hedge that surrounded number 12's small courtyard. The person had lit a match, to light a pipe. As Nelly looked down, the person, a man, looked up.

She closed the curtains at once, stepped back against the bedroom wall, and stood quite still, holding her breath, hoping that her heart would calm. Was it the watchman who stood outside the house? The very man she had been warned to beware?

Nelly could not be sure, but even the familiar room no longer felt like a sanctuary. If it was him, it meant he knew where she lived; where she slept. Nowhere was safe for Nelly any longer.

Nowhere.

After a few moments, she moved, taking care to keep to the other side of the lamp so she would not cast shadows visible to anyone watching from outside.

Nelly was shivering now with cold.

She poked the coals in the fireplace, but there was little residual heat left. She wrapped a blanket around her shoulders, got back into bed and propped herself up on the pillows with the bedclothes pulled up high. She leaned on the side closest to the lamp, opened the copy of the novel she had borrowed from Eveline, *The Small House at Allington,* and tried to concentrate on the story, and not on the brief letter signed *Eliza M.* that lay on the table.

She kept turning the pages, straining her eyes to read, until sleep at last took hold of her and when it came, she gave in to it gratefully; the flame at the wick of the lamp still burning, the open book on the pillow beside her and she not knowing if the man outside was the watchman, or merely a stranger pausing to smoke his tobacco.

30

SUNDAY 30 OCTOBER

Every Sunday morning Nelly went to St Andrew's, the church closest to Redfield House school. Her intention was to catch a glimpse of Harriet, and to be close to her for the duration of the service. These Sunday expeditions were the nadirs of Nelly's week, and also the zeniths. It hurt to be so close to Harriet, yet at the same time, so distant. But it was reassuring to see that, mostly, she appeared, if not happy, then not actively miserable. Sometimes, Nelly observed her daughter whispering with her friends, or she put a hand over her mouth to hide her smile, and it was for these precious moments that Nelly lived.

That morning, she drank a cup of coffee, ate some bread and butter, conversed briefly with Miss Norton and Miss Sylvester, then made her excuses and left.

Outside the house, she looked left and right, but nobody was about; there was no smell of pipe smoke; no man with a broken nose watching her.

The quiet of the Sunday morning city was interrupted by the peal of church bells ringing out from different parishes. It was another bitterly cold day, though the wind that had kept Nelly awake in the night had also kept the frost away. Nelly was huddled in her cloak, the paving stones beneath her boots hard as iron; the filth on the streets turned to black ice. The sky above glowered and the sound of the wind whistling around the chimney pots and roof tiles was threatening too. She saw a robin perched amongst the empty twigs of a garden bush, saw how it had puffed itself up, to try to keep warm, and how the wind ruffled its tiny feathers, and she felt pity for all people and creatures obliged to be out in this punishing temperature.

* * *

The girls of Redfield House were filing through the churchyard when Nelly arrived. She stood beneath the boughs of the yew tree, wrapped in her cloak, the wind flapping the fabric about her legs, and watched. Some of the pupils were taller than others, but, that aside, they looked almost identical in their oxblood-coloured cloaks, faces and hair hidden by the hoods. Today, the girls seemed subdued, their heads held low. Nelly could not pick out Harriet. She felt the beginnings of panic. Was Harriet not there?

She counted the girls: there should be thirty-six. Today, she counted thirty-three, then thirty-four, and then thirty-three again.

So at least two were missing.

She counted again: thirty-four.

You're too tired to think, she told herself, but it was not merely tiredness, her nerves were stretched tight as tenterhooks, so desperate was she to see Harriet.

Where was she?

The other members of the congregation, waiting amongst the gravestones, stared at the Redfield House girls with undisguised curiosity as they entered the church. There was something compelling about the daughters of the middle classes being sent to reform school – almost as compelling as those committed to the asylum.

Nelly was feeling edgy and anxious, almost beside herself with worry.

She counted again: thirty-four. She'd had thirty-four three times now. Two pupils were definitely missing.

When the children had all filed through the porch into the church, Nelly followed. She took a space at the end of a pew, her eyes fixed on the girls lined up ahead of her. As they lowered their hoods, Nelly's heart lifted. The child at the far end of the second row was the right size to be Harriet, and her hair was the right colour, parted in the middle, and tightly plaited.

At nine o'clock, the church door was pushed shut with a dreadful groan.

The girl at the end of the pew turned to watch the vicar's progress up the aisle, and Nelly saw that she wasn't Harriet after all.

Her heart sank. If Harriet wasn't here, then where was she?

The vicar walked to the front and greeted the congregation. The service began. Nelly stood up, sat down and knelt in the appropriate places, but her heart was not in it.

They had come to the last hymn, 'Now Thank We All Our God', when the child who resembled Harriet began to sway on her feet, and then collapsed. A small bundle, wrapped in a dark red cloak, she lay crumpled on the floor and the girl beside her was torn between the urge to kneel down to care for her friend and being afraid of being scolded for doing so.

Nelly was with the child in an instant, helping her up. She took her to the back of the church. The girl was shivering, but her skin was hot to the touch.

'I'm going to be sick,' she said.

'It's all right,' Nelly replied. 'I'll look after you. Let's try and get you outside.'

From the corner of Nelly's eye, she could see a large woman in a black dress making her way past the girls who were sitting on that pew – the same woman from Redfield House who had challenged Nelly earlier in the week.

The child Nelly was holding retched, threw up a pitiful amount of watery vomit and began to cry.

Nelly helped her out via the church door. The big woman lumbered down the aisle after them. The rest of the congregation continued to sing, but eyes were swivelling.

Nelly and the child went out into the cold.

Amongst the gravestones, the girl was sick again. Nelly took her in her arms. Behind them, the Redfield House staff member huffed as she approached.

The child clung to Nelly. 'I don't want to go back to school. Please don't make me go back!'

'Sybille Montgomery, what are you doing?' exclaimed the big woman, looming now over Nelly and the girl.

'I'm sick, Mrs Garrow,' said the child.

'She has a burning fever.'

'For goodness' sake,' Mrs Garrow said. 'Not another one!' She leaned over, grabbed the girl's chin between her thumb and forefinger and tilted her head back. Her throat and chin were covered in an ugly rash.

'Scarlet fever,' the woman muttered. She reached for the child's hand. 'Come, Sybille. We must get you to the hospital.'

Nelly knew she shouldn't ask. She *knew* she shouldn't, because she was jeopardising Harriet's future at the school and her own future contact with her daughter by doing so – but she had to know. 'Is Harriet Brooks one of those afflicted?'

Mrs Garrow tensed but it was the expression on the girl's face that confirmed what Nelly feared.

'Yes,' the girl murmured.

Mrs Garrow peered closely at Nelly. 'You're the woman who loiters outside the school gates, aren't you?'

'I do not loiter...'

'You've been warned to stay away, yet you persist in harassing pupils at the church.'

'I harassed nobody. I helped this child.'

'There's something amiss about you.'

'I mean no harm to anyone,' Nelly said.

Mrs Garrow pointed her finger at Nelly. 'Stay away,' she said. 'Stay away from the school, from the church, from our pupils. If I see you again, near any of the children, I'll have you arrested and thrown into gaol. Do I make myself clear?'

Nelly nodded.

Reluctantly she moved away from the ailing Sybille.

'Pray God you are soon recovered,' she said. And then she left.

31

MONDAY, 31 OCTOBER

All Hallows' Eve

Monday dawned dark and gloomy, heavy grey clouds looming above Bristol.

Outside 12 Orchard Hill, Nelly saw a playing card, face down on the pavement beside the yew hedge. She let it lie.

All her thoughts were of Harriet.

On the way to work, she was startled by urchins who jumped out from behind a wall then ran down the street screaming like banshees.

Three men walked along Park Row, hands in prayer, hoods covering their faces, murmuring Latin incantations. Nelly could not tell if they were real monks, or Hallowe'en pranksters. Older children pushed an effigy of Satan, complete with a rusty scythe and a skull-mask, in a wheelbarrow.

'Penny for the devil,' they cried, holding out their palms towards Nelly. She shook her head and pulled her cloak tighter.

She kept her eyes low. The clouds were reflected in puddles.

She knew how dangerous scarlet fever could be, especially for children.

It did not always kill, but often it did. It had taken over two hundred lives in Bristol during the last outbreak, and many of those who survived the initial onslaught were left weakened, subsequently struck down by other illnesses. The thought of Harriet enduring the pain and sickness alone in some miserable hospital ward was dreadful. Knowing that she could die, unbearable.

* * *

Nelly was present in body, but barely in spirit when she joined the rest of the *Courier*'s editorial team for the morning conference.

It was a busy meeting, with updates on the imminent completion of work on the Clifton Suspension Bridge, plans for its opening; progress reports on the commemorative supplement and two major criminal cases.

Will updated the team on the events of the trip he and Nelly had made to Keynsham. He was generous in his account, giving Nelly full credit for progressing the story.

Nelly struggled to concentrate as Will told his colleagues he'd been to Bridewell station to make a report to the police, and that an investigation into the theft of Gerty Skinner's corpse would be launched. The medical schools would be asked to look out for a body matching the description of Gerty's being offered for sale. The more established reporters were sceptical.

They said the medical schools would turn a blind eye. Trainee surgeons were so short of dead people on whom to practise that huge sums of money – in excess of £300 – were being paid for bodies in good condition with no signs of decomposition. The only legal source of relatively undamaged human remains were the prisons, but fewer convicts were being hung these days, and women were rarely given death sentences, which meant the supply of female bodies came nowhere near to meeting the demand. Without corpses, medicine could not progress. The reporters talked about this in matter-of-fact voices, as if they were discussing an illicit trade in gin or diamonds. Meanwhile Nelly wondered how she might find out about Harriet's condition. Could she ask Maud to enquire on her behalf?

The older reporters had heard and written so much about grave-robbing and its associated crimes that they had become inured to the horror of what they were saying and indeed discussed it with the blackest humour until George Boldwood noticed the pallor of Nelly's face, unaware it had little to do with the matter at hand, and told them to desist.

* * *

When the conference was finished, Nelly went back to her cubbyhole. She had barely taken her seat before Sam, the errand boy, appeared at her shoulder.

'Excuse me, Miss Brooks, but there's a gentleman downstairs to see you.'

'Do you know who it is, Sam?'

The boy passed a card to Nelly. The name on the card was Sir Edward Fairfield.

'He definitely asked for me?' Nelly asked anxiously.

'Yes, Miss Brooks. It's you the gentleman wants to see.'

* * *

The Emerald Shawl

Nelly went down the stairs slowly, to give herself time to think and to compose herself. Duncan had taught her it was always prudent, no matter what the situation, not to appear too keen as a reporter.

At the bottom of the stairs, she turned and walked towards the man who was standing gazing out of the window onto the street beyond. He heard her footsteps approaching, turned and regarded her. She recognised him, of course. He was an old man, but he was impeccably dressed and groomed, with well-formed features and dark eyes; a thin face framed by sideburns. His presence was strong. He wore a black band around his hat and was holding a leather bag beneath his arm. He seemed a suitable ghoul for All Hallows' Eve. His very presence repulsed her.

Nelly saw how the backs of his hands and wrists were covered with dark grey hair, and remembered how his touch had made her feel the first time they met. She pictured him holding a pillow over his wife's face and she recoiled further. She did not like to be anywhere near him.

'Miss Brooks?' He made a slight bow.

'Good morning, Sir Edward.' Nelly stood straight. Her contempt gave her courage. 'May I offer my condolences to you on the loss of your wife and child.'

He did not acknowledge her words, nor thank her for them; rather his expression became more severe, his posture stiffer. Nelly was gratified that, even though he tried to hide it, she had managed to rile him.

'What can I do for you?' she continued, her tone matching the coldness of his eyes.

'Nothing at all,' he said. 'It is I who must return something to you.'

He put the bag on the table, opened it, and removed a notebook. 'I believe this is yours.'

Nelly caught her breath. 'Oh, it is!'

'An associate of mine found it,' said Sir Edward, 'and asked if I might return it to you.'

Nelly took the notebook from him.

'I assume the associate was Mr Scarrat,' she said. 'It was he who caused me to drop my bag in a public house, which is how the notebook came to be mislaid in the first place.'

'I am sure his clumsiness was unintentional.'

'Perhaps he had taken one glass too many,' said Nelly.

'Mr Scarrat is entitled to a nip or two, after a busy afternoon's rent-collecting, don't you think?'

'It must be exhausting,' said Nelly, 'relieving the poor of what little they have.'

Sir Edward narrowed his eyes; and Nelly remembered that he was one of the *Courier*'s major shareholders. She tempered her attitude a little.

'I appreciate you returning the notebook, Sir Edward. Now I must return to my desk.'

She went to leave, but Sir Edward took hold of her arm. She turned towards him and at once he removed his hand, the whole manoeuvre conducted so swiftly that Nelly was not sure if it had been as threatening as it had felt.

'I would like to talk to you, Miss Brooks,' he said. 'Perhaps you would be gracious enough to join me for a cup of coffee. My carriage is waiting outside.'

Nelly felt the first stirrings of panic. She did not wish to spend a second longer with this man than was necessary. But then again, when else would she have an opportunity to question him about Priscilla?

She hesitated, reluctant to accept his invitation but loath to waste this chance. Besides, she was curious about what he wanted to say to her.

'Very well,' she said. 'Excuse me for a moment, while I let my colleagues know that I am going with you, and then I'll be back.'

In truth, she had no intention of telling anyone that she was going to take refreshment with Sir Edward Fairfield – were she to do that, she would have to tell them everything. But as long as Sir Edward believed her colleagues thought her to be with him, she was confident he would not dare harm her.

Nelly took the notebook back to her cubbyhole, leaving it on her desk.

Her blood was thrumming through her veins. She was excited, she was scared, she was buzzing with vigour.

She opened the desk drawer.

The green velvet shawl was folded at the bottom. She wondered if she should wear it as a means of taking both Priscilla and Eliza with her. But there was a chance that Sir Edward would recognise it, and ask for it back, and he was the last person on Earth who should have it. Also, Nelly couldn't help feeling superstitious about the shawl, especially today, on All Hallows' Eve. The last two women who had worn it were both dead, and Nelly had been told all her life that terrible events always moved in threes.

* * *

Sir Edward's carriage was waiting on the street outside the *Courier* offices. His driver helped Nelly into the compartment, and then Sir Edward climbed up. The carriage was comfortable; the journey smooth; Sir Edward did not speak, but looked out of the window, both hands folded neatly on the brass knob of his cane, avoiding Nelly's eye, and any kind of communication with her.

Nelly tried to enjoy the luxury of the ride and the sight of the faces of the pedestrians they passed looking at the carriage with admiration as the horses trotted by, but her nerves were on edge. She didn't trust Sir Edward. He didn't know precisely what she knew about him; she did not know how much he knew about her. It was a dangerous game she was playing and she was not familiar with the rules.

32

Sir Edward took Nelly to a part of Bristol she did not know. They climbed out of the carriage into a narrow alleyway. Sir Edward's driver rapped on an unremarkable door at the side of a tall, brick-built warehouse. They were admitted by a doorman onto a small landing.

'Welcome to the Venus Club,' he said.

Nelly and Sir Edward were standing at the top of a steep staircase that descended to a heavy, purple curtain at the bottom. The wallpaper at the side of the stairs featured a swirling pattern of exotic birds and flowers; something about it disturbed Nelly. It took her a moment to realise what it was. The flora on the wallpaper, the opening buds, stamens and seedpods, resembled the private parts of men and women, but depicted lasciviously, in a manner Nelly had never seen before.

What is this place? she wondered. *What happens here?*

Sir Edward's hand in the small of her back pushed her forwards.

A plump woman dressed in silk and feathers held the curtain open for them at the bottom of the steps.

'Good morning, Sir Edward,' she said. 'It's good to see you again.' She indicated a small table beside her, its top covered with glasses of drink. 'Would you care for some wine?'

'Is this really a coffee house?' Nelly asked.

'Venus is an exclusive club for gentlemen of standing,' the woman answered, looking Nelly up and down with a disparaging eye as she handed a glass to Sir Edward. Her face was lip-sticked and rouged, her flesh soft and milky. How could one so young have eyes so hard?

'Few people know of its existence,' said Sir Edward. 'One has to meet certain criteria to join. We members help one another where we can. Here, the wheels of law, commerce and industry are oiled.'

'In a delightful environment,' said the waitress with a coy smile.

'Exactly so,' said Sir Edward.

A different woman came, curtseyed, and said, 'Follow me, sir, I'll show you to your table.'

The décor was theatrical: heavy velvet swags and gilt sconces; ornately framed mirrors and lamps perched on marbled plinths. They were below ground, so there were no windows. A fine carpet covered the polished floorboards, and smoke from dozens of pipes and cigars wreathed the air, which seemed heavier than normal; musty; corrupt.

The clientele was male, although several were accompanied by women who did not look like wives. These couples were sitting in booths, which afforded an element of privacy. The men's hands were on the women's flesh. The women laughed loudly and often. As Nelly watched, one of the couples stood up. The woman took the man's hand and led him further into the bowels of the club. They disappeared through a door at the back.

The man had grey hair and a stoop. The woman was younger than Nelly.

The air was so warm, so thick with smoke and perfume, that Nelly struggled to breathe.

She and Sir Edward were shown to a table, amongst other tables occupied exclusively by men. The clientele stared at Nelly. She, without cosmetic adornment, in her plain clothing, could hardly have been more out of place. She realised the very act of bringing her here was not mere thoughtlessness, but an act of subjugation. What man would bring a woman here unless it was to humiliate her?

A waitress came. The look she gave Nelly was not particularly friendly.

'Is Mrs Hogarth not joining you today?' she asked Sir Edward.

'Mrs Hogarth is otherwise engaged,' he replied. 'Bring us a pot of coffee, if you will, and a plate of cold meats.'

* * *

'Tell me about yourself, Miss Brooks,' said Sir Edward a little later, as the waitress poured cream into their cups.

'There's little to tell,' said Nelly, who had the distinct sensation of being scrutinised, as if she were a smear on a slide placed under a microscope.

'How long have you been with the *Courier*?'

'One year and a half.'

'And what did you do before that?'

'I was a writer.'

'For whom did you work?'

'I was not directly employed. I submitted stories and articles to various publications.'

'Did you draw on your own experiences for inspiration?'

Sir Edward took a slice of cold beef from the plate, folded it between his fingers, and then put the whole piece into his mouth. He ate it, dabbed his lips with his napkin, and stared at Nelly. She wondered if he knew about her pregnancy and the asylum; if, when he'd discovered she had been investigating him, he had initiated investigations into her.

Or perhaps his arrogance and confidence were making her feel vulnerable. Perhaps he knew nothing.

She had to hold her nerve. She had to stay calm.

'I prefer to write about other people,' she said.

'I suppose prying into the private affairs of others is the main preoccupation of reporters.'

'One could describe it thus, or one could say we are committed to the uncovering of the truth.'

A woman wearing a dress that pinched her waist and pushed up her breasts to the point of indecency came to stand by Sir Edward and opened a wooden box that contained cigars. Sir Edward peered inside and then took one. A man on the table behind theirs turned to try to attract her attention. Nelly recognised him, but could not place him.

'What do you think of George Boldwood?' Sir Edward asked as he examined the cigar.

'He's a brilliant editor and a good man. He has integrity.'

'Integrity,' Sir Edward repeated.

He sniffed the cigar, then put it between his lips, and leaned forward so that the waitress might light the end. He inhaled deeply, and the exhaled smoke streamed through his nostrils. The waitress turned to the other man. It was frustrating Nelly that she could not recall where she had seen him before.

'Do you believe integrity is important, Miss Brooks?'

'I believe it's the most important quality any newspaperman

can have. What about you, Sir Edward? Do you enjoy being a member of parliament?'

'Very much so. There is no greater privilege than serving one's constituents...' he paused '...other than serving one's country, of course.'

'I understand you travel abroad a great deal.' Two could play the dissemination game.

She did not quite dare ask if the 'Mrs Hogarth' to whom the waitress had referred was his travelling companion.

For a moment, Sir Edward did not answer. He puffed on his cigar.

'I am obliged to spend long spells in India,' he said at last. 'It is a place that is close to my heart. I enjoy shooting tigers.'

'What do the tigers do to make you so pleased by their killing?'

'Unless you have experienced the thrill of hunting big game, Miss Brooks, you cannot possibly understand the pleasure of it.'

The man on the table behind laughed at something his companion said, and at last Nelly recognised him. He was Inspector Vardy, the police officer to whom she'd spoken after Eliza Morgan's death. She looked around her cautiously. Who else was a member of this club? Who else was involved in oiling the wheels?

Sir Edward was still speaking about trophy hunting.

Nelly couldn't bear it. Besides, the tension of what they were not saying to one another was becoming unbearable.

33

'I suppose you looked in my notebook, Sir Edward,' Nelly said casually, when he paused to puff on his cigar, 'and that is why we are here together now.'

He blew smoke from the sides of his mouth.

'You suppose correctly, Miss Brooks.'

'So you are aware that I met Eliza Morgan?'

'What did she tell you?'

'That a woman and child had been murdered, although she did not give me any names,' said Nelly.

'But still you investigated?'

'I was duty-bound to find out whether or not this was true – especially when Eliza herself was found drowned the very next day.'

'Working for a newspaper is making you cynical, Miss Brooks. You make it sound as if Eliza Morgan's death was suspicious. The fact is, she was a gin-sot – an accident waiting to happen.'

Dear God, thought Nelly, *what a merciless man he is.* Hadn't

Eliza been with him only hours before her death, measuring him for alterations to his coat?

She took a sip of coffee, to buy herself a moment to collect her thoughts. Should she let him know that she knew Scarrat had been complicit in Eliza's drowning?

She decided instead to go directly to the heart of the matter, and said: 'I have subsequently established that, when she spoke of the murders of the woman and child, Miss Morgan meant your wife and her child.'

Nelly was watching Sir Edward closely. He did not react outwardly to this, although it must have felt like a punch to the belly to have Eliza's accusation spelled out so bluntly to him. He was a politician of course. He took a drink, and smoked, while he considered his next move. After a moment, he reached into the inside of his jacket, and withdrew an envelope. He laid it on the table before Nelly.

'What is it?' she asked.

'It is a copy of the letter written by the eminent physician who attended my wife's confinement, the letter that was presented to the registrar. It clearly states that the causes of death were haemorrhage, in the case of my wife, and that the child was too feeble to survive.'

Nelly took the envelope, opened it, and read the enclosed letter, signed Jacob Thorpe-Thompson. It was as Sir Edward had said. She replaced it into the envelope.

'Does that settle the matter?' asked Sir Edward.

'Is the physician a friend of yours?' Nelly asked. 'Does he frequent this club?'

Sir Edward laughed. 'Such distrust is most unbecoming in a woman.'

'You have not answered my question.'

'I refuse to pander to paranoid fantasies. You are almost as unhinged as my wife.'

His lack of manners was astounding, although the words were gentled by the polite, quiet way in which they were delivered.

When next he spoke, the tone had changed. 'I know that you went to Miss Morgan's lodgings,' he said. 'I presume you were searching for my wife's diary?'

'It had already been removed from the room by the time I got there.'

Sir Edward sat back in his chair. 'So you never read it. Never were horrified by what you found within its pages.'

'What would I have found?'

'My wife's pathetic bleating about me forcing myself upon her in my desperation for her to give me a child. Details of supposed cruelties and assaults inflicted by me upon her when she failed to do so. It is fortunate for you, Miss Brooks, that you did not read these allegations.'

'Fortunate for *you*, surely?'

He laughed, as a fond uncle might chuckle at his niece's girlish innocence. 'Oh Miss Brooks! I can see you now, poring over the diary! You would have been fascinated and horrified by my wife's colourful testimony. You'd have taken her scribblings as the truth, written your feature in a rush of womanly affinity, and had Mr Boldwood been rash enough to publish, then I'd have sued the *Courier* for every penny it had. Furthermore, I'd have done my utmost to persuade my fellow shareholders to withdraw their money and invest it elsewhere. I'm not teasing, Miss Brooks. It is quite within my power to bankrupt the newspaper for which you work.'

'Libel is only effective if what is published is untrue,' said Nelly.

He leaned towards her, so close that she could see the pores in the skin of his nose. The cigar-stink of his exhaled breath was repulsive. 'Precisely. What you may not know about my wife Priscilla, Miss Brooks, is that she was quite mad.

'She had hysterical episodes,' he continued, 'and was afflicted by them randomly during the day and night. I had no idea what I was marrying,' he said, his voice becoming softer, self-pitying. 'I soon became afraid of her, this beautiful young woman. When she was having one of her turns, she would threaten me: with knives, with the fire poker, once with a brass sculpture. She was aggressive, and paranoid. She would accuse me of behaving as she was behaving.' He exhaled slowly. 'Once, she accused me of cutting the girth of her horse's saddle, in an attempt to kill her. It was utter nonsense.'

He pushed away his cup, as if his appetite for coffee was gone.

'Yes, my wife's diary contains a number of stories that paint me in a bad light. But they are untrue, Miss Brooks. Just as it is untrue that she was murdered. My wife and the infant died of natural causes.'

The infant, he'd said. Not *my child*.

'Obviously,' Sir Edward said, 'I would prefer for none of this to be made public. It would be embarrassing for me, as an MP, a baronet, and the High Sheriff of Gloucestershire, to have my poor wife's tragic affliction exposed in the press. I don't believe it would harm my career, but I am not a man who welcomes pity or sympathy. If I am to be completely honest with you, Miss Brooks, there is, mingled with my grief, an element of relief that my wife is gone. She would never have been happy and God knows what damage she might have inflicted on the poor child had they both survived. Apart from my reputation, there is also the matter of my wife's dignity at stake.'

'Her dignity?'

'She was an insane young woman who struggled to discriminate between real life and fantasy, who bore a child and died as a result of that. She is in a better place now, and her suffering is over. Do you understand?'

Nelly nodded.

'Give me your word,' said Sir Edward, 'that there'll be no more "investigating" a non-existent crime.'

Nelly was silent.

He leaned in closer still.

'Are you not prepared to leave this alone?' he asked.

'I owe it to Eliza Morgan to...'

He made a fist of his hand and put it on the table in front of Nelly. The movement was not violent, but she found it deeply intimidating.

'The bottom line is this, Miss Brooks,' he said, in a harsh whisper. 'You keep your nose out of my business, and I'll stay away from Redfield House school.'

She felt a dread bloom within her.

'What is Redfield House school to you?' she asked.

'I'm the chairman of the governors.' He paused, drinking in Nelly's shock, enjoying the moment. 'There's a pupil there with the same surname as you,' he continued, his tone now warm, almost conversational. 'She even looks rather like you. Harriet is her name. When I was there last week, the girls read some of their work to me. Harriet's writing is rather good.'

Nelly felt as if all the blood had drained from her body.

Harriet. He'd said: 'Harriet.' Edward Fairfield knew her daughter's name.

Sir Edward smiled: 'It's interesting, isn't it, Miss Brooks, how everything is connected to everything else?'

He watched her.

'If one searches diligently enough, one can always expose secrets and lies.'

He took a deep drag on his cigar, then waved it towards Nelly. 'I will share with you, Miss Brooks, a lesson I have learned.' The false benevolence in his eyes belied their viciousness. 'It is all too easy to endanger the ones we love for the sake of our own selfish ambition.'

34

By the time Nelly returned to her cubbyhole, the experience with Edward Fairfield was taking on the qualities of a nightmare. She had a splitting headache, her clothes reeked of smoke, and she felt as if her very skin had been tainted by that claustrophobic underground club.

Sir Edward's threats had been subtle, and implicit. He had said nothing definitive; nonetheless Nelly was left with the uncomfortable feeling that something awful might happen to her, or to Harriet, if she continued her investigation. She felt angry and chastened and belittled. She did not know if she should keep going. If it was true, that Priscilla was insane, it put a different slant on everything. And the doctor's letter would stand in a court of law as proof of the causes of the deaths.

Perhaps she had been foolish to commit so much time and energy to the story already.

Perhaps there was even an innocent explanation for Eliza Morgan's death although for the life of her, Nelly could not see that there was.

Nelly's instinct now was to leave the Fairfield story well alone.

Too much was at stake to persist in following leads that might only take her to dead ends.

She had settled down to finish off the next day's women's page, a task she did not relish, but which had to be done, when Will Delane came over.

'You've been elusive today, Nelly,' he said. 'I came looking for you earlier and you'd disappeared. Nobody knew where you were.'

'Is Mr Bagnet on the warpath?'

'I made an excuse for you.'

She looked up at Will with heartfelt gratitude. 'Thank you.'

'It was my pleasure. But now I need to ask a favour of you. I'm heading to the mortuary to ask about the women who collected Gerty's body, and then I'm going to see Mr and Mrs Skinner. I'd like you to come with me.'

'I'm sure you don't need me, Will.'

'This is your story as much as mine, and besides, the Skinners trust you. I'm dreading telling them what happened in Keynsham on Saturday. You have a more sympathetic touch. So, if it's not too much trouble, I *do* need you to come with me, Nelly, please, to help break the news.'

Nelly looked up at Will; his gentle face, his hair uncombed, his fingers blackened with ink, and a coffee stain on the front of his shirt. He needed a shave, and one of the buttons was missing from his jacket. His spectacles were wonky, and there was a tic in the corner of his left eye.

She pushed back her chair and stood up. She clipped the papers on which she'd been writing together, and waved to Sam to come to collect them, and take them to the copy editors' desk.

'You're coming?' Will asked, relief flooding his face.

'Of course, I am,' she replied. 'It's the least I can do.'

***

At the mortuary, Will and Nelly were shown into a waiting room. A cheerful fire in the grate gave off warmth and light, the chairs were cushioned and there was a small table with periodicals, newspapers and leaflets on the top. Bunches of dried herbs had been placed in glass jars on the window ledges; they subdued but failed to mask the smell of death.

At the opposite side of the room was a hatch, with a handbell on the ledge. Will crossed to this and rang the bell.

'Be with you in a minute!' a disembodied voice answered.

Nelly stood by the fire, leaning down to warm her hands. The Skinners had been here, twice. How anxious they must have felt, believing that Gerty's body lay beneath a shroud in the post-mortem room next door. How desperate when they learned she had been taken.

There was a mirror hanging over the fire and, as she straightened, Nelly thought she glimpsed the face of a woman standing behind her. It was only a flicker, a trick of the light, but it looked like Eliza. She turned sharply, but nobody was there.

She looked again. Nothing.

Stop this foolishness, Nelly told herself firmly.

Will paced the perimeter of the waiting room, an indication, Nelly realised, that he too was on edge.

After a while, a short, portly man appeared at the hatch. He was wearing a long apron that was horribly stained, and his shirt sleeves were rolled up. He brought with him the smell of carbolic. What was left of his hair was standing on end over a pate that was mostly bald. His eyebrows made up for what his head lacked in hirsuteness. He appeared genuinely delighted to see Will.

'Mr Delane!' he exclaimed. 'What can I do for you?'

'I'm after some information, Mr Squires,' Will replied.

'Give me two minutes, then. I've been cleaning the corpse of a poor old derelict who expired by the cathedral door. I'll wash the grime from my hands then I'll be with you.'

The mortuary attendant disappeared, and re-appeared a few moments later through the internal door with a cup of steaming tea in his hand. He took a seat next to Will. Nelly sat on Will's other side, took out her notebook, and waited.

'Well, Mr Squires,' Will said, pushing his glasses up the bridge of his nose. 'I suspect you know why we're here.'

'Gerty Skinner?'

'Yes.'

Mr Squires ran his hand over the top of his head. 'I assume you're aware of what happened?'

'We know that Mr and Mrs Skinner showed you a photograph of their daughter, and that you recognised her.'

'Sadly, yes. She was definitely the same corpse we'd released to the two ladies from Keynsham. I gave Mr and Mrs Skinner their address, hoping they could sort it out between them. It's not the usual course, but we believed there'd been an honest mistake.'

'The address was fake,' said Will.

'We know that *now* – the police have been here asking for descriptions and the such-like.'

Mr Squires took a drink from his cup. Nelly tried not to look at the dirt caked beneath his nails; tried not to imagine those stubby hands on poor Gerty Skinner's flesh – or Eliza's, come to that.

'Those two ladies took us in, good and proper,' Mr Squires said. 'When they observed the body they were shocked – it's difficult to fake that kind of sentiment. And the one was to the other: "There, there, Anne my dear, you must be brave for the sake of our darling girl," and the other was, "Really, Martha, I didn't expect this to be so harrowing! I don't know if I can go through with it!" and the other said, "But you must, Anne, you must!" Damn it – excuse me, miss. They had us! Played us for fools!'

Will leaned forward, forearms on his thighs, hands clasped, his expression one of complete empathy. 'They must have been very convincing.'

'Well, that's it, see, they were! Convincing! Yes, that's exactly it.'

'What did they look like, this fraudulent pair?'

'Like I told the police detective, they were normal. Unassuming. One was fairish, slender, quite tall; about my daughter's age, I'd say. Late twenties. The other was darker, shorter with a womanly figure. Few years older.' He made a vague, hourglass shape with his hands. 'They were both well dressed. The shorter one had nice eyes; kindly.' He paused, then he added, 'She smelled sweet. The woman. You notice nice smells in this place. And she smelled warm and... *sweet*. Like cake.'

'Cake?'

'Cake.'

'Thank you,' said Will. 'That's really helpful.'

Mr Squires sniffed. 'I can't believe it,' he muttered. 'Pair of conniving witches.'

* * *

Will and Nelly left the mortuary and walked a little way along the side of the road before hailing a cab to take them to Bedminster, to where the Skinners lived. It was one of the poorest, and filthiest, parts of the city. The closer they came, the stronger the combined stinks of the slaughterhouse and the associated tannery and glue-making factory.

The Emerald Shawl

The cab dropped them on the outskirts of the district; the driver said he wouldn't go any further, the next streets were renowned as the haunts of criminals and scoundrels. The very air seemed darker and colder here. The faces of some of the people were skeletal. Children were barefoot despite the cold, dressed in scraps and rags. Small girls, no more than seven or eight years in age, were holding onto babies and watching toddlers, calling them away from carriage wheels and feral dogs. Boys were gathering what scraps of wood and other rubbish they could find to add to the pile they were building in the centre of a small courtyard. It was a bonfire, Nelly realised. It was difficult to conceive a less suitable environment for a large, uncontrolled fire.

Soon Will and Nelly found themselves in a street full of filth.

Buildings had been constructed in the yards and gardens of existing buildings. They were precarious, three storeys high, and leaning over one another, with a warren of alleyways connecting them. Smoke from a multitude of chimneys dirtied the sky and clogged the air.

There were no birds; no plants; nothing natural or lovely.

Nelly held up her skirts as best she could but the hem was already soiled by the disgusting black slime on the surface of the street.

She walked slightly behind Will, ignoring a drunk woman, propped against a wall, and shouting obscenities while a younger woman attempted to calm her. 'Mother, Mother, hush your voice! You don't want to be arrested again!'

Nelly ignored the dreadful sounds emanating from the direction of the tannery to her right, although the smells of death, urine and lye were more difficult to discount.

'This way,' Will said. He waited until Nelly was beside him, then put a hand about her waist to guide her through a sharp turn into the narrowest and darkest of alleyways. Normally, Nelly would have objected to his touch, but that day she was grateful for it. A little gaggle of children was following them now, begging for money.

Nobody was dressed up for All Hallows' Eve here; the suffering, the rags, the dirt, the horror – all of it was real.

Small fingers pecked at Nelly's skirt. 'Please, miss, please, miss, it's my little brother, he needs medicine, he's terribly sick! It's the scarlatina!'

Nelly gave the child a coin, and was then swamped by a dozen others; filthy, little hands all around her and dirty, desperate faces.

'Please, miss, please, miss!'

Nelly put her hand in her pocket, removed the few coins that were left, and tossed them into the street. Will, observing her, sighed, and did the same.

While the children were occupied, he checked the number scratched into the plaster on the wall.

'This way, Nelly,' he said, before turning again, up a dark, enclosed stairwell. Again, Nelly followed. At the top was a door, ajar, and Will knocked on this door. He looked at Nelly, tension etched on his features. 'Ready?' he asked.

Nelly nodded.

Mrs Skinner opened the door.

35

A little over an hour later, Nelly and Will were back outside the *Courier* building. Before they entered, they cleaned their boots as best they could, turning their ankles to wipe the leather of their soles and heels on clumps of grass on the small lawned area outside. Then, hoping the omnipresent odour of pipe smoke inside the offices would mask anything worse that lingered on their clothing, they went upstairs.

Will returned to his desk. Nelly went to the cloakroom and washed her hands with soap and water until the skin was dry and red. Then she went back to her desk, and considered the events of the afternoon.

The Skinners had been touchingly pleased when they saw Nelly and Will on the landing beyond their door. Their faces had lit up in recognition, and in anticipation of good news – if the recovery of a missing daughter's body could be called that.

The couple were so dignified in their grief; so polite and welcoming.

'Come in, come in!' Mr Skinner cried.

He insisted that Nelly took the only chair in the single room where the whole family lived, a miserable room with bare floorboards, plaster crumbling from the walls.

Archie was playing with pebbles in one corner. The little girl who had come to the *Courier* to look after him was curled up, feverish, on a thin mattress on the floor. Nelly looked at her and felt a pang of guilt. So many children in this city were caught in lives they did not choose.

'She's not well,' Mrs Skinner said, apologetically. 'It's not the scarlatina,' she added hurriedly. 'Nothing that will infect you. Only an earache and a runny nose.'

She offered tea to Will and Nelly, but both were reluctant to deplete the Skinners' meagre resources, so they declined. Instead, gently, they related their experiences of the past days: the trip to Keynsham, the involvement of the police when they discovered the Keynsham address was fake; the interview with the mortician.

Mr and Mrs Skinner listened, their expressions becoming more downcast as the story progressed.

'So, we still don't know where our Gerty is?' asked Mr Skinner, when Will and Nelly had told all they knew.

Nelly shook her head. 'I'm so sorry,' she said, and she meant it.

Gerty's parents remained stoic. They did not blame the morticians for their loss and had no intention of seeking retribution or compensation; all they wanted was to have their girl returned to them. 'So we can take Archie to visit his mama's grave.'

'What do we do now?' asked Mr Skinner.

'We have to put our trust in the police,' said Nelly, 'and pray the trail has not gone cold.'

She spoke with hope in her voice, but, in her heart, she knew there was very little reason for it.

* * *

The Skinners had been embarrassingly grateful when Will had returned the tobacco factory photograph to them. He'd had the original cleaned, then copied, enlarged and framed and Mrs Skinner had held it to her chest as if it were a direct connection to Gerty.

'We shall hang it on the wall,' she said, 'so our Archie can look at it every day.'

'I felt awful when you gave it to them,' Nelly had said to Will, as they'd walked into the office. 'They behaved as if you had reincarnated their daughter.'

'It was better than giving them nothing,' Will had said.

'I know. You're right. It's just... those poor people.'

'I know, Nelly. I know.'

* * *

Before she left the office that evening, Nelly went into the archive, removed the envelope that contained the cuttings about the previous year's scarlet fever outbreak and put the envelope into her satchel. Then, with her skirt soiled, and her hair and cloak still reeking of slaughterhouse and tannery, she headed back to her lodgings, avoiding the merrymakers dressed as ghouls and ghosts trying to scare passers-by as the night of All Hallows' Eve settled in.

* * *

Nelly knocked on the door to the Augurs' private quarters as soon as she was back in 12 Orchard Hill. Mrs Augur was out, so she explained to Eveline that she was in need of a bath and wondered if she might take one in advance of her appointed time. When Eveline heard where Nelly had been, she agreed that she must have a bath immediately, and asked Ida to warm some water. Sarah drew the curtain between the kitchen and the scullery, where the bath was kept, and once it was full, Nelly took off her soiled clothes and stepped into the tub.

The water was deliciously hot, and Ida had added lavender oil and oatmeal so it was milky and smelled wonderful too. Nelly sank in, bending her knees until the back of her head and all her hair was submerged, and it was heavenly to lose the combined smells of the claustrophobic gentlemen's club and the slums.

She felt tendrils of her own hair float about her shoulders and she closed her eyes and sank further into the water, so that her face was entirely submerged, and she thought about all she must do in the morning, and knowing she was going to be fully occupied was a kind of solace.

It would stop her being angry.

It would stop her from thinking constantly about Harriet.

36

Nelly sat on the rug in her room to let her hair finish drying by the fire.

She had put the clothes she'd been wearing that day in the laundry bag, and her cloak was airing outside in the tiny courtyard.

As the flames crackled and spat companionably beside her, Nelly looked in the envelope that contained the cuttings pertaining to the scarlet fever epidemic.

She read that all children under the age of fourteen who had been affected last year had been taken to, and treated at, the specially constructed Children's Hospital for Infectious Diseases in the countryside of North Somerset. There had been four dedicated wards for scarlatina patients, and a specialised team of medical staff to take care of them.

A doctor was quoted as saying it was important to remove children showing symptoms of the illness from their environments, to limit the spread of the disease.

Nelly thought it likely that Harriet had been taken to that

same hospital. She would go there as soon as she reasonably could. Nobody would recognise her there.

* * *

That night, Nelly dreamed that she was back in her childhood home. She found herself in the hallway – knowing it at once by the dark wood of the banister and the elephant's foot umbrella stand. The door was closed, but she could hear Sir Edward in the drawing room, talking to her parents. Nelly, hovering at the keyhole, trying to eavesdrop, caught only the odd word: *disobedient, wilful, hysterical, insane.*

She turned and climbed the staircase before her. She opened the door to her old bedroom, and stood stock-still, startled by the blast of heat that came from within.

She looked around the room and recognised the scene.

Mrs Winter, her parents' housekeeper, was standing beside the window. On the sill was a wicker bassinet. A fire burned in the grate, and the room was hot as an oven. The doctor, who stood in the corner, was dabbing sweat from his forehead with a handkerchief.

A young girl lay on her back, on the bed, her nightgown and the sheets around and beneath her soaked with blood. Her skin was blueish in colour, dark bruises beneath her eyes, and her hair was stuck to her skull and neck with sweat. Her legs were bent at the knees and splayed like a frog's. She was trying to cover herself with her nightgown. She was opened up; segmented like an orange.

In her dream, Nelly observed the young mother. She was her own, young self.

She tried to go into the room, to comfort the fifteen-year-old Nelly, but she could not cross the threshold.

The doctor walked to the window and peered into the bassinet.

'It's a good colour,' he said to Mrs Winter.

'It's a shame,' said the woman, 'for it would be best for everyone if it died.'

All the young Nelly had seen of her daughter was a floppy thing, waxy and bloodied, head lolling forward as the doctor lifted her from between her legs and passed her to Mrs Winter.

'Please,' she'd cried, holding out her arms, 'let me have her!' But the doctor had told her to be quiet in a tone so quietly threatening that she had obeyed.

The adult Nelly could see, silhouetted against the watery light coming through the window, covered in raindrops, part of one tiny hand protruding above the rim of the bassinet. She could hear her daughter's little, furious cries.

A maid came into the room, ignoring the adult Nelly standing at the door. She moved around the bed, collecting the sweat and blood-soaked rags and towels.

'Can you pass my baby to me?' the girl on the bed asked, quietly, so the doctor would not hear. 'Let me hold her for a minute.'

'I can't,' said the maid.

'Please!'

'Don't carry on, now. You're in enough trouble as it is.'

'She's crying!'

'You need to sleep.'

'I don't want to sleep. I want to hold my baby!'

The maid looked about her, then leaned in close to the girl. 'Listen to me,' she said, 'for your own sake, keep quiet. Do as you're told. It'll be better for everyone.'

Adult Nelly covered her face with her hands. She could hear Sir Edward downstairs, talking to her parents. A carriage was waiting outside to take the girl who had just given birth to Holywell Asylum.

'We will take care of her now,' Sir Edward said. 'The burden of your daughter is no longer yours to bear.'

Nelly knew what was about to happen to her fifteen-year-old self.

She would not see the outside world again for ten years.

37

TUESDAY, 1 NOVEMBER

At the morning conference, George Boldwood was the worse for wear. He had been to a dinner to celebrate a new shipbuilding project the previous evening, and consumed a combination of the finest porter, champagne and brandy, 'because it would have been impolite to refuse'. He had also partaken of rather too much of the wonderfully rich food on offer. He apologised for belching – 'I am afraid I cannot control it' – as he went round the table giving everyone the chance to share the news of the stories on which they were working. The editor remained unusually subdued throughout the entire meeting, apart from his burps, which were sonorous.

When it was Nelly's turn to tell the other reporters her plans for the day, she prevaricated; she was going to write a feature about decorating one's home on a budget, she said, together with tips for emulating the latest Scandinavian home-styling fashions. Since Princess Alexandra had arrived in England, the middle classes couldn't get enough of all things Danish and it was difficult to find affordable items in the shops. George Boldwood liked this idea so much that he clapped his hands with delight.

'My good lady wife would like nothing better than a Scandinavian-style drawing room,' he said. 'Furthermore, she cannot read enough about Princess Alexandra! If you wrote about that woman every day, Nelly, Mrs Boldwood still wouldn't be satisfied. Well done! Really excellent work!'

Nelly was embarrassed by the praise. She saw the scorn in the eyes of the older reporters. If only they knew, she thought, what she had been working on: if only she could tell them about Sir Edward Fairfield and his allegedly mad, young wife.

The dream last night, the memory of how vulnerable women were when they had just given birth, had made her revisit her intention to give up the Fairfield story. If only there were some way to confirm, or disprove what Sir Edward had told her.

When the conference was over, she returned to her cubbyhole. She drafted the feature about Scandinavian home décor – pastel colours, less clutter, avoiding the over-ornate flourishes that had been popular in middle-class English homes for so long.

'One would never see an elephant's foot umbrella stand in a refined household in Copenhagen,' she wrote, with some satisfaction.

Next, she went into the archive. She replaced the envelope that contained the scarlet fever cuttings, and searched for those pertaining to Edward Fairfield, which she took back to her cubbyhole. She did not know what she was looking for, but there might be something.

She opened the first, in which were some two dozen clippings: most of them reports from Parliament, concerning bills brought before the House of Commons and suchlike. She found the reports of all the general elections from 1837, when Sir Edward was first chosen as one of the two MPs to represent Bristol in Parliament. His work in India was mentioned many times. He represented the interests of various businesses, and worked for and with the East India Company. He had been on several long trips to the continent of Asia, the most recent being a six-month stint from November 1863 to May 1864.

Eliza Morgan had mentioned something about Sir Edward travelling a great deal, with his mistress, and leaving Priscilla behind, alone. Hadn't she intimated that a long business trip had been at the root of the couple's problems? Was this what she'd been referring to? Was jealousy the cause of Priscilla's instability?

In the second envelope were numerous – mostly small – cuttings from local events and meetings where Sir Edward Fairfield had had a say or become involved. He had been present at the launchings of new ships constructed in the building yards at Bristol docks, and had sided with local businesses in disputes between the fleet owners and insurance companies.

Interestingly, to Nelly, there was a batch of cuttings, clipped together, all concerning the same matter: the purchasing by the city council of patches of land currently occupied by 'insanitary housing' and owned by slum landlords. It seemed the council was paying landlords, including Obadiah Scarrat – who was mentioned by name several times – 'over seven times the amount the property is expected to realise' for the land. In one letter to the *Courier*, the author had written: 'Slum landlords are incessantly active in influence to bear in favour of their own interests.'

Sir Edward Fairfield had responded to this with a staunch defence of the landlords who, he said, were providing roofs over the heads of people who would otherwise be sleeping 'with their children' on the streets. He had said that it was 'only right and proper' that the landlords be fairly remunerated for their service to the city and its population.

The third envelope contained cuttings about Sir Edward that were to do with his status as '10th baronet' and High Sheriff of

Gloucestershire, his grand home, Mordaunt Hall, and various social events. There was an etching of the hall, which looked an enormous country pile, with a severe façade and far more rooms than any single family could ever require. Nelly had heard from both Eliza and Duncan Coulson that the place was gloomy and uncomfortable and that was exactly the impression given by the illustration.

The accompanying caption described Mordaunt Hall as: 'An excellent example of an extended, moated early Tudor manor house that remains in superb condition. The house has been owned and preserved by the Fairfield family for nearly four centuries.'

The gardens had been designed by someone famous. There was special woodland for breeding game birds for the shoot 'thick with foliage', hares were raised for coursing and deer for chasing. As if those were not enough animals to terrify and kill, there was apparently 'good angling' to be had in the portion of river that curled its way through Sir Edward's vast estate.

Several times the first wife, Maria, was mentioned as having been present at events with Sir Edward, and there was a clipping of her death notice. She had died of 'a damaged heart' at the age of forty-four. Her daughter, Madeleine Avery, aged twenty-four, was present at her funeral, along with her stepfather, Sir Edward.

All of this correlated with what Nelly already knew.

That Sir Edward Fairfield was interested in hunting, shooting and fishing. That he was friends with and supportive of slum landlords in general and Obadiah Scarrat in particular. That Mordaunt Hall was as depressing a place as Eliza had intimated.

And that Sir Edward's marriage to Priscilla Statton had been one of convenience. There was nothing, beyond the notice that Nelly had already found to say that Sir Edward had ever been married for a second time.

Nelly sat back in her chair. On a whim, she opened the drawer that contained the green velvet shawl. She reached down for it, and then withdrew her hand in horror as if she'd been stung.

There, on top of the shawl, was an upturned playing card.

The ace of spades.

38

Nelly picked up the card. She turned it over. On the back was an etching of a ship at sea. Printed in small letters at the bottom of the card were the words: O. Scarrat Esq. Property Management & Letting. Bristol.

Nelly didn't know if this card was part of the pack the man in The Trooper had been using to play Solitaire, but she was certain it was a threat. She recalled the card she'd noticed outside 12 Orchard Hill – that cannot have been a coincidence after all. Scarrat's watchman was warning Nelly that he knew where she lived, and where she worked. If he could put a card in a drawer in her desk in the *Courier* offices, then he could get to her anywhere.

She could do nothing about it. She could hardly take it to George Boldwood, or to the police, and expect them to understand its significance.

'It's just a playing card,' they would say and then they might roll their eyes Heavenward as if to say: 'Here is another superstitious woman becoming hysterical over nothing.'

Besides, she now knew the police, or some of them, were colluding with Fairfield.

How had the watchman got into the office, Nelly wondered. Perhaps he had an ally within the *Courier*. Maybe one of the older journalists was being blackmailed by Scarrat, or working with him. Perhaps one of them was a regular at the Venus Club. Nelly looked cautiously behind her, to see if anyone was watching her.

It was impossible to tell.

To desecrate the ace of spades was said to invoke further ill fortune, so rather than tearing it up, she put it into the wastepaper basket in the farthest corner of the office, beneath scraps of newsprint.

She was afraid, but more than that, she was angry.

If Edward Fairfield was innocent, why was he so committed to intimidating Nelly?

She wished she could ask him directly.

Instead, she returned to her desk and removed the green velvet shawl from the drawer. She laid it over her lap. She pushed the nap of the velvet one way, so that it appeared to be a darker colour, then pushed it back. She wrote the letter 'P' with her index finger, and then smoothed the fabric again to make it disappear.

The Edward Fairfield cuttings envelope was still on her desk.

'What is it you're afraid of?' she asked him silently, inside her head. 'What do you think I might find?'

She peered inside the envelope to see if she'd missed anything. Stuck inside was a folded sheet of paper that was thicker and of a better quality than that used for the newspaper. It was a page from a magazine, Nelly realised, as she opened it out: a photograph.

The accompanying text said the image had been taken to commemorate a Valentine's Day party in London, earlier in the year. Albert Edward, Prince of Wales, was there, but not his 'beloved wife' Princess Alexandra of Denmark. The couple's first child was only a few weeks old, and the princess was occupied with the duties of motherhood.

The prince was centre front of the photograph, surrounded by various 'close friends'. Nelly studied the faces, at least twenty of them. She could not see anyone she recognised; certainly not Sir Edward – he'd have been in India at that time and would remain there for several more months.

But his name was in the caption, and it was circled: that was why the cutting had been put in the envelope. Why was Edward Fairfield named, when he wasn't in the picture? The caption was printed in the tiniest typeface. Nelly picked up her magnifying glass and looked through it. She squinted, and read: 'centre row, fifth from left: Lady Edward Fairfield, of Mordaunt Hall, Bristol'.

It was a photograph of Priscilla!

Nelly counted faces from the left, and found herself, for the first time, looking into the eyes of Priscilla Fairfield, standing directly behind the right shoulder of the Prince of Wales.

* * *

Up until that moment, in Nelly's mind's eye, Priscilla Fairfield had been a delicate woman – if she'd been a flower, she would have been a harebell. She had imagined someone slight and slender, fair-haired, pale, with large eyes and a fragile appearance, shy of demeanour.

The woman in this photograph, if the caption was to be believed, was nothing of the kind. Priscilla was taller than the other women in the image. She wasn't exactly plump, but she was well built, with broad shoulders and a good bust. It looked as if she had been caught mid-laugh, for the features of her face were slightly blurred. Her eyes were half closed, because her chin was tilted upwards, her head tipped back. Her hair was dark, beautifully coiffed, and she was wearing a fine dress, in the French style, cut low on the shoulder with a fringed bodice and a wide skirt with a scalloped hem showing behind the prince's legs. The fabric seemed to gleam in the light, so it was almost certainly satin, and it was intercut with sections of lace.

Priscilla did not look as if she was missing her husband; on the contrary, she appeared to be in excellent spirits: dressed up, with her gloves and her jewels and her hair in ringlets sharing a joke with the other partygoers.

She most certainly did not appear insane.

And then the penny dropped.

In February, Priscilla had been in London, enjoying herself with the Prince of Wales and his entourage: men and women far closer in age to her than the man she had married. The people were handsome and appeared to be having a good time. No doubt there had been drinking and dancing and games.

Nelly counted on her fingers: mid-February to late October.

Eight and a half months after that party, Priscilla had given birth to a child.

Eight and a half months. And her husband had been away for at least half that time.

Nelly knew how it felt to find out one was carrying a baby, when to carry a baby was absolutely the worst thing that one could do.

She could imagine how appalled Priscilla must have felt when she discovered her condition.

She wondered which, if any, of those men in the photograph was responsible.

* * *

Nelly put the cuttings back into the correct envelopes, all except the photograph that featured Priscilla Fairfield, which she hid in her drawer, beneath the green velvet shawl. She was reluctant to put that one back in the archive: it was the only proof she had that Priscilla had been in London while her husband was with his mistress in some far-flung corner of the British Raj.

It must have been obvious to all who were close to Priscilla that the child she was carrying could not have been her husband's... but then how many people were close to her? She had no family left, no parents nor siblings to question her. Probably only those servants who cared for her physical needs would have been aware. Her lady's maid, certainly, and the woman who made her dresses for her: Eliza Morgan. Hadn't Eliza specifically hinted at such a situation, only Nelly had been too slow to pick up the clue?

And when Sir Edward returned from India that summer, did he realise at once that Priscilla was in a delicate condition? If the couple were not being intimate together, then perhaps not. Perhaps he found out only later. Perhaps he did not have time to come up with a sensible plan to resolve the matter, and instead had panicked, and resorted to the murder of Priscilla Fairfield and her baby – quicker, cleaner, far less trouble than any of the alternative routes out of the situation.

If only Nelly had known this yesterday, when she was alone with Sir Edward!

She remembered how he had not referred to the baby as his own child. She recalled how embedded he was in his lifestyle and his traditions, how genuinely proud of his role as an MP. The absolute last thing he would have wanted was a scandal of huge proportions. A divorce would have sullied his reputation and he, being the cuckolded spouse, would have had to endure what a man of his standing might perceive as unendurable public speculation and humiliation.

'You almost had me, Sir Edward,' she thought. 'I almost believed what you told me about Priscilla.'

But now she was certain that he had lied.

Nelly was committed to the chase. The time for letting go of the story was gone. Never mind the watchman and his playing cards. She owed it to those who had died.

She had no choice but to see it through to the end.

39

Nelly's next task was to study the funeral list for Arnos Vale cemetery, where most bodies from north Bristol were interred, now that the local churchyards were full. She wanted to check if Priscilla Fairfield's funeral had already taken place. It had not. It was listed for 3 p.m. the following day.

'P. Fairfield, aged 19,' the notice read, '& stillborn son, Arnos Vale cemetery'. The name of the funeral director listed beneath was M Surguy of Commercial Road, Bristol.

You must not even think about going to the funeral, Nelly told herself sternly. If Sir Edward spotted her, and recognised her, the consequences would be unthinkable.

But she *had* to go. It was the perfect opportunity to observe the people who had been present in Mordaunt Hall when Priscilla and the infant, which Nelly now knew had been a boy, died. The stepdaughter, Madeleine Avery, would almost certainly be present. And presumably some close members of the household staff – key witnesses to the case.

It was an investigative opportunity too important to squander.

*　*　*

The rest of the day passed quietly. But when Nelly left to walk home to 12 Orchard Hill that evening, she could not shrug off the fear that she was being followed. She knew now that the sensation was not simply the work of an overwrought imagination; the playing card she'd found in her desk was proof that the watchman was observing her closely. That night, the threat became tangible. Footsteps behind her slowed when she slowed; quickened when she speeded up. Several times she heard a muffled cough. She found herself looking ahead for escape routes; for people she might ask for help if she was accosted and dark patches that she must avoid.

She took care not to walk close to the street, with the carriages rattling by, in case she was pushed into their path. When she came to the harbourside, she stayed near to the buildings, literally holding onto the stone, so afraid was she of being bundled into the filthy water.

At the bottom of the Christmas Steps, she turned, suddenly, and saw a man she had seen before. Broken nose. Flat cap. The Solitaire player, the watchman, the man Eliza had warned of, from beyond the grave.

And he was staring right into her eyes.

Nelly's instinct was to scream, but her throat constricted and her lungs wouldn't work. She looked around in panic, and at once a woman came to her aid.

'Are you sick, dear?'

'That man with the broken nose,' Nelly said, her voice pitched high in fear, 'he's following me! He means me harm.'

'Which man?'

'That one! Him! In the cap!'

Heads turned. People moved closer to Nelly, protecting her. The watchman stepped backwards. He faded into the darkness.

'Was that man troubling you?' Nelly was asked. 'Did he pester you? Did he hurt you, miss?'

She exhaled shakily. 'He did not touch me,' she said, 'although he shadowed me for some time. I was afraid, but I shall be perfectly fine now he is gone.'

Nonetheless, she was more than grateful when a group of shop-women going the same way offered to climb the Steps with her.

* * *

The first thing Nelly saw when she reached home, making sure the door was shut properly behind her, was an envelope with her name upon it lying face up on the polished top of the walnut sideboard in the hallway.

Nelly recognised the elaborately cursive writing; it was Angel's. Normally, Nelly would be glad to see a letter from her aunt, but the timing of this one pained her heart.

'Dear God,' she whispered, 'please, please, please let it not be bad news about Harriet.'

She picked the envelope up and took it with her into the dining room.

It had been a long day. Nelly's head and eyes ached. She put the letter face down on the table, and sat in an easy chair, close to the fire.

She could not think why Angel would be writing now unless it was to inform her that Harriet had succumbed to the fever.

If Harriet was dead, wouldn't the world feel different? Wouldn't there be a wound in Nelly's heart where her daughter normally resided?

If Harriet was dead, what was the point of anything?

Nelly dropped her head, and sat stooped, exhausted.

She wanted to cry. Crying would be cathartic; it might loosen the knots of emotion inside Nelly, knots that had been pulled so tight over the years that they were hard as stone. But Nelly could not cry. She had pledged as a child never to show her hurt, and she had kept her vow for so long that she no longer knew how to weep.

The fire crackled. There were footsteps above, Miss Norton and Miss Sylvester making themselves comfortable.

Nelly felt a sudden longing for her life to be normal. She was sick of having to lie about her past; of having to disown her daughter over and over, of having to pretend to be someone she was not.

She was not a wicked person.

All she had done was lie with Sidney, who she'd loved. And he had loved her.

Nobody had been hurt – her mother would deny that, but Nelly had not fallen pregnant to hurt her mother. She and Sidney had not understood the consequences of their actions.

Nobody had been humiliated or had suffered by what they did. All the pain had come afterwards, and none of that could be laid at Nelly or Sidney's door.

He had been packed off overseas, she to the asylum. As if ten years of punishment were not enough, she was now committed to a lifetime of dishonesty, always fearing the truth would come out. A lifetime of having to act as if she had not laboured while the rain slashed against the window of the bedroom in her parents' home; a lifetime of pretending she had neither wanted, nor loved, the infant they took away before Nelly even had a chance to hold her.

And if Harriet had died of the scarlet fever, what was left?

A lifetime of emptiness.

Nelly gave a quiet sigh.

Winter was here. Things always seemed worse when the days were short and the nights were long.

There was no use prevaricating. It would change nothing.

'Please God,' she whispered, 'let Harriet not be dead.'

She sat up straight and opened the envelope. She took out the paper inside, unfolded it, hardly daring to look at it. But there was no black border around the writing, as one might expect if it was news of a death; indeed, the corners of the notepaper were embossed with a pretty floral design quite inappropriate to the bearing of bad tidings.

Nelly relaxed a little, and read:

My dearest niece,

I trust this letter finds you in good health and good spirits.

I am writing to you, darling girl, because I have had a letter from your mother, who, in turn, received a missive from the governor of a school in Bristol. I shall not mention its name, in case you are innocent of the behaviour I am about to detail.

It seems a woman of your physical likeness, has been seen on several occasions outside the school and at a nearby church.

Darling, I do not know if this mystery woman is you, but Maud told me she feared she might have let slip where your daughter is. If it is you, then I urge you with all my heart to stay away. No good can come of it. Your parents are considering sending the child abroad to put her entirely beyond your reach, and they won't stop there. I am not at all sure I would be able to engineer your release from Holywell for a second time.

Write back to me. Promise me, as you promised before, to

put the past behind you. Let go of the child. You cannot have her, Nelly. She is not yours.

With fondest affection from your devoted aunt,
Angel.

Nelly sighed and dropped her head into her arms.

She would not think about the implications of the contents of the letter. Not now.

Harriet was not dead.

That was all that mattered.

40

WEDNESDAY, 2 NOVEMBER

Fog was like snow in that it changed the atmosphere of the city. Only, unlike snow, it did not make everything bright and beautiful, obscuring ugliness and hiding filth, rather it changed the landscape for the worse.

Nelly was unsettled from the moment she opened her eyes that morning. The light in her room was different: murky. She was cold. She felt anxious and unsettled, as if everything was out of sorts.

She remembered the man who had followed her to the foot of the Christmas Steps.

She recalled the playing card she had found in her office drawer.

And the contents of Angel's letter played through her mind.

She picked up the locket with the daisy and Harriet's hair wound in it, and held it to her lips.

'Be well, my darling,' she whispered.

She'd had an awfully peculiar dream. She and Will Delane had been lying together on a grassy bank beside a stream, in the sunshine. Nelly recognised the place: it was in Essex, across the fields where she and Sidney used to go. In the dream, Nelly had closed her eyes and Will thought she was sleeping. He took her hand in his and Nelly had a longing, like a weight, inside her. If Will knew she was awake, he would not have touched her, but because he thought she was drowsing, he lifted her hand and kissed the palm. Nelly had turned towards him and he had whispered, 'I know everything about you, Nelly Brooks!' and when she opened her eyes, she was lying, not beside Will, but beside the man who had threatened her child: Sir Edward Fairfield.

Nelly felt tainted by the dream.

She realised what she had missed when she first read Angel's letter last night: that it must surely have been Sir Edward Fairfield who had written to her parents. He was demonstrating his power to Nelly; the ease with which he could interfere with her life; controlling the people to whom she was connected as easily as if they were pieces on a chess board.

What would Nelly do if Harriet really were sent overseas?

Would she be able to find her a second time?

She clasped the locket, slid out of bed, and wandered to the window.

The floorboards were cold against the bare soles of her feet. She drew back the curtains and looked out. The world had turned grey. The fog was so thick that it masked everything, even the buildings on the other side of the road; the walls, the trees; everything.

If the watchman was there, she could not see him.

She crossed the room, knelt at the fireplace, and poked the ashes. Tiny embers glowed, but not enough heat was left to make a difference.

Nelly shivered. Here came the season of chilblains, of coughs and colds and chills. Here came winter, long and dreary. She must make sure she was prepared for whatever next was thrown at her.

* * *

Everything was wrong that Wednesday, right from the start.

Sarah had a sore throat, so had stayed in bed, which meant nothing was prepared for breakfast: there was not even any water boiled for coffee.

As soon as she left the relative warmth and comfort of 12 Orchard Hill, Nelly was assaulted by the cold and damp. The cobblestones had been made slippery by the moisture in the air and the fog was so thick that she could not see ahead of her. She did not know if the watchman was present. She was startled by the sudden appearance of a horse, a child, even a lamp post, from the depths of the gloom. Several times she heard a cough, she thought she recognised as the watchman's, but how could she know if it was him? The soles of her boots betrayed her on the greasy streets. She was afraid of falling. The city that she normally loved had turned into a sinister place; a place where bad things might happen; did happen; would happen again.

She did what she always did when emotion took over: rationalised. The watchman was a puppet controlled by Scarrat, whose own strings were pulled by Sir Edward Fairfield. Sir Edward was using the other men to frighten her into leaving the Fairfield story alone because he was guilty. He was deploying every weapon in his arsenal.

But she could not, *would* not leave it. Nothing Fairfield had told her about Priscilla could be true. A madwoman would not be invited to London to spend time merrymaking with the Prince of Wales. Fairfield had lied through his teeth to Nelly, and assumed she'd be gullible enough to accept his word.

Rage simmered inside her. This wasn't the first time she'd come across a powerful man using bullying tactics to force a woman to bend to his will. Her dearest friend in the asylum was a woman called Constance Parr. Constance had been sent to Holywell by her aristocratic husband because she had asked him for a divorce. As far as Nelly knew, Constance was still there.

Nelly had written to Constance, but never received anything in return. Constance would have replied if she could: in all likelihood, her husband had requested that she be refused the privilege of contact with the outside world. Nelly ought to go to see Constance in person, but she didn't feel strong enough to go back into the asylum; not even to visit the woman who had, for ten years, been her closest friend. She could not entirely shake off the fear that the door might be locked behind her; that she might be trapped once again.

The older Nelly became, and the longer she lived in the world, the more angered she was by it. Young women, especially if they were headstrong and happy, were punished by men, and by society. And, it seemed to Nelly, there was no reason for it save a deep fear inside men that if women were not subjugated and controlled, they would show their true strength.

She muttered to herself as she walked. People glanced at her. Nelly did not care. So what if she became one of those eccentric old ladies who went about shouting at people?

So what?

And as she walked through the fog, and she thought of all the wrongs that had been done to women like herself, and Constance, and all those other souls growing old on the ward for fallen women because they'd had the courage to cross the entirely fabricated moral lines drawn for them by the judgemental and the repressed, something changed inside Nelly Brooks.

Angel's letter had intimated that if she did not let go of Harriet, she would end up back in the asylum.

Sir Edward Fairfield had warned that if she did not abandon her investigation, he would use her affection for Harriet as a weapon against her.

One was acting out of love, the other was driven by cruelty; but both were attempting to corrupt the only thing in her life that was absolutely pure: her love for her daughter.

She would not let go and she would not give up, simply because that was what she had been told she must do.

Instead, she would relinquish her fear, and go forward with renewed determination!

41

Will came to stand by Nelly in the queue for the tea trolley. 'Are you quite well, Nelly?' he asked.

'Yes.'

'Only you seemed a little distracted in conference.'

'I don't know what you mean, Will. Really, I'm fine.' She looked at him. He had combed his hair and appeared tidier than usual. 'Are you going out somewhere?'

'I'm accompanying Harry Roscoe up to Clifton so he can take some atmospheric images of the bridge.'

Mr Roscoe was the *Courier*'s newest team member, a photographer. The *Courier*'s directors were on the brink of investing in expensive new machinery so that photographs might be reproduced in the newspaper. The new equipment wouldn't be ready for some weeks, but its installation was eagerly anticipated. Mr Roscoe had been employed in advance, so that he could get to know the reporters, the newspaper, and the topics it covered.

The images being taken today would be printed and sold to readers of the *Courier* as souvenirs upon the opening of the suspension bridge. Mr Boldwood had been delighted by this fine example of timely enterprise.

Nelly suspected it would be too foggy for Will and Mr Roscoe to see anything up above the gorge, but the photographer was hoping beams of light would shine through the mist and give him the best pictures.

Mr Boldwood and Mr Bagnet were attending a board meeting held on the top floor of the building. These meetings tended to go on for several hours and included a long lunch. Consequently, nobody paid any attention to Nelly when she slipped out of the office just after 9 a.m. She hurried through the foggy streets to Temple Meads station, stopping to buy a velvet toy fashioned into the shape of a rabbit, and a book of adventure stories for girls. Harriet was a little old for the toy, but soft things were a known comfort to the sick. At Temple Meads, Nelly bought a ticket for the next train to North Somerset.

She alighted at Backwell, a low-lying village surrounded by countryside. Nelly could see very little of the place through the mist that lay like a blanket over the fields and moorland.

She had been counting on there being cabs available at the station; there were not. But when she asked the stationmaster how she might find her way to the Children's Hospital for Infectious Diseases, he indicated a person loading potato sacks into the back of a small wooden cart to which a donkey was harnessed.

'My wife will take you there,' he said.

'It's no trouble, I'm going there anyway,' said the wife, who Nelly had not recognised as a woman because she was wearing a woollen scarf around her head, a man's jacket and thick trousers. She heaved the last of the vegetables into the cart, while the donkey, a dear creature with only one eye, waited patiently. Then

Nelly climbed up beside the stationmaster's wife, and she clicked her tongue, and the little cart was on its way.

The cart was rickety and the lane had been built on boggy ground, and undulated dreadfully, so that at times one wheel went up as the other went down. Nelly found herself swaying on the wooden bench as if on some reckless amusement at a country fair. She genuinely feared the whole contraption would tip over.

'It feels rather unsteady,' Nelly said, holding on for dear life, with her satchel bumping at her side.

'You're safe enough, my dear. We goes to the hospital almost every day, don't we, Dobbin? He's a good lad. He could do it blindfold.'

Before long, the cart turned into the hospital drive; a better road, inclining uphill, with trees on either side, whose leafless branches seemed to gather the fog and hold it. When they emerged, the hospital was in front of them. Large, Gothic, with a clocktower in the middle, and a wing on either side, each dissolving into the murk. Nelly was awed by the size and grandeur of the place.

The stationmaster's wife said her business would take a half-hour – the kitchen staff always gave her a cup of hot milk to thank her for her trouble – so if Nelly was back at the front entrance by a quarter to twelve, they could ride back together. Otherwise, Nelly would have to find her way back to the station herself.

Half an hour.

It was no time at all.

Nelly climbed the steps to the entrance to the hospital and asked for directions at the reception desk in the foyer. The nurse explained that the hospital was divided, boys on the left wing, girls on the right. The scarlet fever wards were on the ground floor.

'Go through those doors, and keep walking,' the nurse told Nelly. 'There's a list of names outside each ward.' She hesitated. 'You know, don't you, that you can look through the windows into the scarlatina ward, but you can't go in? We don't want the infection spreading.'

Nelly clutched her satchel and hurried along the central corridor. She came to the first scarlet fever ward soon enough.

Harriet's name was not on the patient list but Nelly recognised the name Sybille Montgomery, the Redfield House pupil who had fainted inside the church.

With her heart racing, she hurried to the second ward and ran her finger down the list pinned to the door. Harriet's name was there. She was in bed thirteen.

'Oh, thank God,' Nelly whispered. 'Thank God!'

She took a deep breath, and pushed open the door marked 'Visitors'.

The door opened into a corridor, which ran the length of the ward, with windows all along the partition wall that separated the two. The beds were in a line with their heads against the opposite wall.

Harriet was in the thirteenth bed, lying on her side, the sheets pulled up to her chest.

She no longer had the distinctive red mask of scarlet fever, but she was pale as a ghost. Her eyes were closed, and even from several yards distant, behind the window, Nelly observed the dark circles beneath her eyes.

'Oh, darling,' she whispered.

Other people were in the viewing corridor, other parents. A woman at the far end was weeping. Nelly pressed her hands against the glass, and she looked at her daughter sleeping, and she felt helpless, and empty and, at the same time, full of love.

As she stood watching, a nurse came to Harriet's bed. She roused Harriet gently. Harriet opened her eyes, and the nurse supported her back while she shook and rearranged the pillows, then had Harriet sit up a little. The nurse gave Harriet a cup, and Harriet took it and drank, and the nurse must have said something amusing, because Harriet smiled.

Nelly smiled too. Her exhaled breath clouded the glass. She wiped it away.

Then Harriet passed the cup back to the nurse, and the nurse took it. She put her wrist against Harriet's forehead and seemed to be pleased with what she felt. She spoke to Harriet again, and then she smoothed the child's hair tenderly, and moved to the next bed.

Nelly looked at Harriet. And Harriet, perhaps sensing Nelly's eyes upon her, suddenly looked towards the corridor windows and she squinted, to see more clearly. Nelly smiled and waved.

Harriet smiled and waved feebly in return and then she let her head fall back into the pillow, and she closed her eyes, and went back to sleep.

Nelly stood at the window for ten more minutes, then she walked back to the ward entrance. The nurse who had tended to Harriet was making notes. Nelly approached her.

'I have some gifts for Harriet Brooks,' she said. 'May I leave them with you?'

'You may,' said the nurse. She put down her papers and admired the rabbit. 'He's rather sweet. I'll give him and the book to Harriet when she wakes.'

Nelly hesitated. Then she asked quietly: 'Will she be well again – Harriet, I mean. Do you think she'll make a full recovery?'

'She is over the worst of it,' said the nurse. 'She's stronger than she looks, that child.'

'May I visit again, in a day or two?'

'You may come, but Harriet won't be here,' said the nurse.

'Where will she be?'

'Her parents have arranged for her to be sent to a sanatorium in the Swiss Alps.'

The news delivered so gently felt like a punch to Nelly's stomach. Even though Angel's letter had warned of this possibility, Nelly had not thought for one moment that it might happen so quickly.

'Surely they can't send her away like that!' she cried.

'They're her parents and they can do as they will.'

'But she's been so poorly!'

'She's ready to start a programme of recuperation now.' The nurse hesitated. 'Besides, we need the bed; so many children are afflicted.'

Nelly could hardly hold a thought in her mind.

'When does she go?' she asked, desperately.

'She leaves tomorrow morning, in the care of a private nurse.'

'No,' Nelly said, 'no! She cannot! The seas are dangerous at this time of year. It's not safe.'

The nurse put a calming hand on Nelly's arm.

'Don't distress yourself, miss. Harriet will be travelling on a reputable ship. She will be well cared for. And the sanatorium has a fine reputation. The mountain air will do her good.' The nurse looked closely at Harriet. 'I can see a likeness between you. Are you Harriet's sister?'

'No,' Nelly said, 'I am not her sister.'

There was a moment's silence, during which Nelly surmised the nurse had worked out the truth; that she understood all the truths that could not be spoken. There was pity in her eyes but pity changed nothing.

She gave a small sigh.

'Who should I say left the gifts, then?' she asked.

'A friend,' Nelly said. 'Tell Harriet it was a loving friend.'

42

All the way back on the train, Nelly's heart twisted itself in knots as she attempted to devise a plan to prevent Harriet being taken abroad. No reasonable scheme came to mind. She could not take a sick child on the run at this time of year. Her savings were pitifully meagre, she had no friends outside Bristol to whom she could turn; she could not expect Harriet to sleep beneath hedgerows, like the peddler and his wife. She would do nothing that might hurt Harriet. The only way to do no harm, it seemed, was to stay away.

Nelly leaned her head against the train's window and watched the fog rush by. She could not recall a time when she had felt so unhappy. She was losing Harriet all over again, and nothing had been gained; nothing achieved. She did not know when, or if, she would ever see her daughter again. The loss pained her more than she could say.

And it was because of him: Edward Fairfield. Liar. Philanderer. Murderer.

* * *

The *Courier* offices were on the opposite side of Temple Meads station to Arnos Vale cemetery, where Priscilla Fairfield's funeral was to take place, so it made no sense for Nelly to go back to work on her return from the hospital. Besides, she didn't have time and she wasn't in the mood for the office. During the last part of the train journey, her frustration and despair had transmuted into blade-sharp determination. She would not stop until she had proved Sir Edward had killed his wife and her child, and brought him to justice. She needed to witness the interment.

She knew she was stretching her good fortune. If the board meeting luncheon finished early, and Mr Bagnet realised she was absent without leave, and had been for most of the day, Nelly would be in trouble. But she was tired of obeying restrictive rules; weary of being told what she couldn't do, how she must behave, who she must be.

That day, Nelly felt that everyone who tried to control her could go to hell. She did not care. Let them be damned.

* * *

Arnos Vale cemetery had been created to give Bristolians somewhere safe to bury their loved ones. The persistence of a cholera epidemic some years earlier had been blamed on well water contaminated by disease emanating from the bodies piled into the graves of the city's overcrowded churchyards.

Arnos Vale, physically removed from the city centre, with acres of land and green space all around it, seemed a long way from such dreadfulness.

Modelled on the finest burial grounds in Paris and London, it was an Arcadian garden cemetery, containing thousands of newly planted trees, and Greek-style architecture. In summer, the beds were planted with glorious floral displays, and in springtime, wildflowers filled the sloping woodlands.

Nelly had walked through the grounds on fine days and found them uplifting. But this afternoon, in the fog, the cemetery assumed a different personality. Most of it was hidden behind a curtain of grey. Monuments, crypts and trees faded into the gloom, losing their form until all that was left of them were sinister dark shadows.

Nelly pulled the hood of her cloak over her head and walked forward.

A burial, not Priscilla's, was taking place to one side of the track that led in a circle around the main part of the cemetery. Nelly walked past the mourners as the coffin was removed from the back of the hearse. She kept her distance, hiding herself in the fog.

She was early for Priscilla Fairfield's funeral and it was cold. She went inside the Anglican chapel, but it was barely warmer in there. Chairs had been arranged in lines, with the catafalque prepared to receive a coffin. The chapel was well served with large windows, but on a day like this they did not help brighten the interior. Nelly came out again and returned to hover close to the entrance off Bath Road. She did not know where Priscilla and her baby were to be buried, and if she missed their arrival, she might not find them in the mist.

* * *

By the time she heard the clopping of hooves slow and turn into the cemetery at five minutes to three, Nelly was bitterly cold. She kept her hood low, concealing herself behind a large, stone monument. Two black horses turned onto the track. They were draped in black regalia, with black ostrich plumes attached to the harnesses on top of their heads, and were pulling a closed hearse carriage; the coffin visible through glass windows. A bunch of white lilies lay on top. Nelly peered out from her hiding place. There was a mourning carriage behind.

Nelly waited until the small procession had turned away from her, and then she slipped out, and followed at a distance until the horses stopped. The undertakers removed the coffin from the hearse, and the mourners who had been inside the second carriage stepped down from it.

The first was a woman in her late twenties, or thereabouts, wearing a bonnet with black feathers clipped to its ribbon and a fur-trimmed coat made of bombazine. Both looked of the highest quality, but were old-fashioned and had seen better days. She carried her head slightly forward, like a bird about to peck at something. As she alighted the carriage, she looked about herself anxiously.

After her came another woman, a little shorter and younger; almost certainly a servant, although a high-ranking one, judging by how at ease she was beside her companion. There was no sign of Sir Edward Fairfield.

He must be here, thought Nelly. Surely he would not miss his wife's funeral, even if he had not loved her at all.

But he was not present.

When the two mourners were ready, the undertakers lifted the coffin and carried it on their shoulders, following one of the smaller paths that wound uphill into the forested area. In this weather there was nothing lovely about the path. It was muddy underfoot, with no green left at all; no birdsong; nothing but the wreathing mist.

Nelly waited until the undertakers and the pathetically small funeral party had disappeared into the murkiness of the foggy woodland before she came forward. She walked past the hearse, and the mourning carriage, the horses being held by the undertaker's lad, and followed the procession along the narrow pathway, which bent and twisted uphill for a short distance, before she saw them again. They had stopped before a large stone crypt. It was enclosed by a metal chain strung between small pillars. The edifice was imposing and severe; no angels, no flowers, no tenderness here.

The chief undertaker turned to speak with the woman in the feathered bonnet. They had a brief conversation and then the undertaker said something to his men. Nelly couldn't hear what had been said, but it immediately became clear that there was to be no service for Priscilla Fairfield.

The undertaker had the keys to the crypt; he took them from his pocket. He opened the metal gate that enclosed the wooden door, and then the door itself, and his men, carrying the coffin, followed him inside. The undertaker was carrying a lantern containing a candle, to guide the way.

The two mourners waited outside, blowing on their hands, huddled against the cold. Nelly, with her cloak wrapped tightly around her, came a little closer. She stood behind a copse of young trees, trying not to make a sound.

The taller of the pair, in the threadbare black coat, was comforting the other. 'Oh, Miss Avery,' the shorter woman said, 'this is so sad. I don't know how I shall ever get over it!'

So that was Madeleine Avery, Sir Edward Fairfield's stepdaughter. Nelly felt a twinge of satisfaction at seeing the woman, at last.

Miss Avery put her arms around the other woman and held her close, murmuring consolations.

'Lady Fairfield is at peace now, Violet. Of course, you miss her, we all do, but you know that she is gone to a better place.

You must try to think of what's happened as a blessed escape for her.'

'I cannot, for I am to blame for her death,' the one called Violet said.

'Of course, you're not to blame! What on earth do you mean by that?'

Nelly leaned a little closer.

'The doctor gave me some medicine to give to Lady Fairfield,' said Violet. 'Sophy took it from me. She promised she would give it to Lady Fairfield herself, but she never did. I found the phial in the drawer at the side of Lady Fairfield's bed and the seal unbroken.'

'Ah,' said Miss Avery. 'I see.' She took hold of the young woman's gloved hand and enclosed it between her own, shaking it slightly for emphasis. 'Violet, believe me, that medicine would not have helped Lady Fairfield.'

'Don't you think it would have?'

'I know it would not.'

'That's what Sophy said.'

'Well, there you are, then. You know, don't you, that Sophy is *always* right?'

Violet gave a feeble laugh.

'That's true enough. She used to get on my nerves, but now she's gone, I do miss her.' She paused and sniffed back her tears. 'I miss you too, Miss Avery. Mordaunt Hall was always a bleak place but these days, oh, it's dreadful there.' She lowered her voice. 'If it wasn't for my sister, I would look for another position in a heartbeat.'

Madeleine Avery held Violet's hand to her heart.

'When you are ready, Violet, I shall help you escape! You shall come and work for me.' She glanced over Violet's shoulder. 'Oh, they are coming back out.'

The two women turned back towards the crypt as the undertakers emerged without the coffin.

The chief undertaker, who had a hawkish nose that lent him a sombre air, bowed solemnly.

He passed the lilies that had been on top of the coffin to Madeleine Avery, who laid them on the ground.

'The coffin is in its final resting place, Madam,' the undertaker said. 'We have left the candles alight, if you would care to go down to pay your last respects.'

'I think not,' said Miss Avery, 'but let the candles burn awhile to keep her company.'

Then the small group turned and walked away, back down towards the waiting hearse, Madeleine's arm around Violet's waist.

Nelly stepped out of her hiding place.

The doors to the crypt were still open.

43

Nelly didn't have time to think; if she had, she would never have done what she did next. She acted on instinct, compelled to see for herself what lay within.

She waited until the mourners had passed, then she crept forward, following the little path through the chippings, and on in through the mausoleum door.

Beyond, steps led down to an opening, flickering shadows on the floor proof that the candles were still lit. Gathering her skirts and cloak, she went down the stone stairs, and found herself in an underground room, a cellar really, that was about twice as large as the edifice above it though not as tall with metal sconces built into the walls and a hook in the ceiling from which a lamp might be suspended. This cellar was lined with stone shelves, ready to receive the coffins that held the mortal remains of members of the Fairfield family. For now, it contained only three. One, labelled Lady Frances Fairfield, was covered in dust and cobwebs. Lady Frances, 'mother to Edward', had died in 1838, a year after Arnos Vale opened. The second, on the shelf beneath, was more recent and although Nelly could not see the plaque, she guessed it belonged to Lady Maria Fairfield. The third was new. It was on the other side of the crypt, on the floor, against the wall, almost hidden beneath the shelf above it.

Nelly picked a candle from a sconce and went over to the coffin.

'Priscilla?' she whispered, crouching down, at last close to the one for whom she had been searching.

She closed her eyes and brought to mind the face of the young woman in the photograph: that vivid, vital girl whose life had been taken when she was at her most vulnerable. Nelly was silent for a moment. Then she whispered: 'I will expose the truth, Priscilla. I won't let him do this to anyone else.'

And then she heard a noise behind her, and she dropped the candle, feeling as if her heart would stop.

She turned slowly, her pulse galloping.

Sir Edward Fairfield stood stooped before her, tall and wan as a summonsed apparition. His face, awfully shadowed, had an expression of horror, and he was holding one hand to his heart.

'Oh, dear God!' he muttered. 'I thought you were she! I thought you were Priscilla!'

He staggered, and for a terrible moment Nelly thought he might collapse. He leaned against the wall, breathing deeply and blocking the stairs, so she had no means of escaping him.

When he had recovered his equilibrium, he slowly removed the hand from his chest. His face was skull-like, his eyes reflecting pinpricks of candlelight. He was hunched like a crow because of the crypt's low ceiling. There was something cruel and murderous about him.

Nelly stood before him, the coffins of his mother and first wife to one side, and Priscilla's to the other. The candles flickered, as if holding their breaths, casting weird and ghastly shadows.

'Miss Brooks,' Sir Edward said at last, his voice dry and cold. 'How dare you intrude on the sacred resting place of the dead? How dare you contaminate a funeral with such discourtesy? Such lack of respect?'

He appeared composed but Nelly sensed a great violence within him. She was afraid to turn her back to him. If he were to kill her, no court in the land would blame him for lashing out in such circumstances.

She was paralysed by fear.

'Get out!' he cried. 'Get out of here, damn you! You shall answer for this!'

She walked past him slowly, holding tight to her skirts, climbed the steps back to the tiny upper chamber of the crypt, expecting a blow to the head with every heartbeat. She stepped out through the door into the cold and the fog.

And then she ran.

44

Nelly did not know how or when retribution would come, but she knew that it would come, and that it would be unforgiving. She decided to take a pre-emptive approach and confess what she had done to George Boldwood before Sir Edward made a complaint, either directly or via the board of directors.

Back at the *Courier* offices, she combed her hair and tidied herself, standing at the cloakroom mirror. She looked into her own face and saw the faces of Priscilla Fairfield and Eliza Morgan looking back. And there would be others, she was sure of it.

Still, she dreaded what she must do because she knew George Boldwood would be hurt by what he would see as her betrayal. He had shown her nothing but respect and kindness, taken a risk with her and made her his protégée, and she had let him down.

Heart pounding, she approached Mr Bagnet. 'May I have a word with Mr Boldwood, please?'

The secretary checked the clock. 'He'll be going home shortly. Can't it wait until tomorrow?'

'I'm afraid that it can't.'

'Send her in, Jeremiah!' Mr Boldwood called. 'I've always got time for my fifth daughter.'

That was what he called Nelly when he was in a particularly buoyant mood. On this occasion, his kindliness twisted Nelly's heart.

Mr Bagnet opened the door, and she stepped inside.

'Nelly!' said Mr Boldwood, in his delighted-to-see-you, avuncular way. His smile faded when he saw her expression. 'What is it? Is something wrong?'

All Nelly's confidence drained. She wanted to run and hide, or to become very small and disappear – but she must do the opposite. She straightened her shoulders and lifted her chin. 'I fear I have upset an important man in pursuit of a story, Mr Boldwood. I wanted to tell you myself before you heard it from any other source, and before a complaint is made.'

'You? Upset somebody? Oh, Nelly dear, I think that's unlikely.' He indicated that she should sit down. 'Now, tell me what happened.'

Nelly took a deep breath. 'I went to an interment, today, at Arnos Vale.' She hesitated. 'It was that of Sir Edward Fairfield's wife, Priscilla.'

A shadow crossed Mr Boldwood's face.

'Did you know this Priscilla?'

'No.'

'Then why did you go to her funeral?'

Nelly could feel the blood drain from her cheeks.

'Nelly?' Mr Boldwood asked, sitting opposite her and leaning forwards across the round table.

'I had been told on what I believed to be good authority,' Nelly said, 'that Lady Fairfield and her child had been murdered.'

'You mean you'd heard a rumour?'

'I thought it was true. I still think—'

Mr Boldwood stood up and put a hand to his forehead. 'Have you ever heard me say, Nelly, never to chase a rumour? They are shadows cast by the spiteful, the revengeful, the stupid. No reporter should ever follow a rumour, for it will only ever lead to court.'

'I have heard you say that, yes.'

'But you didn't listen.'

'I did, but—'

'And, Nelly, I am tired of saying it, but why were you concerning yourself with a rumour about a murder in the first place? Your remit is the women's page, no more and no less. You know perfectly well that you should have passed the rumour, if you believed it had any validity, on to Will, or Duncan or one of the others.'

'Yes, sir, I know that's what I should have done. But I have been yearning after an opportunity to write a strong news story.'

'We have sufficient well-trained and experienced male reporters to cover the news.'

He strode over to the window and gazed out. 'You were not invited to this funeral, I assume?' he asked, with his back to Nelly.

'No, sir.'

'Of course, you weren't. Sir Edward is a very private man. What did you do, Nelly, at this funeral?'

'I observed discreetly, from a distance.'

'You did not intrude upon it?'

'No, sir.'

Mr Boldwood looked immensely relieved. 'Well, then, there is no harm done. You must stop whatever it is you are doing with regards to the deaths of Lady Fairfield and her child right now, Nelly, and hopefully we'll hear no more of it.'

'I'm afraid, sir, that there is more.'

George Boldwood was relaxing. Nelly could tell that whatever he thought she was about to confess would be something trivial. His expression now was one of a parent being bothered by a troublesome child.

'Out with it,' he said. 'Let's get this over with.'

Nelly cleared her throat. 'When the mourners had moved away, I...'

She hesitated. Mr Boldwood leaned forward.

'Yes?'

She clenched her fists. She wished for an interruption, anything to stop her having to say the fateful words.

'I went into the Fairfield family crypt,' she said.

'You did *what*?'

'I ventured into the crypt, sir.'

Mr Boldwood struggled to comprehend the gravity of what Nelly was saying.

'Why, Nelly? Why would you do such a thing?'

'I felt compelled, sir. I was following the story and... Well... The long and short of it is, Sir Edward Fairfield found me there.'

'In the crypt?'

'Yes, sir. I startled him. He thought I was the ghost of his dead wife.'

'Oh, Nelly,' said George Boldwood.

'I'm sorry,' Nelly said. 'I'm truly sorry, Mr Boldwood. Not for what I did, but for betraying your trust.'

'What were you thinking of? *Why*, Nelly? Why would you do something so reckless?'

'As I told you, sir, I believed, I still believe, that Lady Fairfield and the child were murdered.'

He shook his head as he battled to contain his frustration.

'How many times have I warned you against interfering in the lives of these people?'

'Many times,' Nelly answered.

George Boldwood's eyes were heavy.

'You have gone too far, Nelly. Far too far. I do not know how I, or anyone else, can protect you from the consequences of this.'

45

Nelly was suspended from work with immediate effect.

She was told to collect her personal belongings and go home.

George Boldwood would not wait for a complaint to come in; he would write to Sir Edward himself, and invite him to a meeting to discuss the matter. Depending on the outcome of that, he would decide whether or not to raise what had happened with the directors at the next board meeting. Both Mr Boldwood and Nelly knew that he would have to give Edward Fairfield whatever he demanded to compensate for Nelly's indiscretion, and that would almost certainly mean dismissal. Her future at the *Courier* hung in the balance and the weights were tipped against her.

Will, back from the photography expedition to the bridge, saw Nelly coming out of the editor's office and came over to her.

'Is everything all right?' he asked.

Mr Boldwood had told her not to say anything to anyone, but Nelly was in so much trouble already that she didn't think one further act of insubordination would make much difference.

'I've been suspended.'

'Suspended? Why?'

'I got involved with something that Mr Boldwood thinks I should have left well alone.'

'You're always doing that.'

'I have overstepped this time. Let me be, Will. I have to pick up my things and leave.'

'Nelly, tell me what it was that you did!'

'I'm not even supposed to be talking to you.'

She gave him an apologetic smile, to show that she was not being purposefully evasive, then began to collect her belongings. She deliberated over her notebook – officially *Courier* property – and the green velvet shawl, but in the end took both and walked out of the office. She could not bring herself to say goodbye to anyone because that would mean explaining.

It would mean shame. It would mean the vindication of their opinions that a newspaper office was no place for a woman.

Maud raised her head from her desk as Nelly walked past. *What's going on?* she mouthed.

Nelly did not respond.

Duncan frowned to see Nelly leaving, but was deep in conversation with the political editor and could not break away.

Will walked down the stairs with Nelly. 'If there's anything I can do...'

'There isn't,' Nelly said.

At the bottom of the stairs, they crossed the foyer.

'Does this trouble concern Sir Edward Fairfield?' Will asked. 'You've shown an uncommon interest in him lately. And I noticed you'd been studying his cuttings.'

'I can't tell you, Will.'

She hitched her satchel onto her shoulder and reached for the doorknob.

'It looks cold out there,' said Will. 'Why don't you wear the shawl?'

'It's not mine to wear,' said Nelly. 'Goodbye, Will.'

She pulled up her hood, pushed open the door, and stepped outside.

The fog, now it was meshed with the smoke issuing from chimneys across the city, was worse than it had been earlier. Nelly held a handkerchief to her mouth and breathed through that, for the filthy air hurt her lungs.

Is this how my career ends? she wondered. A solitary walk of shame away from the job she adored, and the friends she had made, having broken the heart of the editor who'd taken a chance on her, she having lied, deceived and disobeyed him.

She remembered her mother telling her: 'There's something wrong with you, Helen Brooks, something missing.'

Mrs Brooks had meant that Nelly was deficient in femininity, but was that all Nelly lacked? Was there some intrinsic part of her personality that had failed to develop, which meant she was destined to keep building the life she thought she desired, and then destroying it?

She stopped outside The Three Horseshoes, thinking that a drink would be a nice restorative before she walked up the hill. Two drinks would be better. Three drinks and, if she spotted the watchman, she would give him a piece of her mind. Four drinks and she might stop despairing about Harriet.

She opened the door and went inside. It was warm, and fuggy, little lamps making reflections on the tankards and glasses. The bottles lined up behind the bar sparkled.

Nelly smiled at the barmaid. She opened her satchel and took out her purse. And there was the folded piece of paper inside on which Nelly had written the details of Priscilla's funeral, with the name and address of the undertaker's.

M Surguy. Commercial Road.

'Yes, miss,' said the barmaid. 'What can I get for you?'

'Sorry,' Nelly said, 'I've just remembered; I have a job to do.'

46

Nelly was out of breath when she reached her destination on the Commercial Road. She found herself at the side of a busy thoroughfare, lined with an assortment of shops, their façades blackened by smoke and dirt. A butcher's shop, its window hung with carcasses, was beside an ironmongery. There was an establishment that sold haberdashery, a furrier's, a second-hand book store.

Nelly soon found the place she was seeking. A board above the front announced:

M Surguy. Funeral Director, Undertaker, Embalmer, Cremator, Hearses, Gothic and Classic Carriages.

Beneath that was the script:

Private mortuary for the reception of remains.

Nelly opened the door, heard the ringing of a bell in the back, and stepped inside.

The interior was pleasantly warm, and decorated like a stage set, with black gauze swags draped across the windows and walls, a display of plaster-of-Paris memorials and an urn containing strongly scented white lilies. Nelly had been expecting to be greeted by the beak-nosed undertaker she'd seen at the cemetery earlier, but instead a rosy-cheeked woman appeared from the back.

'Good afternoon,' she said. 'How can I help you, miss...?'

'My name is Nelly Brooks.'

'And I'm Mrs Surguy, the funeral director's wife.' She tipped her head, eyes full of sympathy. 'Have you suffered a bereavement?'

'No,' said Nelly. 'I have deep concerns about a young woman and child who were brought to you some days ago, and who were interred today at Arnos Vale.'

The woman blanched.

'Deep concerns?' she repeated. 'Oh goodness! Won't you take a seat, dear, and we can talk? Would you like some tea? I have a fresh pot made out the back.'

Nelly said she would very much like some tea, and she sat on one of the chairs by the desk, upholstered in black, and most comfortable. Behind the desk, a bronze cage was suspended from a hook and inside it, a little bird fluttered from perch to perch and sang. The bird made Nelly feel sad – she believed no creature should be caged – until she realised it was an automaton, a clockwork bird. It was not, on closer inspection, particularly realistic, although the feathers with which it was adorned appeared to be real. Strange how the mind made assumptions. Just because something looked like a wren, and sounded like a wren, it didn't mean it was a wren.

Mrs Surguy returned with a tray. She placed two cups and saucers on the polished surface of the occasional table beside

Nelly's chair and came to sit beside her. Nelly took a sip of the tea, hot and strong, from the rim of a delicate bone-china cup. It was delicious – she had gone all day without sustenance and would happily have consumed the entire cupful in one go if she weren't being observed.

'Now, tell me about these concerns you mentioned,' said Mrs Surguy. 'I assume the funeral to which you referred was that of Lady Priscilla Fairfield, as that was the only one of ours at Arnos Vale today. Was there a problem with the coffin, perhaps?'

'Oh, no, the concerns have nothing to do with the service provided. The funeral went to plan as far as I could tell. I'm sorry, I should have made myself clear.'

Nelly took a deep breath.

'Mrs Surguy, I cannot think of a courteous or sensitive way to ask this question, so I will simply ask it. I heard from somebody close to Lady Fairfield that her death was not natural. And I wondered if you, or your husband, had noticed anything peculiar about her corpse.'

'Oh,' said Mrs Surguy. The question had clearly made her uncomfortable. After a moment's deliberation, she answered carefully: 'I didn't see anything untoward, and my husband didn't say anything.'

Nelly understood that she was asking the woman to betray the trust of an enormously important client. She asked the next question as gently as she possibly could.

'But an undertaker as experienced as your husband would have observed, if, for example, the skin of the face was discoloured in a manner that might have indicated foul play?'

'Of course!'

Mrs Surguy paused, then added: 'Lady Fairfield's corpse came to us already dressed in a delightful gown, her hair arranged and her skin powdered and rouged. Mr Surguy and me both looked at it, to admire her beauty. I am certain that, had there been any bruises on the face, we would have noticed them.'

'What if there had been small, red marks?'

'As I said, the face had been prettified before the body came to us. But there was nothing obvious.'

Nelly nodded and looked into her teacup. She had been so hoping for a breakthrough – some kind of evidence that could not be disputed. This had turned out to be a wasted journey.

'Were you friends with the deceased?' Mrs Surguy asked.

'I did not know her. But she means a great deal to me.' Now Nelly deliberated about how much to give away. 'If harm was done to her,' she said, 'I am committed to exposing it.'

Mrs Surguy sighed.

'The sudden loss of one so young is always shocking,' she said. 'It's human nature to want to blame someone. But sometimes, these things just happen. Childbirth is a dangerous time for women.'

'Yes,' said Nelly.

'Try not to dwell on it,' said the woman, tenderness in her eyes. 'Look to the joys still left to you, my dear. It is the only way my husband and I can remain cheerful in a world with so much sorrow.'

There was a silence, during which the little mechanical bird stopped singing, and the heavy wooden clock on the wall ticked, its pendulum swinging back and forth as if to demonstrate the speed with which time, and life, slipped by.

Then, unprompted, the undertaker's wife spoke again. 'Of course, we were surprised to be asked to take care of poor Lady Fairfield in the first place.'

Nelly paused, the teacup halfway to her lips. 'Why was that?'

'Because, normally, Fairfield funerals are handled by Glanvilles – they're a far grander and bigger undertakers than we are, and based just round the corner from Mordaunt Hall. They've looked after all the Fairfield deaths for as long as anyone can remember. Miss Avery – it was Miss Avery who approached us – never explained why she wanted us to take care of Lady Fairfield. We're only a small business and we've never looked after anyone as well-to-do as that before, but we weren't going to say "no", were we? It wasn't a big funeral, nor a showy one, so we could manage it perfectly well. And I'd be lying if I didn't say we were astounded by the fee Miss Avery offered to pay. She said it was only fair, given that the situation was a little out of the ordinary.'

'In what way was it out of the ordinary?'

'Well, for a start, Miss Avery brought the body to us, in a carriage, and it was already dressed and ready for the coffin. And we didn't look after the infant at all. He only came, entirely swaddled, this very morning, and was placed in the crook of his mother's arms before the coffin was sealed. Miss Avery said she had wished to take care of the child's remains herself. You should've seen the tenderness with which she laid him down, Miss Brooks. It was evident to those of us present how dearly she must have loved him.'

47

Nelly was late for supper again that evening and so ate alone by the fire in the dining room. It was only leftovers, poor Sarah still was not feeling well. Leftovers suited Nelly's mood, for she was still fretting dreadfully over Harriet. Her heart was telling her to return to the hospital while she still could; her head reminded her that any kind of disruption or distress would only hurt her daughter.

Let go of the child, Angel had written. You cannot have her.

Last time, the letting go had been violently enforced. Now Nelly had to make a choice to stay away from her daughter, the conflicting emotions she was enduring were almost unbearable.

When she had finished eating, Nelly took her tray down to the kitchen, to save Ida the journey up, and found she and Sarah sitting close to the kitchen hearth. Ida was knitting, and Sarah was in the rocking chair with Flossy on her lap and a camphorated cloth around her neck.

'How is your throat?' Nelly asked.

'It feels as if it's been brushed with wire.'

'Sip your cordial and don't talk,' said Ida. 'It's most likely an excess of chatting that's given you the bad throat in the first place.'

Sarah rolled her eyes. Ida smiled.

Nelly poured herself some coffee from the pot and pulled up a chair beside them. Ida and Sarah were close friends, and they were kind enough not to exclude Nelly when she came to sit with them like this, on a cold evening. She knew they moderated their conversation when she was present, but there was no tension between the three of them. This was one of the small pleasures Nelly had come to take for granted as part of her life in the Orchard Hill house. But if she had no job, she would not be able to afford to stay here. Now she risked losing these small moments of companionship, she realised how much she appreciated them and how they added to the sum of good in her life. She tucked her feet up beneath her on the chair and listened to the women's voices and the crackling of the logs in the fireplace. She felt as if she was on the brink of losing everything.

It was past eight o'clock when the knock came at the door.

Ida grumbled as she got up, putting on the boots she had taken off to give her poor feet a breather.

'Who's that,' she muttered, 'disturbing people at a time when respectable people are tucked up safe inside their homes?'

She climbed the stairs up to the ground floor with deliberate slowness and before she'd reached the top, the knock came again.

'Patience!' she called. 'I'm coming.'

She opened the door, and said irritably, 'Yes? Can I help you?'

A male voice replied. 'I was wondering if I might have a word with Miss Nelly Brooks.'

Nelly untangled her legs from her petticoats and stood up.

It was Will.

* * *

They sat together in the dining room, Nelly and Will. He had brought a bottle of Maud's home-made cherry wine as a gift.

'Maud says it is very good,' he said. 'She says that, in moderation, its properties are medicinal.' He coughed nervously. 'She insists it's not as strong as it tastes. What I can confirm is that it's utterly delicious.' He looked at Nelly. 'Right now, you look as if you could do with a nip of something strong.'

Nelly took two glasses from the sideboard and put them on the table. Will poured the wine and passed a glass to Nelly.

'Here's to you,' he said.

They clinked glasses. There was an awkward pause. Then Nelly asked, 'Why are you here?'

'Partly to assure you of my unfailing moral support. And partly because I'd like you to tell me about this Fairfield story you've been working on. The one for which you were prepared to risk your job.'

'I can't, Will.'

'Why can't you? Are you worried I'll steal it from you?'

She gave a small laugh. 'I was, but no, it's not that. Sir Edward is on the warpath. He has his sights on me at the moment, but I don't want your career to be threatened also.'

'Tell me the story,' Will said. 'Perhaps the situation can still be salvaged.'

'Too much damage has been done.'

'What is this?' Will exclaimed, in mock astonishment. 'Nelly Brooks, giving up?'

This time she did not smile.

'You cannot stop now,' said Will. 'You have the time and liberty to investigate with every ounce of your being. I will help you where I can.'

'Will, you mustn't. You are a good friend to me, but I cannot allow you to risk all that you have achieved simply to help me out of a hole which I dug myself.'

'With all due respect, Nelly, what I do with my life is my choice, not yours.'

Will pushed up his glasses. He cleared his throat. 'I trust you are aware that I think very highly of you, Nelly Brooks.'

Nelly did not know how to respond to this, so she took a sip of her drink. It was sweet and strong. She coughed.

'Medicinal?' she asked.

'Medicinal,' Will confirmed. 'Now, tell me about the Fairfields.'

Nelly put more coal on the fire, and then she talked. She told Will how she was adamant, now, that Sir Edward Fairfield had gone into Priscilla's room while she was sleeping on the night of Sunday, 23 October and held a pillow over her face until she was dead, and then he'd done the same to the infant she'd delivered hours earlier. She believed the evidence of the murder on Priscilla's body had been concealed by Madeleine Avery, working with the maid, Sophy.

'You genuinely believe Sir Edward killed his wife and the baby?' asked Will.

'To protect himself from a huge scandal, yes.'

'I've never heard of a man of his standing committing such a crime.'

'Because usually,' said Nelly, 'such crimes are concealed behind insurmountable walls of respectability. Nobody ever challenges men like Sir Edward on account of their power and influence.'

She thought of the courage of poor Eliza Morgan with a pang of regret.

Will remained unconvinced.

'He could have divorced Priscilla.'

'And exposed all the family secrets, including the fact that he'd been cuckolded by this young woman, to the public and the press? A man such as he could not have borne the shame.'

'Or he could have sent her to the asylum.'

'But for as long as Priscilla was alive in an asylum, he would not be free of her. A woman's insanity is not grounds for divorce. And there would remain the possibility of the scandal coming to light.'

'Why harm the baby?'

'If the baby survived, then Sir Edward would have no choice but to acknowledge him as his own progeny. That would have meant bringing him up, caring for him *and* the infant would become heir to the Fairfield fortune.'

She took a drink. 'You have met Sir Edward, haven't you, Will?'

'Several times. He's ruthless, certainly. Not a man you'd want to cross. Not if you valued your livelihood or your reputation.'

'Priscilla crossed him.'

'And now you have too.'

Nelly nodded regretfully.

'Although, to be truthful, Will, it was not Sir Edward who was my undoing, but me. I was so close to finding the answers I needed, and then I ruined everything. I still don't know what impulse drove me to enter that crypt.'

'I do.'

'You do?'

'You had to see everything, Nelly Brooks. You had to know. You are a real reporter, through and through,' said Will. 'It's in your blood.'

48

THURSDAY, 3 NOVEMBER

Nelly's sleep had been fractured; she'd sweated and tossed and turned within the sheets that tangled around her legs. She believed the watchman was standing beside her bed, holding the shawl taut between his hands, intending to strangle her. She woke from the dream screaming – the pitch of her own voice woke her, and when she opened her eyes, heart pounding in panic, and saw that she was alone in her quiet, safe room on the top floor of number 12 Orchard Hill, her relief was immense. She was thirsty, after drinking so much of Maud's cherry wine, so she got up and padded across the floor, to pour herself a glass of water from the jug. She looked out of the window and saw a figure lurking at the periphery of the light from the street lamp.

Nelly shivered. She climbed back into bed and pulled the covers over her.

She could hear murmuring noises from the misses below, and glimmers of light shone through the cracks in the floorboards. Her screams must have woken them. Nelly was sorry, but that night, in the cold, dead hours before dawn, she was grateful for their voices, and their presence.

* * *

That was the night's trauma, and now it was morning and Nelly was awake early and the prospect of a day with nothing to do was strange: she felt unanchored, as if, without the usual structure and customs, she might drift away. She hadn't only lost her job yesterday, but she'd also lost Harriet again.

It was too much, all at once.

She dressed and went down to eat breakfast with Miss Sylvester and Miss Norton, so that she might apologise for disturbing them in the night.

'We wondered if the house spirit had stirred from its slumbers,' said Miss Norton, catching Miss Sylvester's eye to share some private joke that made Nelly feel excluded. She was fond of the two misses, but that morning their twittering irritated her heavy heart. She was relieved when Mrs Augur came in, but that was only to say that she and Eveline were going to visit friends in Exeter and would not be back for several days. She trusted her lodgers would be taken care of in her absence by Sarah and Ida, but if they had any concerns, it would be prudent to address them now.

None of the three lodgers had concerns.

After breakfast, Nelly returned to her room, and while Ida cleaned around her, she wrote down the notes from her encounter with the funeral director's wife, and then she read through all the notes about the Priscilla Fairfield case to refresh her memory and to see if there was anything she had missed.

Keeping her mind occupied in this manner prevented it from dwelling on Harriet, and what might be happening to her that morning. Also, Will's encouragement had renewed her enthusiasm for the story.

There was one question that Nelly, try as she might, could

not answer. She was certain now that Madeleine Avery was involved, if not in the actual murder of Priscilla Fairfield, then in the covering up of it. But why? And why had she chosen to use the services of Mr Surguy, rather than the undertakers traditionally used by the Fairfields?

Nelly drummed her fingers on the tabletop.

Ida was cleaning the fireplace. She tipped the ashes from the dustpan into a sheet of newspaper and folded it over. She was humming to herself.

'Ida,' Nelly said, 'will you help me with something?'

'If I can.'

'Why might people choose to use the services of a business who were strangers to them, over one they'd always used before?'

'Why?' Ida took the question seriously. She sat back on her heels and scratched her neck beneath the ear. 'Well, maybe they'd fallen out over something. Perhaps the old business had short-changed the people, or sold them something poor-quality.'

'Yes.'

'Or, they might've become greedy, charging too much. Or they could have employed new staff who the people didn't like.'

'Possibly.'

'Or...' Ida said, 'perhaps it's the people that's the problem.'

'What do you mean?'

'Maybe they're ashamed of something they've done. Maybe they stole from the business, or maligned them and they decided to go somewhere new, where they wouldn't be recognised.'

Nelly had not considered that final point but it was a good one. Perhaps Miss Avery hadn't wanted to use the Fairfields' usual undertakers because they were more likely to notice that something was amiss with Priscilla's body.

Nelly drew a large question mark in her notebook.

What she needed was an independent witness; someone

who'd been at Mordaunt Hall on the night of Priscilla's death but was not involved in it. Violet, the young woman who had accompanied Madeleine Avery to Priscilla's funeral, fitted the bill perfectly.

Nelly needed to speak to Violet.

49

Before she left the house on Orchard Hill, Nelly told Sarah not to worry if she wasn't back for a day or two, and suggested to Ida that she leave the fire in her room unlit, rather than waste good coal.

'Where are you going?' Sarah asked.

'It's an assignment for the newspaper,' said Nelly.

'My!' said Sarah, 'how thrilling!'

Nelly packed a comb, a small piece of soap wrapped in a handkerchief, a brush for her teeth, a wrap of tooth-powder, some money, her notebook and several pencils into her satchel. She folded the green velvet shawl and put that on top of the other items. She pinned up her hair so that it was neat, and fastened the chain that held the locket that contained Harriet's hair, and the daisy, around her neck.

Nelly regarded herself in the mirror and thought: *You must stand up for yourself, and for what is right, for there is no one else to do it for you.*

She hoped that she might one day look her daughter in the

eye and say, 'Look what I did, Harriet. The odds were not in my favour, but I persisted.'

* * *

The fog had lifted now. The sun was shining brightly, and a thick frost had settled.

Nelly did not see the watchman that morning, but she sensed he was nearby and heard his muffled cough. She dawdled, giving him a chance to get close to her, then went into a milliner's shop. She asked the owner, who was a friend of Mrs Augur's, if she might exit through the living quarters to the back of the premises. Trusting that the watchman would be waiting at the front, she hurried to the carriage rank, where she caught the first available coach that could take her close to Mordaunt Hall.

The carriage dropped Nelly in the main street of what had once been an independent village, now subsumed into the city of Bristol. It was, she was advised, a short walk to the hall. Nelly hitched the strap of the satchel onto her shoulder, and set forth.

The nerves did not set in until Nelly reached the entrance to the estate: a pair of large, ornate, wrought-iron gates set into a tall wall. Ahead was a long drive, gravelled, with frozen pastureland between the trees on either side.

Nelly walked between the gates, enjoying the long shadows cast by the great, established trees, and the sight of fine, fat cattle seeking out the grass where the sun was melting the frost, their breath making clouds around their heads.

She reached the hall itself without incident. A sign affixed to the wall read 'Tradesmen's Entrance', and Nelly followed the pointed finger across a yard and into a service area. Washing was hanging on lines fixed to high poles at either side; there was an enormous coal-shed, an even bigger wood-store and other outbuildings. Chickens were pecking about an enclosed run on a lawned area with a pathway across it leading to a gate set into a wall. The gate was open and Nelly could see a magnificent kitchen garden beyond.

It was ordered and tidy; Sir Edward's staff clearly ran a tight ship.

The door into the main house was painted green. Nelly knocked and the door was opened by a plump woman with flushed cheeks with a cloth in her hands.

'Oh,' she said when she saw Nelly. 'I was expecting a delivery from the mill. You're not from the mill, are you?'

'I'm not,' said Nelly.

'What is it you want, then?'

Nelly adopted her most personable smile. 'I'm looking for a job. Do you have any work going?'

'Well, it's no good asking me, is it?' the woman said. 'It's not up to me.' She looked around to see if anyone else was in earshot, then said in a low voice, 'There's always people coming and going at the hall. It's not the cheeriest place, if you take my meaning. If I were you, I'd look elsewhere.'

Nelly's face must have fallen, for her expression softened.

'You've tried everywhere else, have you?'

'I have.'

The woman sighed. 'I'll see if I can find the housekeeper. She might have something she can offer you. What's your name?'

'Constance Parr.' Nelly had decided already to take on the name of her beloved friend from the asylum.

'Do people call you Connie?'

'Yes.'

'I'm Betty. I knew a Connie once. Great lazy lump of a girl she was. Come in, let me get that door shut before we all freeze to death.'

50

Nelly followed Betty through a kitchen where two women were so hard at work they barely glanced at her, and into a scullery, warmed by the hot water pipes running through it.

There was a large sink, and a pile of dead pheasants lying on sheets of newspaper on the wooden worktop. A young woman, with her sleeves rolled up, was spreading sacking over the floor, to catch the stray feathers when she plucked the fowl.

Betty asked this woman, 'Do you know where Mrs Lavant is?'

'She's about somewhere, all in a tizzy about the shooting party. Have you tried her room?'

'I haven't. This way, Connie,' Betty said.

At the end of the corridor, Betty knocked on a door labelled 'Housekeeper', and, when there was no answer, put her head around and peered in.

'She's not there,' she said. She was becoming flustered; all this was taking up her precious time.

'Shall I come back later?' Nelly asked.

'You're here now, aren't you?'

She showed Nelly into a small room that contained an assortment of old chairs and little else. It smelled of damp.

'This is the servants' lounge. Wait here,' Betty said, and disappeared.

Nelly looked around the dismal room. Perhaps the staff who came in here for a respite from their chores were too tired to care about their surroundings, for no effort had been made to make it more cheery. A soiled apron was draped over the back of one of the chairs, and an old pair of slippers had been discarded beneath another. Nelly perched on the edge of a seat. A clock ticked on the wall above the tiny fireplace where a few coals glowed.

Minutes went by. Quarter of an hour. Half an hour. Nelly became anxious. Had Betty forgotten her?

The door opened. Nelly looked up; it was not Betty, but Violet, the young woman who had accompanied Madeleine Avery at Priscilla's funeral.

'Oh,' she said, seeing Nelly on the chair by the fire. 'I didn't know anyone was here.'

'Don't mind me,' said Nelly.

'Well, then, I won't!'

Violet took a book out of her apron pocket, curled up on a chair, and, without saying another word, began to read.

Nelly studied the young woman surreptitiously. She was slender of build, with a small, pretty face; a thin nose, small mouth, light hair. She twisted a loose strand around one finger as she read. The skin on her hands was chapped; red-raw in places.

Nelly was loath to interrupt her, but she might not have another opportunity like this.

'I'm looking for work,' she began tentatively.

Violet looked at her over the book. 'And you've come here? Are you desperate or insane?'

'Is it so bad at Mordaunt Hall?'

Violet shrugged. 'The master of the house, Sir Edward Fairfield, has a most dreadful temper. None of us would stay if we didn't have to. My sister's married to the gamekeeper. If it wasn't for her, I'd have been out of here long since.'

She exhaled a puff of air and looked back to her book.

Nelly interrupted again. 'Was it better when the lady of the house was alive?'

'Yes,' said Violet.

She did not say anything else, so Nelly prompted: 'I heard she died in childbed.'

Violet nodded.

Keep talking, Nelly begged silently. *Tell me what happened.*

Violet opened her mouth to speak, then, as if she had perceived Nelly's desperation, suddenly stopped herself. She looked at Nelly through narrowed eyes. 'Why do you ask so many questions? What is all this to you? Who are you?'

Nelly felt a rush of panic. Had she gone too far?

'My name is Constance Parr – Connie,' she said calmly. 'I'm hoping to get a job at Mordaunt Hall, but I would like to know first what I'm coming into. If you feel I am prying, then I'll ask no more. The last thing I want is for us to start off on the wrong foot for, if I am employed here, I'd like us to be friends.'

'I understand,' Violet said resignedly. 'I would be the same. And, to tell the truth, Connie, it's a relief for me to talk. I used to have friends here, but they are all gone and now there is nobody in whom I can confide.'

She took a gulp of air. 'What was I saying?' she asked.

'That Lady Fairfield died after giving birth.'

'That's right.'

'Were you with her?'

'During the confinement I was.'

'She must have trusted you deeply.'

'She did. Me and Lady Fairfield's maid, Sophy, took it in turns to watch over her.'

'Just the two of you?'

'The doctor was there too.'

'Of course.' Nelly paused for a moment. Then she asked: 'Was it a difficult birth?'

'Not really. The baby birthed beautifully, a good, strong boy,' said Violet. 'And she, Lady Priscilla, she lost blood, but I've seen women survive far worse. When I went to bed that night, I was confident all was well.'

'When did you discover something was wrong?'

'I woke in the early hours. I went downstairs, and I saw Miss Avery coming out of Lady Fairfield's room and securing the door behind her. Miss Avery is Sir Edward's stepdaughter. She near jumped out of her skin when she saw me. "Why, Violet!" she said. "You gave me such a fright! What are you doing?" I said, "I've come to see if there's anything Lady Fairfield needs," and she said, "Oh, Violet, dear... A terrible tragedy has occurred," and my heart near stopped beating, "What has happened?" I asked and she replied: "Lady Fairfield is gone to a better place. She will never need anything from you again!" and I said, "What about the baby, madam?" and she said, "Neither will he, poor little mite."'

Violet had struggled to tell the last part of her story, and the sorrow behind her last words affected Nelly deeply. For a moment she could not speak. At last she said: 'How dreadful that must have been for you.'

Violet sniffed. Tears were spilling from her eyes. 'It was one of the worst moments of my life! I could barely believe it! Even now I struggle to comprehend how quickly they were lost.'

She was hunched over herself; her grief obvious. 'I did not

see Lady Fairfield, nor the baby, again,' she continued. 'Miss Avery had them removed to the undertaker's the very next morning.'

Only the infant hadn't been taken directly thence. Where had Miss Avery kept his body in the interim?

Violet sighed and wiped her eyes with the heels of her hands. 'Lady Fairfield was a ray of sunshine in this gloomy place, and now I spend most of every day missing her dreadfully. Sophy too.'

'Where has Sophy gone?'

'To work for Miss Avery in Clevedon.'

'I understand now why you must feel so alone,' Nelly said. She passed her own handkerchief to Violet, who took it and dabbed at her eyes.

'Thank you for your kindness,' Violet said.

'It's nothing. I'm sorry to have upset you.'

'That's not your fault.' She gathered herself a little. 'If you do come to work here, I will show you the ropes.'

She glanced up at the clock. 'I'd better go back to work. The first of the shooting party will be here this evening. We need to have all the rooms ready.' She hesitated. 'It's been nice talking with you, Connie. I hope we shall be friends.'

Nelly said, 'I hope so too.'

51

Violet stood up to leave just as Betty came back into the room. She took one look at Violet's face and sighed. 'You've been getting yourself all worked up about Lady Fairfield's death again, haven't you?'

Violet nodded. She was still clutching Nelly's handkerchief.

Betty squeezed Violet's shoulder. 'Go on, you great, soft thing,' she said, 'back to work.'

Violet disappeared and Betty perched on the chair beside Nelly's.

'Now then, Connie, I've had a word with Mrs Lavant,' she said. 'We've had a difficult couple of weeks: first the lady of the house passed away, God bless her soul, and then we lost Sophy, one of the maids.'

'Violet told me.'

'But Sir Edward is going ahead with a shooting party as planned, and there's a great deal of work needs doing in preparation. You speak nicely and you don't seem the flighty sort. So Mrs Lavant has suggested we give you a trial. You help prepare the house, show that you are capable and can follow orders, and in return we'll give you food and a bed for tonight. What happens after that depends on how well you conduct yourself in the meantime.'

Nelly nodded demurely, but inside she danced with delight. This was absolutely the best outcome for which she could have hoped.

'That sounds perfectly fair,' she said. 'Thank you.'

'Good,' said Betty. She hesitated a moment. 'I don't know what Violet told you about Lady Fairfield's death, but there are some wild rumours circulating. I'd be grateful if you wouldn't participate in the scandal-mongering, and let poor Lady Fairfield and her little child rest in peace.'

'Of course.'

'Violet's head is full of nonsense. She reads too many novels. Come on, then, Connie, come with me.'

Nelly followed Betty through a number of different corridors, each painted the same shade of dark green and as poorly lit as the next. Betty found a uniform for Nelly in the airing cupboard – a plain black dress and a white apron, both recently laundered. They had belonged to Sophy and fitted Nelly well. Betty also helped her arrange her hair into the mobcap – black, to indicate mourning, rather than the traditional white – and suggested she polish her boots in the scullery and make sure there was no grit stuck into the soles that might scratch or otherwise mark the polished oak floors of the grand rooms.

'Sir Edward is particular about his floors,' Betty said.

After this, there was a whistlestop tour of the back corridors and stairways that provided the servants with routes into the various parts of Mordaunt Hall without ever showing themselves to the resident aristocracy or their guests. Nelly realised how easy it would be for the servants to eavesdrop or spy on those they served, behind doors that looked as if they opened into cupboards, and passageways tucked away around corners, behind curtains or large items of furniture. She understood now why people like Eliza Morgan, who had moved between the upstairs and the downstairs, had such a clear and full picture of what was going on in a household such as this one.

* * *

Soon enough, Nelly found herself dispatched to the first floor of Mordaunt Hall, working with Violet in the guest bedrooms. Their first task was to remove all the evidence that a member of the household had recently died.

This meant drawing back the curtains that had been kept closed for the period between Priscilla's death and the funeral, to let the light in again. The curtains were old, heavy and dusty. Beyond were ancient mullioned windows, with small leaded panes. They wound the clocks, which had been stopped, and took the black cloths from the mirrors, and folded them into drawers.

'It's not even two weeks since Lady Fairfield died, is it?' Nelly asked. 'I should have thought the household would be in mourning for longer.'

'It should be,' Violet said. 'But Sir Edward didn't want to cancel his precious shooting party. Couldn't countenance the possibility of disappointing his business associates; them as sponsor his career.' She flicked a loose feather on the side table. 'Mrs Lavant says the shooting-party gentlemen won't want to be thinking of morbid matters while they're downing pheasants by the dozen.'

They collected brushes, cloths and mops from the store cupboard, and set to sweeping the floors, cleaning the furniture, clearing the fireplaces and preparing the fires in the guest rooms.

Linen for each bed was stored on its own individual shelf in a giant linen store.

The rooms were large, dark and panelled, the furniture ugly, although the view beyond the windows was glorious: a pastoral landscape of pale green horizontals interspersed with the black uprights of winter trees and fence-posts. Still, it was a long way to anywhere. Nelly, putting herself in Priscilla's shoes, could imagine how lonely the young woman must have felt. She must have drifted through the house, weary with the dullness of it all and dreading the return of her vicious husband.

Some of the shooting party were bringing their valets, and Violet had a list of who was expected and where they were to sleep. Nelly saw how skilled she was at her work; how quickly and precisely she laboured. She was meticulous in checking that every nook and cranny was free of dust and hair; that no dead fly lay on any windowsill, that every lavatory bowl was immaculate. She worked so hard that she didn't have the breath left for chatting, so Nelly was sparing with her questions.

'I suppose it was in one of these rooms that Lady Fairfield died?' she asked as they made up yet another bed.

'Sir Edward and Lady Fairfield's private rooms are down the end of the landing,' said Violet. 'Lady Fairfield's is the one beyond the fancy peacock vase.' She paused, one hand in the small of her back, stretching. 'Mrs Lavant generally takes care of those rooms. Sir Edward doesn't like to see the staff if he can help it.' She sniffed. 'He regards us as barely human.'

She ran a finger along the top of a headboard to check it for dust.

'Were you here when his first wife was alive?' Nelly asked.

'I was.'

'What was she like?'

'Lady Maria? Anxious.'

Anxious, Nelly noted, was a word often used to describe the women close to Sir Edward.

'She used to say he only married her because he knew she was capable of giving him children,' Violet said.

'But she never did? Give him children, I mean.'

'No, God bless her soul.'

Violet smoothed the bedsheet. 'I am of an opinion that's why, when Lady Maria was in her grave, he married a woman so much younger than himself. He was expecting Lady Priscilla to be with child almost at once, and, of course, she wasn't, so that made him angry. And then he went to India and she—'

Violet stopped herself from finishing the sentence. Her cheeks flushed a deep pink.

She finished with the bed, then stood back, hands on hips, casting an eye over the room, to make sure all was as it should be.

52

Nelly worked with Violet for the rest of the day, exploring Mordaunt Hall.

She saw the dining room where Duncan Coulson had dined with Sir Edward and the merchants, traders and entrepreneurs who funded his political campaigns. She peeped into the reception rooms: grand and imposing; the walls draped with faded tapestries depicting battles won by Britain; the great brown furniture replete with enormous clocks and bronze busts of fierce-eyed statesmen on top of marble stands. She walked past the peacock vase on the landing; an ugly, ostentatious thing, tall as Nelly's waist, full of dusty old dried flowers. She tried the handle of the door behind it – the door to Priscilla Fairfield's old room. The handle moved. The door was not locked.

Nelly and Violet used the back stairs, but when it was time to make up the fire in the great fireplace in the hallway, Nelly glimpsed the main staircase, a monstrosity in carved and polished wood, changing direction twice as it made its way up to the first-floor landing. Portraits of ancient male Fairfields, their faces uniformly thin in shape, with hard eyes and soft chins, gazed down from the walls.

There was one large, empty space.

'That's where *she* used to be,' said Violet.

'Lady Priscilla?'

Violet nodded. 'Sir Edward had a full-length portrait made of her as a wedding gift, to replace the picture of Lady Maria that used to hang there.'

'What did her ladyship look like?'

'In the painting? Her hair was ringleted and she was wearing an ivory gown, and her green velvet shawl. She was so beautiful!'

'Then they were happy in the beginning?'

'Hmm,' said Violet. 'I wouldn't call it "happy". By the time they came back from their honeymoon, she didn't like him being anywhere near her. She used to wince if he raised his hand.'

Nelly felt a pain inside her, empathy for Priscilla. Perhaps death was a kinder outcome for her than a lifetime of abuse at the hands of her husband.

'What became of the portrait?' she asked Violet.

'He took it down when he returned from India. Had it put in the attic, covered in sacking.'

When he returned from India, thought Nelly, *and realised Priscilla's condition.*

And the removal of the portrait, wasn't that, in itself, an obscure threat? Maria had died, and her portrait had been taken from the wall. Priscilla's image had been taken away while she still lived – the implication being that she would not live for long and some other woman's image would take her place.

Nelly had believed, before she came here, that Priscilla's life was difficult. She was realising now that, when Sir Edward was present, it must have been a living hell.

***

The longer the day drew on, the more anxious Nelly became about being in Mordaunt Hall. The atmosphere amongst the staff changed as the hour for Sir Edward's return drew closer. They became tense, and irritable with one another, anxious that everything be just as the master of the house preferred it to be. More than once, Nelly was spoken to in a sharp voice.

She tried to keep out of the way. She knew she wouldn't be serving dinner that evening, nor welcoming the shooting-party guests as they arrived, nor showing them to their rooms. Her tasks were limited to the most menial household work, emptying dustpans and the like, and, as the afternoon drew to a close, helping light the fires in the upstairs rooms.

Evening approached. Long, horizontal shadows appeared inside Mordaunt Hall. They broke where the walls met the floorboards, and slanted vertically. The rooms to the north and east of the hall became dark and chilly.

By the time the sun had disappeared into the icy haze of cloud above the horizon, the kitchen was hectic with preparations for the evening meal that Sir Edward had ordered to be served to him and his guests. Now the domestic staff's chores were completed, they helped the kitchen staff tackle the monumental task of preparing and serving five courses of food to more than forty people.

Nelly found herself, sleeves rolled up, at the sink in the scullery, scrubbing congealed meat fat from the sides and bottoms of venerable old roasting pans.

There was a brief interlude for the staff to eat, at least those not involved with serving drinks and canapés to the gentlemen preparing for dinner upstairs, nor seeing to their horses, or their carriages, their guns, their dogs and their own personal servants, all of whom required feeding and watering too. The busyness, the constant comings and goings, made Nelly wonder at the stamina of the staff, some of whom were no longer young, who undertook this hard labour day after day. By now, her hands – unused to manual work – were red raw, and every muscle in her back and shoulders was aching. She glimpsed herself in a mirror, and saw that she was wan with tiredness.

Her expression was one she'd seen on the faces of countless working-class women before, but never her own face. This was a new kind of labour for Nelly and her exhaustion was interspersed with dread at the knowledge she must spend a night in this ancient old house, unhappiness, infidelity and cruelty absorbed into the plasterwork; misery in the very fabric of its stones.

* * *

Nelly observed that Mordaunt Hall's domestic staff did not go up to their beds until the early hours of the following morning, after the last of the gentlemen had finished smoking in the billiards room and drinking in the drawing room. Then, and only then, could the staff scuttle in to clear away the ashtrays and the glasses; to sweep up the spilled ash and wipe away the sticky whisky marks on the floorboards; to rearrange the chairs and plump up the cushions and dampen down the fires and polish the greasy finger-marks from the furniture. When the guests came down in the morning, the curtains would be drawn back and fastened with their swags, the fires would be burning; newspapers would be on the tables and fresh coffee and tea brewed. Everywhere would be aired, would smell clean, and look as good as new.

Sir Edward Fairfield's visitors would take their comfort for granted. It would be the staff whose backs ached, whose eyes were dry with weariness, who must labour through yet another, relentless day.

53

That night, Nelly was to share Violet's room in the eaves, sleeping in the bed where Priscilla's lady's maid, Sophy, used to sleep. While Violet changed into her nightgown, Nelly splashed her face with cold water, trying to keep herself awake, for she was so tired by now that she could have slept on a clothes' line.

Nelly took her time removing her outer garments, and Violet was already asleep by the time she was done. She looked longingly at the empty bed that Violet had kindly made up for her. How she longed to crawl beneath the blankets.

The prospect of going back down into that awful, gloomy house, alone, filled Nelly with dread. It wasn't the darkness nor the fear of becoming lost in the warren of corridors. It was knowing that less than two weeks earlier a woman and child had been murdered in these rooms and that the killer; Edward Fairfield, a man whose violence was without boundaries, was nearby.

But Nelly was here now. She must go.

She picked up the little lamp with the candle in it, and crept from the room. On the landing, she listened hard, her senses on full alert, but all she could hear were snores, dream murmurs and the occasional cough from the other servants.

The corridor through the attic was narrow and dark with staircases at either end; Nelly took the left-hand option, this being the one that would take her closest to the room beyond the peacock vase.

She reached the stairs without incident, and crept down, soft-footed, blood pulsing in her ears. At the bottom was a door that opened behind a heavy drape on the first-floor landing. Nelly put her hand on the knob and turned it slowly. The door opened with a quiet creak. Then she stood for a moment, inhaling the dusty smell of the curtain, shafts of moonlight falling through the staircase windows, sliding in oblongs across the floor.

Nelly could hear an orchestra of male snores from behind the closed bedroom doors.

'Please, God,' she whispered, 'let them sleep on.'

She crept forward, stymied now by her unfamiliarity with the hall. She listened at the door of the first room she came to and heard a definite snoring within. It was the same at the next, and a crack of light at the base of the third door informed Nelly that whoever was in that room was still awake, even at this ungodly hour.

Nelly walked soft-footed to the vase, praying none of the doors would open. The face of the peacock, illuminated by candlelight, appeared evil in its expression. It looked as if it was guarding the room; as if it might fly at her. She reached for the handle of the door behind it, touched it, then let it go. She stepped back, afraid; her heart pounding so strongly she feared it might burst from her body.

Go on, open it! she told herself. *You can't give up now!*

She took hold of the handle, and carefully she turned it. The latch clicked and the door opened. Nelly pushed it and peeped around. The air inside the room was cold; no fire had been lit within for some time, and the curtains were open, letting in the moonlight.

Nelly stepped inside, pushing the door shut behind her, but not closing it fully. She held the lamp in front of her. She found herself in a dressing room with a large wardrobe, a dressing table; a full-length mirror, a washstand and a commode.

This was where Priscilla had come each morning, to dress and to attend to her toilette. The mirror was tilted at an angle to suit Priscilla. Her dressing gown was folded over the back of the chair and a pair of pink silk slippers lay tumbled beneath the washstand. The room smelled of lavender and was still full of Priscilla's presence, as if she had simply walked out to fetch something.

On the seat of the dressing-table chair was a tiny gown, beautifully sewn, and beneath it a pair of socks. These must be the clothes Eliza had made for Priscilla's baby. All that Nelly had been told was proving itself to be true.

She stepped towards a second door, one that must connect this room to the bedroom beyond, and as she passed the mirror, she glimpsed a tall woman with dark, ringleted hair and broad shoulders in the glass looking, not at her, but through her, for the woman's eyes were dead and her cheeks and chin were covered in the pinprick blemishes that signalled she had been suffocated.

'Priscilla?' Nelly gasped. But when she looked again, all she saw was her own reflection in a mirror that had spotted with age, distorted by the double brightness of the reflected candle.

Cautiously, Nelly walked through into a large bedroom, with moonlight making a ghostly shine on the polished floorboards and the panelling on the walls.

A window had been partly opened, no doubt to air the room

after the deaths, and the draught that sidled through it was like ice.

The bed, a stately four-poster with hunting scenes carved into its panels, was up against the far wall. An old, mahogany cradle stood beneath the window and a well-worn carpet lay in the centre of the floorboards. Nelly's toes curled as she thought of all the bare feet that must have stepped upon that carpet, and all the ancient shed hair and dandruff and nail clippings and flakes of skin amongst its fibres.

Oh, but it was cold in that room. All Nelly wore was a woollen chemise; warm beneath a dress, but offering no protection from the biting chill she encountered now.

She walked carefully to the bed, holding the lamp high. The draught licked around her ankles. Her feet were cold as stone. She imagined Priscilla labouring on this huge, ancient bed. How impersonal it was; how oppressive; a monstrous piece better suited to a mausoleum.

She dared not look too closely in case she saw the imprint of Priscilla's head still on the pillow, a dark hair snaking on the pillowcase. The pillow beside it might have been the one used to kill her. It was not hard to imagine Sir Edward leaning over his wife, pressing down, the old goose-down feathers suffocating the young mother who writhed beneath him, until she struggled no longer.

Nelly tugged at the neck of her chemise, for she herself now felt as if her throat were constricted and her lungs no longer seemed to operate of their own volition. What if she were to cease breathing? What if she were to fall, insensible, onto the bed and Sir Edward were to find her there? How easy it would be for him to finish her off with the same pillow. Nelly felt the old asylum panic in her fingertips, the tingling, the dizziness, the loss of control...

Stop it! she told herself sternly. *Stop, now!*

She couldn't afford to succumb to the terror; she must keep hold of her senses. But even as she fought to bring herself back, the lamp slipped from her grasp and clattered to the floor. The candle was extinguished. The lamp rolled under the bed.

Nelly stood stock-still, her every sense now alert.

She listened for the sound of voices, and footsteps; looked towards the doors for any new kind of light. She heard and saw nothing.

'Be quick, Nelly Brooks,' she told herself. 'Hurry!'

A small chest stood beside the bed. Nelly opened the top drawer. It contained a book, hairclips, and pots of cosmetic creams and lotions. As she searched through the clutter, Nelly heard a noise. Turning, she saw a flicker of light beyond the open door – someone was in Priscilla's dressing room.

Nelly dropped to her knees, crouching beside the bed. She clenched her jaw to stop her teeth from chattering with cold and fear and held tightly to the bedspread to keep herself still. She had not felt such terror, except in nightmares, since she left the asylum.

She heard footsteps, the creak of floorboards. Whoever it was was standing at the connecting door between the dressing room and the bedroom.

Oh, please, Nelly begged silently, *please don't let it be Sir Edward!*

If it was anyone else but he, she might talk her way out of her predicament. If it was Sir Edward, she was done for.

'Who's there?' a voice growled. It was Sir Edward. 'God damn you to hell. I heard you. Who is it?'

The door swung open. Light shone in. Nelly crouched lower. Could Sir Edward see the open drawer from where he stood?

'Show yourself, you thieving cove, you fucking coward! I'll beat you to buggery and then I'll have you hung!'

Nelly bit her knuckles to stop herself from whimpering. Her hair hung over her face, and she felt sick with fear. Sir Edward took a step into the room – she could see his be-slippered feet from beneath the bed, and the end of the metal fire-poker that he was brandishing.

The lamp that she had dropped was there too, under the bed, out of reach.

'This is your last chance!' Sir Edward said in a threatening whisper.

Another pace forward and he would surely see her.

Nelly imagined the noise the poker would make when it cracked against her skull. She pictured herself curled on the dirty old carpet, blood seeping from the fatal wound. Oh, the irony of dying in the same room where Priscilla died! What would Will say when he found out? What would he do?

Just as she braced herself for the inevitable beating, the cradle lurched. Nelly cringed as something dark and dread rose from within it and she must have cried out, but her scream was lost in the cacophony and confusion, for Sir Edward screamed too and dropped the poker. The thing from the crib spread its wings, and made a dreadful caw. Nelly, curled with her hands over her head, recognised that it was not a ghost, but a crow, which flew directly towards Sir Edward and the lamp he'd left behind him. He retreated through the door, slamming it shut, and the bird flew around the room several times, bumping into the window, before perching up high on the frame of a picture.

Nelly did not know if Sir Edward would wake the servants now to have them remove the corvid from the bedroom of his deceased wife, or if he would leave it until the morning, or if he might return with a gun or a net to trap or kill the creature. Either way, she knew she could not leave through the door.

And she had to be quick.

She stood again, her knees stiff and she numb with cold and trembling with fear. She turned her attention back to the drawer. She found a pocket handkerchief, its four corners knotted together; something solid was inside. She put the handkerchief in her pocket and explored the drawer with her fingers. There, at the back, they encountered a small, cold tube. Carefully, Nelly removed it and held it up to the light. It was a glass phial, the cork stopper sealed with wax.

The crow startled her as it flapped from the picture frame to the mirror above the fireplace. Nelly put the phial in her pocket, with the handkerchief. It was proof that Priscilla hadn't been given the medicine she needed. She reached under the bed for the lamp; it was Violet's and she did not want the other woman to be accused of trespass when it was found. Then she went to the window and looked out. Beyond was the nightscape of Mordaunt Hall's grounds: a dark expanse of countryside with only the branches of the trees silhouetted darkly against a sky full of stars.

Closer to, directly beneath the window on the outside, was a stone ledge that stretched the length of the wing of the hall.

Nelly turned to the bird.

'If you have any sense, you'll flee this place too,' she told it. And she hitched up her chemise and climbed out.

54

FRIDAY, 4 NOVEMBER

It felt as if Nelly had barely been in bed at all when she was woken by Violet, shaking her by the shoulders.

'Come on, sleepyhead, it's time to get up.'

Oh, please, no! Not yet!

'Connie! *Constance!* Wake up!'

Nelly opened her eyes. Dawn hadn't even broken. The little room in the eaves was so cold that the view from the window was obscured by frost and Nelly could see Violet's exhaled breath.

'What happened to your hands?' Violet asked. 'You washed them last night, and now they're all scratched and dirty.'

Nelly looked at her palms and remembered.

After she'd climbed out of the open window in Priscilla's bedroom in the early hours, she'd made her way along the ledge until she'd reached the corner of the building. From there, she'd managed to climb down a drainpipe – a skill she'd learned in childhood.

Getting back into Mordaunt Hall had been more difficult, but she had found an unlocked door to one side of the laundry.

She could not think of an explanation for her dirty hands, but fortunately Violet had more pressing concerns on her mind.

'We need to get the fires going downstairs,' she said, 'so it's warm when the guests come down for breakfast. I'll wash first.'

She poured fresh water into the bowl, and Nelly closed her eyes again.

Two minutes more sleep, she pleaded, but no sooner had she had the thought than Violet was telling her to hurry up and get dressed.

Nelly climbed out of bed, arms wrapped around herself, huddled against the cold.

Violet was hopping about in the middle of the room doing up her stays.

'Quick!' she urged. 'And you need to be presentable. Sir Edward likes to see all the staff in the entrance hall before the party sets out to shoot.'

'Why?'

'It's a tradition to wish them well. We always do it. We serve the men a snifter of whisky and Sir Edward has the gamekeeper say a poem asking the game to be obliging.'

Nelly recalled the bird that had found its way into Priscilla's room – the crow that had saved her. She hoped it had found its way back out through the window.

'Do I have to be there, in the hallway?' she asked.

'Everyone has to be there, Connie. That's the rule. Otherwise we'll get the blame if they have a bad day's hunting.'

* * *

Nelly knew she had to get out of Mordaunt Hall before the hallway ceremony, but she did not want to sneak away and leave the domestic staff in the lurch, after they had been so kind and accommodating to her. So, when she was ready, she went downstairs with Violet and drank a cup of weak coffee, before she was set to work washing up again. Through the scullery window, small and steamy as it was, she saw the horses being led out through the yard and put into the paddocks to stretch their legs. A few minutes later, Sir Edward came out into the courtyard, deep in conversation with another man. He was looking at the window, directly towards Nelly, and although she knew the sun was shining on the glass, and he could not see her, still her legs felt feeble.

Sir Edward looked angry. He pointed up towards the upper storeys of Mordaunt Hall.

The bird, thought Nelly. *He is angry about the bird.* He was telling the gamekeeper, if that was the other man's role, to ensure that it was gone.

After the guests had been served their breakfast – an enormous and complex meal that the cooks had been preparing since well before dawn – the shooting party prepared for their day's sport. Nelly became more tense as the time for them to leave approached. Eventually, a bell rang three times: the sign that the staff were to assemble for the hallway ritual. Nelly stayed in the scullery, keeping still and quiet, while the kitchen emptied, all save the young lad who was tasked with watching the stove. She walked past him, holding a finger to her lips, then trotted up the back stairs to the staff quarters on the top floor. She took off her uniform – Sophy's clothes – folded them on the bed, and put her own clothes back on. Then she gathered together her possessions, making sure she had the knotted handkerchief and the unopened phial, buttoned her boots, and went back down.

She tore a page from her notebook, and wrote a brief thank you note, and an apology, to Violet, Betty and Mrs Lavant.

I appreciate you giving me the opportunity, but I do not feel this is the job for me. Thank you for all your kindnesses.
   Constance Parr

Then she fastened the buttons of her cloak, made sure her bonnet was securely in place, and left by the same door by which she had entered.

* * *

Nelly was more anxious leaving Mordaunt Hall that morning than she had been when she arrived. The gamekeepers would be out preparing for the shoot, and the kitchen was expecting deliveries, so there was a good chance she might encounter someone on the drive. She walked quickly, her breath streaming behind her. The under-gardeners had already been out to sweep the gravel and clear away the manure left by the horses yesterday, and the grounds were pristine. A peacock and a peahen were patrolling – the male bringing back unpleasant memories of the previous night's adventure. Nelly gave the strutting birds a wide berth and they ignored her. The leaves that had fallen on this part of the Mordaunt estate had been either blown away by the wind or cleared away by the staff. The grounds to the great house were lovely, but when she turned back, to check that nobody was following her, Nelly saw the façade glowering after her, the stone dark and grey and the countenance of the building severe and threatening.

She saw the ledge on which she'd made her escape a few hours previously, and she felt a twang of pride deep inside; pride that she had had the courage to do what she had done and pride that she had, seemingly, successfully evaded detection.

55

Outside the *Courier* building, Nelly walked up and down for a few moments, plucking up the courage to go inside, and when she finally did, the first thing she saw was the smirk on Mr Snitch's face. Behind him, Sam was sweeping the floor. He glanced up at Nelly, and she gave a quick smile, before proceeding, head held high, to the reception desk.

'I've come to see Mr Delane,' she said to Mr Snitch. 'Would you let him know I'm here, please?'

Mr Snitch raised an eye brow. 'You're not supposed to be inside the building, Miss Brooks. I ought to have you ejected onto the street.'

'Could you just ask Sam to fetch Mr Delane, if you don't mind?'

'Sam's busy,' said Mr Snitch.

Nelly caught her breath, wondering what she should do now, but, behind the receptionist, Sam caught her eye and gave her a thumbs-up.

'I'll wait outside,' she said, and went to stand in the sunshine with her back to the *Courier* office. She used the time to look out for the watchman, but it was a bright day and she observed no patches of darkness that might indicate his presence. Perhaps, now Sir Edward knew she was no longer officially working for the *Courier*, he had called off his dogs. Or maybe she wasn't looking hard enough. It would be a mistake to let down her guard at this point.

Will came to find her. He had come straight down from the office, for his shirt sleeves were rolled up and he wasn't wearing a coat.

'Nelly? What's happened?' he asked, hair dishevelled, glasses askew. 'Are you all right?'

'I need to talk to you... in private.'

They went into The Three Horseshoes. Will ordered ale for himself and porter for Nelly and they sat at the table closest to the window, with a wall to one side of them, where they could neither be overheard, nor overlooked.

'I've been to Mordaunt Hall,' said Nelly, when their drinks were served.

Will leaned closer to her. 'For God's sake, Nelly, you promised me you would do nothing reckless!'

'But I had to, Will. I spoke to a maid who was present during Priscilla Fairfield's labour. She said the baby was a healthy boy, and that the mother was well after the birth. But when she went to check on them during the small hours, she encountered Madeleine Avery—'

'Who?'

'The daughter of Sir Edward's first wife. She was coming out of Priscilla's room and she told the maid that both had expired. Which confirms my instinct, Will, that Miss Avery is working with Sir Edward, and that there must be some evidence of foul play on the corpses. Why else take them away with such indecent haste? Why send Priscilla Fairfield to a funeral director who did not know the family? One who had never met her? One who would be less sensitive to any sign of murder? Why powder Priscilla's face and dress her before she went to the undertaker's? Why go to any of that trouble?'

Will nodded, acknowledging everything she said.

Nelly continued, all tiredness forgotten so immersed was she in her story. 'I am convinced now that Sir Edward was the killer, and that Madeleine Avery and the maid, Sophy, were also complicit. And another thing...'

'Yes?'

'Until last night, I thought Sir Edward's motives for murder were anger and jealousy; that he wanted rid of Priscilla and the baby by the quickest and simplest means and death fitted the bill better than the asylum or the divorce courts. But now, I believe the scandal he was trying to avert was larger than we'd imagined.'

She took the knotted handkerchief out of her pocket, and laid it on the table.

'I found this in the drawer beside Priscilla's bed.'

Will opened the handkerchief. Inside was a gold chain, on the end of which was a finely crafted pendant in the shape of a bee. He weighed it in his palm, letting the chain trickle between his fingers.

'It's pretty but I don't understand the significance...'

'Look at the inscription, Will.'

He turned the pendant over and squinted at the tiny lettering. '"For Priss,"' he read, '"from your adoring Bertie."'

He looked at Nelly over the top of his glasses.

'Priscilla's lover was called Bertie,' he said.

Nelly nodded.

'So?'

'Bertie, Will. Albert. *Bertie!*'

Will frowned.

Nelly glanced around to make sure nobody was close enough to hear, then she leaned closer to Will and whispered, 'I believe the baby's father was Albert, Prince of Wales.'

As she spoke the words aloud, Nelly realised how shocking they were.

'What?'

Nelly nodded.

'Oh, Nelly, surely not! There are many Alberts in this world.'

'But how many would have crossed Priscilla Fairfield's path?'

'Nelly...'

'Listen, Will, it all fits! The prince used to be a regular visitor to Mordaunt Hall but recently he and Sir Edward have ceased to be friends. I have a photograph that proves Priscilla and the prince were together at least once while Sir Edward was in India. And this pendant, it's a beautiful thing...'

'My God,' said Will. He put a hand to his forehead. 'My God! If you're right...'

'Then it's the biggest story ever!' Nelly whispered. 'It is a story for which at least three people have already died.'

'But how do you... *we* prove it?'

'Firstly, we need to talk to Priscilla's lady's maid, Sophy.'

'If she was involved in the conspiracy to murder, she will not want to talk to us.'

'If she refuses to answer our questions, then we will know she is complicit. There is still a chance that she is innocent, and she would have known more about Priscilla than anyone else.'

'Do you know where we might find her?'

'In Clevedon, working for Miss Avery.'

'What is the second thing?'

'That's more difficult. We need to look at Lady Fairfield's body.'

'But she's been buried...'

'Not buried. Her coffin is in the Fairfield crypt. And if she was smothered, as I believe she must have been, when we wipe the face powder and rouge from her face, there will be evidence of suffocation on the skin beneath.'

Will shook his head. 'Nelly, we cannot do that.'

'We must.'

'No! We cannot go creeping into crypts, opening coffins and interfering with human remains. Absolutely not. No. Never.'

56

As Will continued to protest that Nelly's plan was immoral and unworkable, she reached down for her satchel and removed the glass phial.

'Here is more evidence,' she said.

'What's that?' Will asked.

'This is the medicine the doctor gave to the maid, Violet, to give to Priscilla. Sophy took it and hid it.' She paused. 'I suspect she was doing as she was told. I heard Miss Avery say the medicine would not have helped Lady Fairfield. She *knew* she was going to die.'

'We should have it analysed,' said Will, 'for this is vital evidence.'

'How do we do that?'

Will tapped the side of his nose. 'Fortunately,' he said, 'I know just the man.'

* * *

They returned to the *Courier* offices, going directly to the rear of the building and explaining their situation to Cuddy, who had heard of Nelly's suspension and was anxious to help her. He harnessed up the larger horse, and drove Will and Nelly directly to the home of Dr Alexander Blyth, a professor at Bristol University and an esteemed man of science who lived in a grand house built against the cliffs on Hotwell Road. Will, in his role as crime reporter, had spoken to Dr Blyth on many occasions but Nelly had not met him before.

Upon their arrival, Will and Nelly were shown into a light and airy drawing room, adorned with framed watercolours of toxic plants.

Nelly sat politely on the edge of a chair while Will and the professor spoke, catching up on mutual acquaintances, and discussing the ongoing public-health issues caused by contaminated water. Nelly tried to interject, but the professor was not interested in anything she might have to say.

It was only after they were done with this conversation, and an elderly maid whose complexion was as grey as her apron had brought tea, that they turned to the subject of the phial of medicine that was contained within Nelly's satchel.

She gave it to Dr Blyth who held it up to the light and peered through the glass. He withdrew the stopper and sniffed the liquid inside. He frowned.

'You say it's some kind of anti-bleeding potion?'

'That's what we believe.'

'Would you like me to take a look at it now?'

'If that's not too much trouble,' said Will.

'No trouble at all. I'll send a message to your office as soon as I have a result.'

* * *

Outside, Cuddy was waiting for Will and Nelly, the horse standing patiently at the side of the road.

'Where to now?' he asked, as the reporters joined him.

'We need to get to Clevedon,' said Will.

'There and back is too much for this fellow to do in a day,' Cuddy said. 'You'll have to take the stagecoach.'

* * *

Clevedon was an elegant town built on a hill overlooking the Bristol Channel.

The seafront was pretty, although there was not much of a beach, merely a rocky area beneath the promenade where small children and dogs were running about. On the far side of a stony bay was a wooded outcrop, the trees leaning inwards, their spiky black branches forced over by the prevailing winds.

It was evident that this was a fashionable place by the number of well-dressed ladies and well-heeled gentlemen taking the air on that chilly afternoon. The coffee shops, with lights glowing beyond their windows and arrays of cakes and sandwiches on display, seemed doubly appealing.

'Now we are here,' Nelly said, holding the sides of her cloak together to prevent it from billowing in the wind, 'how do we find where Madeleine Avery lives?'

'We ask a reporter,' said Will.

Clevedon had its own newspaper, the *Mercury*, founded the previous year by George Caple, who was only seventeen at the time, and eighteen now. Mr Caple knew everything about everyone in his town, and was able to provide Nelly and Will with Miss Avery's address.

They followed his directions to a quiet road set back from the sea and protected from it by rocky cliffs and woodland.

Madeleine Avery's cottage was surrounded by a wall, and when Will rang the bell to one side, two large dogs ran to the gates, barking and baring their teeth. Nelly stepped back in alarm, but Will spoke calmly to the animals until a woman approached. Nelly recognised her from the funeral: she was Miss Madeleine Avery.

'Good afternoon,' Miss Avery said. 'How may I help you?'

Nelly bowed her head politely.

'My name is Helen Brooks and this is my colleague, Will Delane. We are reporters for the Bristol *Courier*.'

Miss Avery's expression instantly became less friendly.

'Why are you here?' she asked.

'We are investigating the deaths of Priscilla Fairfield and her infant son,' Nelly said.

Madeleine Avery did not flinch. She looked directly at Nelly with a gaze that was bold and strong.

'There is nothing to investigate,' she said. 'Both died of natural causes and I have nothing to say on the matter. Let the dead rest in peace, and leave me alone.'

'If you are not willing to talk, may we have a quick word with Sophy?' Nelly asked.

'Sophy's not here, but if she was, she would not wish to speak with you.'

'Might we wait for her?'

'No!'

'Miss Avery, we do not intend to distress or inconvenience you,' said Will, in his gentlest voice. 'We only wish to uncover the truth.'

Madeleine Avery raised her head and now her eyes were narrowed with anger.

'What's done is done,' she said. 'Nothing you do, or say, or write will change it now. Don't pretend you're motivated by philanthropy, or moral convictions: you're not. You're here because you're jobbing penny-a-liners, the two of you, who want to write a scandalous story to further your own prospects. You don't care about anything, certainly not the memory of poor Lady Fairfield. Remove yourselves from my property, or I shall not hesitate to set the dogs on you.'

57

As they sat in the stagecoach on the way back to Bristol, Nelly and Will discussed Madeleine Avery's behaviour.

'Her unfriendliness and unwillingness to help are proof of her guilt and complicity,' said Nelly.

'She certainly does not like the press,' said Will.

'You have a talent for understatement.'

'Perhaps she had a bad experience in the past.'

'Even if that's true, there was no need for her to be so aggressive!'

'Don't take it personally, Nelly.'

'She accused us of salacity.'

'Mark my words, if you remain a reporter, you'll be accused of worse than that.'

* * *

A little further on, Nelly closed her eyes for a while, wondered if Harriet was at sea yet, and, if she was, prayed for calm weather and smooth waters. Then she dozed, soothed by the rhythmic rocking of the carriage. When she woke, she found her head was leaning on Will's shoulder, and her bonnet was skew-whiff. She sat up and dusted herself off. Will was looking out of the window, acting as if nothing had happened.

'Shall we dine at Pierre's when we are back in Bristol?' he asked in a casual voice.

'That's an excellent idea,' Nelly replied, as if she could not care less.

* * *

Darkness had fallen by the time Nelly and Will were back at the *Courier* offices.

'I'll fetch my bag, then we'll head straight to Pierre's,' said Will.

As he went towards the door, a small figure with protruding ears appeared out of the darkness.

'Mr Delane?'

'Sam? What are you doing here so late?'

'I have an urgent message for you, Mr Delane, sir. The gentleman said it wouldn't wait.'

He passed an envelope into Will's hand.

Will tore open the envelope and removed the paper inside. His eyes flicked over the words.

'Good grief!' he murmured. And he looked up at Nelly. 'My God!'

'What is it?' she asked.

'It's a message from Dr Blyth.'

'And?'

'The liquid in the phial, it's not medicine.'

'No? What is it then?'

'Strychnine.'

* * *

They went to Pierre's and took Sam with them as a thanks to him for waiting for them.

During the short walk, Nelly had the sensation of being observed. She looked over her shoulder and saw a figure step into an alleyway. She walked another few paces and looked again. A shadow moved at the side of the street.

'What is it?' asked Will.

'I am being followed,' she answered in a quiet voice.

'By whom?'

'The man who murdered Eliza Morgan.'

'Is he there now?'

'He is lurking in the recess of that doorway.'

Will doubled back quickly, to check.

'Nobody is there.'

'Are you sure?'

'I'm certain.'

But Nelly knew what she had seen. She'd shaken off the watchman for a while, but he must have known that sooner or later she would return to the *Courier* offices and had been waiting for her there.

A little further along, she heard the watchman's cough.

Damn him, she thought, this shadow man who would not leave her be.

She was immensely relieved when she, Will and Sam reached Pierre's and stepped into its welcoming interior. No person in his right mind would wait outside in the cold for the time it took for a meal to be ordered, served and consumed. Surely, *surely,* the watchman, knowing Nelly was back in Bristol, would stop trailing her now, and return to his own home, and bed.

They sat at a table in a dark nook, and ordered drinks, and meat pies with roasted potatoes and carrots. All Nelly could think of was the poison in the phial, but they did not speak of it at first. Instead, they spoke of trivial, cheerful matters, with their attention upon Sam. He was due to go for his first ever holiday, with Maud, the following morning. They planned to travel by train to Bournemouth, where Maud's sister lived, and spend a few days at the seaside.

Sam was most excited, particularly about the train ride, and the prospect of exploring the pier. He had never seen the sea, and was looking forward to picnicking on the beach, if the weather permitted.

When the meals came, having made Sam promise he would not repeat anything Nelly and Will said, the two reporters tried to make sense of this new development – the phial of poison.

'When I met with Eliza Morgan, ten days ago, she told me Priscilla had overheard Sir Edward speaking of how he might be rid of her,' Nelly said. 'She believed he would suffocate her. But now it seems the physician supplied him with strychnine...'

'He didn't supply it to Sir Edward,' said Will. 'He gave it to the maid and told her it was medicine. The maid was to give it to her mistress, who would die, and Mr Thorpe-Thompson would say she had bled to death and nobody would be any the wiser. If anything went wrong, and suspicions were raised, then it was the maid who had done the deed. The maid would hang, while Sir Edward literally got away with murder.'

Nelly thought of kind, hard-working Violet, a woman who

her employer was quite willing to sacrifice to achieve his own ungodly ends, and she felt first sorrow, then fury.

'The doctor and Sir Edward must have decided that poison would be a safer means to murder than suffocation,' said Nelly.

'And when Priscilla did not die in the night as expected, then Sir Edward resorted to his original plan.'

Will and Nelly decided the most likely scenario, was that Sir Edward came to check on Priscilla during the night, to see if the poison had worked. Finding her still breathing, he put the pillow over her face. Perhaps his intention had always been to suffocate the infant.

It was imperative, now, that they saw Priscilla Fairfield's corpse for themselves; to look for the signature symptoms of suffocation that would confirm that she had been murdered. Even Will agreed it was their only option. But how might they do this?

'What if we visit the crypt early tomorrow,' Nelly suggested as they ate their pudding. The disturbing conversation had not diminished her appetite.

'But the superintendent will be there. We would be seen.'

Will finished off his plum cake.

'We could go now?' he said.

'Now?'

'Well, why not?'

'It's so late, Will.'

'That's an advantage, for nobody will be about.'

'And so cold.'

'It won't take long.'

Sam looked at Nelly, the spoon halfway to his mouth, waiting to see her reaction.

Nelly did not wish to go to the cemetery in the dark, to break into the crypt and open the coffin. It was the last thing on earth she wanted to do.

'How will we get into the crypt?' she asked, a last, desperate attempt to thwart the plan. 'There is an outer gate and an inner door, both locked.'

'I know how to pick locks,' said Will. He winked at Sam. 'It is a skill acquired by every child who has ever lived on the streets.'

58

Sam left to return to Maud's and Nelly and Will walked across Bristol, following the Bath Road towards Arnos Vale cemetery.

At first, Nelly kept checking behind her for the watchman, but the further they walked, and the more tired she became, the less inclined she was to worry. The watchman had to sleep sometimes and she was with Will so there was little point him following her, if his ambition was to make her feel intimidated. She did not hear the telltale cough. She was almost certain they were alone.

Soon, they reached the three lamps junction, with its metal signpost, one arm pointing towards Wells, the other to Bath. They took the Bath turning. Up to this point, their way had been well lit, but now they were leaving the more densely occupied parts of Bristol, the street lights were situated further apart and the further they travelled from the bright lights of Temple Meads station, the quieter it became.

To their left was the river, its smell less pungent this far upstream, and to their right the steeply sloping district of Totterdown where the cottages and small farms were being replaced by streets of new housing, to accommodate the dock and factory workers.

When they reached the cemetery, they found the gates open, lamps burning on either side. Lights were shining in the windows of the gatehouse, where the superintendent and his family resided, and laughter came from within. It was reassuring to witness so much life, close to so much death.

Beyond was the great garden graveyard, clearer in the moonlight than it had been the last time Nelly was here, when the fog had obscured the trees and the monuments. In this silvery light, the paths were picked out like streams, winding through the gravestones and the lovely marble angels and the monumental trees seemed to hold the moon, the planets and the stars in their arms and their boughs.

'Are you afraid?' Will asked.

'No,' Nelly said, and she pulled the hood of her cloak up over her bonnet and walked on ahead of him, into the cemetery. Will had to trot to catch up with her.

There was a wooden lantern store at the place where the track forked. Will took a lantern, checked that it contained a fat stub of candle, and lit the candle with a match from the box he kept in his pocket.

Then they walked on, Will holding the lantern, the flame of the candle drawing moths to the glass. Its light, although feeble, was enough to cast monstrous shadows of the broken marble columns placed on the graves to signify the fragility of life, the shrouded urns and the stone lambs with pierced hearts.

Despite Nelly's assertion that she knew where they were going, it was difficult to identify the correct small path leading into the woods in the dark, and the pair initially went the wrong way. They had to turn around and retrace their footsteps. On the second attempt they found the Fairfield crypt.

Will passed the lantern to Nelly and she stepped carefully over the chain, the marble chips crunching beneath the soles of her boots, and held the lantern at the height of the lock, giving Will the best possible visibility. In the woods, an owl hooted. Bats skimmed the face of the moon.

Harriet came into Nelly's mind, and in that instant, the expediency of what she and Will were doing revealed itself to her. If they were caught breaking into the crypt of one of Bristol's most powerful families, and punished by law, wouldn't it spoil any future opportunity of Nelly laying claim to her daughter?

'Will...' she began.

'Sorry, Nelly, but I need to concentrate.' Will was hunched over the lock, manoeuvring one of the tools on his penknife inside the lock.

'I don't think we should do this.'

'But it is already nearly done.'

'What if we are caught?'

'We shall be in and out in minutes.'

Nelly imagined herself, older than she was now, telling Harriet about this adventure; this story she had been chasing. She imagined saying to Harriet: 'Will and I got as far as the cemetery, at midnight, but then I decided we should stop, and leave well alone.'

'Why would you do such a thing?' Harriet would ask. 'Why give up, when you had gone so far?'

'There!' said Will as the metal gate swung open. 'One down, one to go. What is it that troubles you, Nelly?'

'Oh,' she replied, 'it's nothing.'

The crypt door proved a more difficult challenge for Will to open.

'Hold the light steady,' he said tetchily as he poked the knife's hoof-pick tool into the mechanism.

High above them, clouds, flimsy as gauze, floated over the face of the moon and, above its bright crescent, Venus shone like a diamond.

Nelly's arm was aching.

'Perhaps it's impossible to pick,' she said to Will.

'No lock is impossible,' he answered.

He turned the handle and the door to the Fairfield crypt squeaked open. A draught curled from within – damp, stale, laced with a sickly sweet smell. Nelly held the lantern higher, her breath catching in her throat.

'Are you ready for this?' asked Will, his voice low. Nelly was not ready. Nonetheless, she said that she was.

59

Will turned to Nelly and, in the light of the lantern, she saw his face, and his eyes told her that he was as apprehensive as she.

'This is just the entrance,' she told him. 'There are steps to the left that go down into the crypt. Priscilla's coffin is beneath the lower stone shelf on the far side.'

She passed the lantern to him. She could see the candle flame reflected twice in the lenses of his spectacles.

'It might be best if you stayed out here,' he said, 'to keep watch.'

She knew he was only saying that to be kind, to save her the ordeal of entering the crypt in the dark, and that she should go with him, for this was her story, and she was the one convinced that Priscilla Fairfield had been suffocated and that the evidence would show on the face of her corpse.

'I'll come with you,' she said.

'One of us must stay here,' he said, 'in case someone comes.'

'Be careful, then,' she said. 'The steps are steep and the ceiling is low.'

'Right you are.'

'And you know what to look for? The signs of suffocation?'

'I know. Wait for me,' he said. 'Call if you hear anything.'

Nelly watched as the light receded, disappearing with Will down the steps until there was only a faint glow coming through the frame of the door. She wrapped her arms about herself, looked around. The woodland was full of darkness and moonlight shadows.

A white shape flew silently between the trunks of the trees: a barn owl, hunting. The wind was whispering; there were faint rustles and scuttles from amongst the fallen leaves and twigs on the woodland floor. The temperature was falling. Nelly, weary from the trip to Mordaunt Hall, had a sudden desperate longing for her room in the house at 12 Orchard Hill, the fire burning in the grate, the comfortable bed.

She listened hard, but the only sounds were natural ones; she heard no breaking of twigs underfoot, no cough or sigh, only a faint dragging sound coming from within the crypt, and she knew that was Will, pulling the coffin from beneath the stone shelf.

Nelly was ashamed then for letting him undertake this dreadful task alone. She hesitated, still, to follow, because he was right, one of them should be on watch duty. And then she did hear a movement close by, behind her.

She turned quickly. 'Who's there?' she called and there was a scuffle and a small deer leapt out of the undergrowth and ran downhill, quick as a flash, its white backside bobbing through the dark.

'Oh God!' Nelly put a hand to her pounding heart. 'God, it frightened the life from me!' She looked around, straining her eyes and ears, but she saw and heard nothing. Just when she thought she could bear the silence no longer, she heard Will's voice calling from within the crypt.

'Nelly! You need to come and see this!'

I can't, she thought.

'Nelly! Come!'

'One moment. I'll prop open the door.'

Nelly looked for a large stone, found one, and wedged it against the door so that it could not accidentally close. Then she gathered up her skirts and she stepped over the marble chips and in through the open door to the crypt. She carefully climbed down the flight of steps and went into the low compartment at the bottom. The lamp was hanging from the hook in the ceiling. There was a strong, sweet smell; the smell of an animal that had died in the woods. The two older coffins remained intact, as they had been before, but Priscilla's coffin was in the centre of the room. The lid had been pushed back lengthways on its hinges, like an opened book, and was propped against the side of the shelf.

'Look at the face of the corpse!' Will said.

Nelly turned her head, dreading to look into the coffin; knowing there was a body inside it, one that had been dead for almost two weeks; afraid of seeing it.

She looked at Will, her heart full of fear. He had removed his jacket to save it from the dust, and his hair was disordered from the exertion of removing the coffin lid. He looked young and scared. He took off his spectacles and wiped his eyes with the back of his wrist.

'Look!' he said, again.

Nelly turned her face towards the coffin and immediately looked away.

'You have to see what I see, Nelly.'

She was struggling to breathe. She reached out her hand, and Will took hold of it.

Feeling emboldened by his encouragement, at last she looked into the coffin.

Inside was the body of a woman. She was of medium build, with dark hair. Her eyes and mouth had been sewn closed. Her arms were folded at the chest, and tucked in beside her, to one side, was a fully swaddled bundle, the size of a small baby. The woman was wearing a white dress, an off-the-shoulder dress with puffed sleeves, a powder-blue corset with flecks of blue lace amongst the scalloped satin of the skirt. It was the same dress that Priscilla Fairfield had been wearing in the London photograph. The fabric had been folded carefully into the coffin around the woman's legs, and her hair had been tied back from her face and secured with mother-of-pearl pins, and a blue velvet band.

Her skin was blueish in colour, and mottled, and although she was not as awful a sight as Nelly had imagined, she knew that this dead woman would haunt her dreams for the rest of her life.

'Look at her face,' said Will.

'Are the blemishes of suffocation visible?'

'Look at her.'

Nelly moved a little, so her shadow was no longer falling over the coffin, and leaned closer. She studied the young woman's forehead, her eyelashes, her nose, her cheeks, her chin. For a moment Nelly couldn't see what Will wanted her to see.

And then she did.

The woman in the coffin had an inverted crescent-shaped scar beneath her lower lip.

She turned to Will.

'I don't understand,' she said.

'This isn't Priscilla Fairfield,' said Will. 'This is Gerty Skinner.'

60

The candle flame flickered as if in a draught. There was less than two inches of wax left.

Nelly leaned closer to study the face of the body in the coffin.

It was Gerty's face.

She heard a small sound from outside the crypt, but it was drowned by the noise in her head, a rushing, uncontrolled sound, like the wind in the trees.

'I cannot make sense of it,' she said. 'Perhaps Priscilla had a scar also.'

'No, Nelly. This is Gerty.'

Nelly heard another noise.

'Someone is out there, Will.'

'It's a fox or a deer.'

She looked up the steps. A shadow drew across the entrance.

'Let's go,' she said. 'Let's get out of here.'

'You wait outside, if you wish. I'm going to check the infant.'

'Oh no, Will, no! Don't touch the child.'

'I must.'

Will leaned down and moved the edge of the sheet in which the small bundle was wrapped with his finger.

'Will! Please! Don't!'

'God forgive me,' whispered Will. He took hold of the sheet and pulled it. It unravelled. Nelly was listening out for noises from above. 'Nelly, look.'

Nelly looked. She saw a smooth white cheek with a circle of red in the centre; yellow hair, an open eye, painted blue, surrounded by painted lashes that were thick as spider legs, cherry-red lips forming a cherubic, cupid's bow smile. She saw a hand fashioned from China clay and a cloth body. It took a moment for her brain to understand what her eyes were observing.

'It's a doll.'

From the corner of her eye, she glimpsed something at the entrance to the steps above her.

Will dropped the sheet.

Nelly turned to the steps. The rushing noise inside her head was becoming unbearable.

'Let's get out of here.'

Will reached for the coffin lid.

'I need to replace the coffin.'

'Leave it, Will, just leave it.'

She heard the crunch of a boot on the marble chippings.

Will closed the lid, pushed it into place. He crouched down to push the coffin back under the shelf.

Nelly was becoming desperate. 'Will!'

'I have to put it back as it was.'

'Will, *please!*'

'You go.'

Nelly heard the scrape of stone being dragged, then the thump as it was flung into the undergrowth.

'Someone's up there, Will!'

'I'm almost done.'

Will pushed the head of the coffin under the shelf.

'For pity's sake!'

The candle flame flickered inside the lamp.

Was that a cough Nelly heard?

'Please,' she begged, 'let's go!'

Will dusted his hands on the thighs of his trousers.

'I'm ready.'

The door slammed shut.

'Oh no! Oh God, please, no!'

'It's only the wind,' said Will.

'It's not the wind! I put a stone against the door.'

They both heard the turning of the handle, the latch sliding into the lock.

'Will!'

He ran up the stairs, grabbed at the handle and shook it.

'Wait!' he cried. '*Wait!* We're in the crypt! You have shut us in.'

'*Will!*'

But it was too late.

Whoever had been there was there no longer.

Nelly and Will were locked in the crypt with three coffins. And all they had for light and warmth was an inch and a half of candle wax.

61

Will was further up the steps than Nelly, whose eyes were on a level with his knees. He turned to her, bending down. The planes of his face and his features had been transformed into weird shadows. Nelly could see the shape of his skull behind his eyes and his cheeks; in this light, he seemed monstrous.

'Perhaps that was the superintendent,' he said. 'Perhaps he took us for body-snatchers, and has gone for the police. If that's the case, we should be freed very shortly.'

But Nelly knew it was not the superintendent who had locked them in, but the watchman. He must have followed them. She should never have dropped her guard.

She wrapped her arms about herself.

Now the doors were closed, it was silent inside the crypt. Silent, and cold.

She glanced at the lamp. Was it her imagination or was the flame already beginning to fade? What was left of the candle was certainly slumping.

Oh dear God!

'Can't you pick the lock from this side, Will?'

'A fine thought!' said Will. He put his hand in his pocket and extricated the knife. 'Will you hold the lamp for me?'

She lifted the lamp from the hook, and climbed a few steps, afraid of accidentally obliterating the tiny flame.

What will we do when the light goes out? she wondered. *How can we be here, in the dark, on our own?*

Will was working on the lock, making clicking noises with his tongue.

'There we go.'

He turned the handle and pushed the door. It moved a fraction, not even enough to let in a draught.

'Oh,' he said.

'Oh, what?'

'There is the gate behind the door. I can't open the second lock, Nelly.'

'What does that mean?'

'That we are stuck here until someone comes.'

And with that, the tiny flame in the lamp gave one last flicker, and expired.

'Ah,' Will said. 'That's unfortunate.'

'Will,' Nelly cried, 'I cannot be here in the dark. I cannot.'

He could not see her face. He could not see her fear.

'We don't have any choice, Nelly.'

'You don't understand, Will. I cannot do this; I cannot be shut in! I cannot breathe in small spaces. I shall suffocate and die.'

She tried to come to the top of the steps too, feeling her way on her hands and knees.

'There must be a way to open the gate!' she cried. 'There must be!'

She pushed past Will and patted her hands up the wood until she found the handle, and she pulled and shook it, screaming, 'Help! Help! We are trapped!'

'Nelly, we will be all right. There's nothing here that will hurt us...'

'Help!' Nelly screamed. *'HELP!'*

But she knew that nobody was beyond to hear her; only the deer, jumping through the undergrowth, and the owl, silently hunting, and the bats flitting from their holes, seeking the moths.

The watchman had shut them in, and he was already gone.

* * *

Will tried to console Nelly, and when he realised that was impossible, he waited until she had calmed, and then he said, 'It might help if we sat together, so that we know where the other is. What we do not need now is one or the other of us to tumble down the steps and suffer a broken arm, or concussion.'

Nelly was exhausted and wound so tightly that she did not know how she was still breathing, but this was clearly a sensible strategy. She moved her arm carefully through the dark until she touched Will's hand, and she took it, and she let him guide her to the step beside him.

'Your hand is trembling,' he said.

'I cannot bear to be enclosed.'

'But you *are* bearing it. You are breathing and conversing. As long as we don't fall, we shall be all right. We each need the other to keep our spirits up.'

'Yes,' Nelly said.

She could not recall the last time she felt more dispirited.

Will lit a match. For a few seconds she could see his face, as he moved the small, inconsistent light, looking for a means of escape. He struck a second match, and a third. The air smelled of sulphur and smoke.

'We would be safer at the bottom of the steps,' he said, resigned to their predicament.

'I can't go down there, Will, not with the coffins and the odour and...' She shuddered. She recalled the seance, and Mrs Chauncey saying how the spirits of those who had been wronged could not rest until the wrong had been righted. She pressed the heels of her hands into her eyes to stop herself picturing Gerty Skinner sitting up and pushing at the lid of her coffin. That poor young woman had been wronged so often, it would be a miracle if she were ever to rest.

'We'll stay here, then, until dawn breaks,' said Will, 'and then somebody will come.'

'How will we know when it's dawn?'

'There will be cracks of light around the door.'

They were sitting close together, sharing one another's body heat, but it was cold as death inside the crypt; Nelly could feel the chill coming up from the ground and if she could feel it through her skirts, it must be worse for Will, who had less substantial clothing.

'At least, while we are here, let's try and work out what is going on,' said Will.

And so they talked. They had no means of telling how time was passing beyond their prison – it was too dark to see the face of Will's pocket watch. Nelly told Will what she had not told him before; about the green velvet shawl and Eliza's death, and the note from the seance. She told him how she believed it was the watchman who had shut them in the crypt. They talked about Gerty Skinner, and how it could possibly be that she had come from the city mortuary to the coffin of a different woman altogether.

'I believe the two women who came to claim Gerty's corpse were Madeleine Avery and Sophy,' said Nelly. 'Madeleine matches the description of the older woman and we know that they are working together.'

'But why not put Priscilla in the coffin?'

Nelly considered this for a long time.

'Perhaps Priscilla wasn't suffocated after all,' she said at last. 'Perhaps Sir Edward murdered her in such a brutal and obvious way that Miss Avery dare not bring her body to the undertakers.'

They talked until they were exhausted, and still they could make no sense of it. At least the puzzle occupied their minds.

When they ran out of things to say, they sat in silence and the horror of their situation became clear.

62

SATURDAY, 5 NOVEMBER

Despite everything, Nelly must have dozed for a while. For the second time, she woke with her head on Will Delane's shoulder, and he with his arm around her.

It took her a moment to orientate herself.

'Oh God,' she whispered, 'are we still in the crypt?'

'We are,' said Will.

'Is it morning?'

'It is. It's Guy Fawkes Day.'

A faint light showed around the rim of the door, sliding half an inch across the cold floor. Nelly, frozen half to death, could make out the shape of Will and that was a comfort.

'Did you sleep at all?' Nelly asked him.

'A little.'

'It was a long night,' said Nelly.

'It was.'

She shivered and gazed down into the darkness at the bottom of the steps.

'I'm sorry, Will. Sorry that you became involved, and that I brought you here.'

'Nelly, you've no cause to blame yourself for any of this. I wanted to come. I wanted to help you.'

'Why?'

'Don't you know why, Nelly?'

Nelly understood he was intimating he felt warmly towards her, fonder, perhaps, than a colleague should feel towards another. And she liked him too, but she had vowed, after Sidney, that she would never, ever, become romantically involved with a man again.

When she did not answer, the silence became uncomfortable.

'Have I offended you?' Will asked.

'I am not offended, but I am surprised that you feel this is a suitable location for such a conversation.'

Will withdrew his arm from around her, and stretched it. He was hurt by her words; she could sense his wound although she could not see his face. She wondered what it was within her that made her be so unkind to a man who had been so good to her. And why sour things now, when they were trapped together?

Will took his watch from his pocket and held it against the crack of light coming from beneath the door so he could see the face.

'Half past seven,' he said. 'The cemetery will not be open for another hour and a half but when it is, people will come to visit the graves of their loved ones. Someone will walk this way and if we shout out at the right time, they will hear us.'

'Nobody will come past the crypt,' Nelly said. 'The watchman will have put a barrier across the path, to prevent people coming close.'

'You cannot know that.'

'But I do know. There is no point us sitting here, waiting for help, when it will not come. We must think of another plan.' She sighed. 'I don't suppose Sam will say anything to Maud...'

'We made him swear that he would not. And even if he does, they will soon be en route to Bournemouth. What could they do to help us from there?'

'Nothing,' Nelly said, sadly.

Will patted his pockets. 'I still have half a box of matches.'

But Nelly could not see how the matches would help. They had nothing to burn. And even if they did, the smoke would choke them to death before enough of it made its way out through the tiny cracks around the door to draw attention to their plight.

'I'm so thirsty,' Nelly said.

'What I wouldn't give for a cup of tea.'

'And a bun.'

'A bun with jam inside, and sugar on the top.'

'Jam *and* butter. And cream.'

'Now you're being greedy.'

Nelly leaned her head against Will's shoulder. It felt right, an apology of sorts. She wished she could learn to be less prickly with him.

'At least we are together,' she said.

* * *

Every so often, Will withdrew his watch, so they could read the time and see how the day was progressing. Nothing changed in the crypt save for the angle of the light coming through the cracks around the door. By afternoon, it had disappeared altogether.

Now and then they called, praying that someone would hear them, but nobody responded.

At two o'clock, the rain came. Water crept in. Nelly stopped shouting for help, and slumped in the corner with her knees drawn up and her head in her arms.

Will resumed banging on the door with his fists.

Nelly doubted anybody would walk through the cemetery in the pouring rain, and if they did, the patter of the raindrops would disguise the thump of the wood.

* * *

Time moved oddly in that dark place. Quicker, and also more slowly than normal.

Will and Nelly filled it with talking about their histories.

First Will spoke about his earliest memories, which were few, and sparse, as a child of the streets. And then he spoke of the orphanage.

He answered Nelly's questions as frankly and honestly as he could. She learned a good deal about the man; about his resilience and resourcefulness; his intelligence.

Then, it was her turn. Nelly felt that she owed Will the truth. She spoke of the decade she had spent locked away in the asylum, the wasted years. It was difficult at first. She struggled to find the words, the language, to explain what had happened to her, but she did her best.

It seemed a strange coincidence that both of them had been institutionalised for a large proportion of their lives. They shared anecdotes. They had more in common than they could have imagined.

Then came the inevitable question.

'Why did your parents send you to the asylum, Nelly?' Will asked.

The day was ending. The light at the edge of the door was fading. Another night was beginning.

Nelly was shivering violently. She kept drifting into a kind of half-sleep. Her mouth was dry; her tongue felt thick and sore.

She was too weak to feel the weight of the shame that usually crushed her when she was asked this question. And it was too dark for her to see the contempt in Will's eyes, if there was contempt. Probably they would never leave this place, so there was no risk in telling the truth. Will would never have the opportunity to tell anyone else.

'I birthed a child when I was fifteen years old,' she said.

'Did some man take advantage of you?'

How easy it would be to lie; to retain her virtue by making herself a victim of the action that set the course of her adult life in motion. But Nelly was not a liar.

'No. The father was a friend of mine. A boy I loved.'

'Couldn't you have married him?'

'My parents would not countenance that option.'

'They'd rather send you to an asylum?'

'It was less shameful for them that way.'

'Dear God,' said Will.

There was a long silence.

Then he asked, 'Did your parents ever come to see you, in the asylum?'

'My mother came once.'

'And? Was she sorry?'

'Oh, Will, no! She was not sorry.'

'So bridges were not built?'

'No. It was unbearable, for both of us. She cried, but her tears were for herself, not for me. And I did not know how to comfort her. She recoiled from my touch as if I was something obscene.'

Will was silent.

Nelly was too tired now to think things through logically. Her thoughts were a soup; a mixture of memories and hopes and dreams; of love and loss; of the shame inflicted on her; the stories she'd heard from the fallen women in the asylum; Constance's precious friendship; the constant, ongoing battle to keep one's dignity when those with power over you were trying to take it from you; the absolute subjugation of one's rights, because one had been born female.

Constance. She must do something about Constance. If she were to survive this current ordeal, she vowed to return to Holywell, and find a way to free her friend from the asylum. Constance could come and live with Nelly in Bristol. Nelly would bring her back to life in the same, tender way that Angel had looked after her.

As she mused on this, Will asked, 'What became of your child?'

'Harriet? My parents said she was a foundling and kept her as their own daughter.'

'Would you like to take her back?'

'I have spent years trying to work out how I might do that, Will. I can't think of a way. And it is too late now. She is on the way to Switzerland, to a sanatorium to convalesce from the scarlet fever.'

'It is never too late and Switzerland is not so very far away.'

'She is out of my reach.'

'I will help you reach her,' said Will.

'I do not know what I ever did,' Nelly said quietly, 'to deserve a friend such as you.'

63

SUNDAY, 6 NOVEMBER

Nelly did not know if the cold was worse, or the thirst, or the knowing that Gerty Skinner's body lay just a few feet below where she and Will sat, huddled in the dark. All their physical energy now was taken up in surviving. Their thoughts jumped around. Their talk was fractured.

They slept, curled together like puppies seeking warmth. Nelly dreamed she was a ghost walking amongst the audience at the seance. She was looking for Mrs Augur and Eveline. She wanted to let them know where she was, but before she found them, the other ghost from 12 Orchard Hill came screeching at her, a banshee with claw-like fingers and ghastly teeth. When she woke, disorientated, a puddle of water had seeped under the crack in the door to the crypt and soaked into her skirts, and she found she no longer cared about anything but quenching her thirst. She squeezed the moisture from the fabric so the drops fell into Will's mouth, and he directed her to the puddle, so that she might lap it, like a cat.

In her drowsy and confused state, Nelly saw a figure at the bottom of the steps. She thought it was Gerty, but then her eyes focussed and she saw that it was Harriet. The child was standing there, and her hair was loose about her face, her eyes dark shadows. Her cheeks were flushed and there were red spots on the backs of her hands.

She stared up at Nelly and Nelly looked down to her.

'Darling,' she whispered, 'sweetheart! Come to me!'

The child did not move, so Nelly pushed herself to her feet, and, with one hand steadying herself against the wall, she began to go down the stairs. But with each step, Harriet became fainter, and further away, and then Nelly lost her footing, and she fell, and she was on the crypt floor with her eyes open, but seeing nothing but darkness, and a splitting pain in her head.

Will was beside her, gathering her into his arms. She could not see him, but she could feel him.

'What are you doing?' he asked her. 'Why did you do that?'

'Harriet was here,' Nelly said. 'Didn't you see her?'

* * *

They stayed together, on the crypt floor, with Gerty Skinner's body only a few feet from them. They must have slept again, because neither of them heard the voices outside. They were oblivious to the lockpick rattling in the keyhole of the gate, and did not notice the door at the top of the steps to the crypt creaking open. Neither reacted until Sam called out, 'Will! Are you in there?'

His voice echoed oddly down the stone steps. Will turned towards it but Nelly was convinced it was not real, but part of a dream.

64

Sam was not alone. Maud had accompanied him to the cemetery and was waiting at the top of the crypt steps. She crouched down to take hold of Nelly as Nelly crawled from the darkness into a murky light that was blinding to her eyes.

'Oh!' Maud exclaimed, first recoiling from Nelly, then gathering her into her arms. 'You look dreadful. Here, lean on me, Nelly, let me help you to your feet.'

Nelly was half-laughing with relief at being rescued; half-mute because she did not fully believe it.

'I thought we would die in there,' she told Maud, dry-mouthed, squinting at her friend, holding onto her.

'I'm sure you did, dear, but you mustn't fret, you're quite safe now.'

Maud took Nelly back to the cab that was waiting on the main track through the cemetery, shielding her from the curious glances of visitors. Meanwhile Will and Sam made the crypt secure.

In the comfort of the carriage, Nelly drank from the flask of mineral water that Maud had brought, spilling the water on her chest, so eager was she to consume it.

'It has therapeutic qualities,' Maud said. 'Drink it all.'

'I must save some for Will.'

'I have another flask for him.'

Maud also had bread and cheese. Nelly tried, but found she could not eat.

She allowed Maud to mother her, covering her in a blanket and rubbing her cold hands, until Will and Sam returned. Nelly saw then how haggard Will had become. Stubble covered his chin and his eyes were bloodshot. His clothes were creased and filthy.

'Is the crypt locked?' Maud asked.

'It is,' said Will. He looked so weary. Nelly's heart went out to him.

They took her back to the house on Orchard Hill first. Through the carriage window, she could see people clearing debris from the streets of Bristol. Smoke still curled from the remnants of fires and shop-fronts were boarded over.

'What happened?' Will asked.

'Guy Fawkes celebrations got out of hand,' Sam said. 'Turned into a riot.'

* * *

Back at 12 Orchard Hill, Nelly drank almost an entire pot of tea while she bathed, and then she went to bed. Sarah sent for the doctor. He came and dressed the wound on Nelly's head. He gave her some medicine to help her sleep. Nelly was suspicious of the medicine. How could she know that this doctor was not also a friend of Sir Edward Fairfield?

She did not take it.

She slept anyway.

* * *

On Monday, Will called to see Nelly, and Sam was with him.

Nelly put on her dressing gown and came downstairs to the dining room.

'Have you been to work?' Nelly asked Will.

He nodded. 'I thought it best to carry on as usual. I had to make an excuse to come to visit you.'

Nelly thought of all her own deceptions, and prayed Will wouldn't get into trouble on her account.

Sarah knocked on the door, and then served coffee and sandwiches.

'Now my appetite is restored, I am uncommonly hungry,' said Nelly.

'So am I!' said Will. He clasped Sam's shoulder. 'We are making up for lost time. And you should tuck in, young man, you've more than earned your lunch.'

'What made you come to find us in the crypt?' Nelly asked Sam.

'The trip to Bournemouth was postponed, due to Maud having a terrible headache,' said Sam. 'I was disappointed, and sorry that Maud was unwell, but also glad, for it meant I could enjoy the Guy Fawkes celebrations with my pals.'

He explained how, at first the atmosphere in the city centre had been joyful, but many people had been drunk, and soon the mood had started to change. When Sam had seen men picking up bricks and throwing them at the windows of the houses, he had hurried back to Maud's.

The next morning, Sunday, Sam had ventured out into the rain, to find the city was smouldering. Knowing the Guy Fawkes

Night riots would provide a good deal of copy for the *Courier* reporters, Sam had headed to Will's house to see if he could be of assistance. But Will hadn't been there and his neighbour had said she had not seen him since Friday morning.

'So, what did you do, Sam?' Nelly asked.

'I'd sworn blind I wouldn't spill to anyone at the *Courier* where you'd gone, but I figured you wouldn't mind me telling Maud.'

'Thank God that you did.'

'It was her idea for us to come to the cemetery together.'

'How did you locate the crypt?'

'Maud asked the sexton, who told us where to go. She gave him tuppence for his trouble.'

'And you found it easily?'

'Not easily. The path through the woods was blocked at both ends, and there were *No Entry* signs. Maud was of a mind that we should obey the signs, but there was no-one around to see us creep past. We were at the crypt in no time. And,' his chest swelled a little at this juncture, 'I picked the outer lock and we found you inside.'

'I am proud of you, Sam,' Nelly said. 'If it wasn't for you, we would probably still be trapped. You are our champion.'

Sam blushed all the way from his neck to the tips of his ears.

* * *

Later that day, after work, Will came to 12 Orchard Hill again. This time, Nelly was dressed and ready to greet him by the fire in the dining room. He had brought a book for her, an illustrated guide to the flora and fauna of Switzerland.

'I thought it would make you feel closer to Harriet,' he said.

Nelly did not know how to thank him.

'I shall look at it later,' she said, and she put the book aside.

She went to the window, and looked out. It was dark, but she did not have the feeling she'd had before, when the watchman was there, of being observed. No doubt, he believed her and Will to be still incarcerated in the crypt.

She drew the curtains, and sat again.

'What should we do now?' Will asked. 'Should we tell the police what we know?'

'I am afraid that if we admit to breaking into the crypt, Sir Edward will use his influence to turn us into the criminals of this whole affair,' said Nelly.

'Then we should confront Miss Avery for a second time,' said Will. 'Perhaps she will turn against Sir Edward to save her own skin.'

They decided to go to Clevedon early the next morning, and discussed their strategy until Mrs Augur, newly returned from Exeter, knocked on the door to remind them, gently, of the lateness of the hour.

Before he left, Will examined the bruise on Nelly's head.

'It is more yellow than green now,' he said.

'Oh, Will, don't tease.'

'I'm not teasing, I am observing.'

'Is it dreadfully ugly?'

Will looked genuinely surprised. 'Nelly, nothing about you could be ugly, ever.'

She felt something give inside her.

A softening.

65

TUESDAY, 8 NOVEMBER

Will and Nelly rode together to Clevedon in the early stagecoach.

The rain was still falling, and the countryside beyond was black and bleak and wet; water lying in the fields and in the dips and hollows of the roads, so that often the horses' hooves were splashing rather than clip-clopping. Nelly, still suffering from the chill she'd developed after the cold of the crypt, was wrapped in Eveline Augur's coat, the one with the fur collar, to try to keep warm. The matching hat, which also had a fur trim, covered the worst of her bruising. Eveline had been concerned when she saw Nelly's wound that morning, and had insisted she take the garments.

As the coach rolled through the countryside, Nelly said: 'Miss Avery may refuse to speak to us, and this journey will have been for nothing.'

'My opinion is that she will prefer to talk to you and I, than to the police,' said Will. He considered for a moment. 'Let's see what happens.'

The carriage dropped them in town and they walked to Madeleine Avery's cottage. This time, when they rang the bell, although the dogs barked, they did not come running and snarling. Instead, a woman in middle-age with her dark hair tied back, came to the gates. She was wearing an apron and gloves, and her sleeves were rolled up, as if they had interrupted her whilst undertaking some domestic chore.

'Yes?' she asked abruptly.

'We are William Delane and Helen Brooks,' said Will. 'We are from the *Courier*.'

'The newspaper?'

'Yes. Are you Sophy?'

The woman nodded. She had become very pale, obviously disturbed by their presence.

'We came before,' Nelly said, 'a few days ago. Miss Avery told us you weren't here.'

'She didn't say anything to me.'

'May we come in?'

'I don't know, I...'

At this point Madeleine Avery herself emerged from the cottage with the dogs, quiet, at her side. She too was wearing an apron over her dress.

She came to stand beside Sophy and put a hand on her waist.

'Good morning, Miss Brooks, Mr Delane,' she said. 'I feared I had not seen the last of you.'

'It has become imperative that we speak to you, Miss Avery,' said Will. 'Matters have taken a significant turn and I'm afraid that if you cannot answer our questions, we shall be obliged to refer our investigation to the police.'

Sophy looked as if she might faint. Nelly felt pity for her. Was she imagining the spectre of the hangman's noose, picturing herself, hooded at the gallows?

Madeleine Avery sighed.

'You had better come inside,' she said. 'This way, if you please.'

Will opened the gate and he and Nelly followed the two women along a gravelled path to the cottage, which was stone-built and modest, surrounded by a most pleasant garden.

Sophy opened the door and stood to the side while they entered.

'Let me take your coats,' she said. 'Please go into the sitting room. I'll bring some refreshments.'

Nelly observed the crates piled in the hallway. On the table visible through the open kitchen door was glassware and crockery, some of it wrapped in newspaper.

Sophy took their outer garments, and then disappeared with the dogs.

Nelly and Will followed Madeleine Avery into a small living room. A fire was crackling in the hearth. The furniture was old, but of good quality; everything a little shabby but comfortable. There were crates in this room also, and a pile of folded dustsheets.

Madeleine Avery held out her slender hand, and indicated where they should sit.

As she took her place to one side of a small sofa, Nelly heard footsteps above. She saw Will stiffen slightly, and knew that he had heard them too. The two women were not alone in this isolated cottage.

Nelly had a dreadful thought. Might it be the watchman, upstairs? Or Scarrat? Or Sir Edward? Or all three of them?

Had she and Will walked into a trap?

Madeleine Avery sat down. She was apparently composed, but Nelly noticed how she turned the ring she was wearing round and round her index finger. A tic twitched in the corner of her right eye.

'I have heard tell how persistent newspaper men, and women, can be,' she said. 'Please tell me why you have returned?'

'You are aware that Miss Brooks and I have been looking into the deaths of Lady Fairfield and her infant,' said Will. 'We have also been investigating the disappearance of the human remains of a woman named Gerty Skinner from the city mortuary.'

At this, Madeleine Avery flinched. She recovered quickly, but for a moment her discomfort was obvious.

Will continued: 'We have established that it is Miss Skinner's body which lies within Lady Fairfield's coffin. We know, Miss Avery, that you and an accomplice claimed Miss Skinner's body from the mortuary, and that you yourself oversaw its delivery to the undertaker's.'

Madeleine Avery did not say a word.

'You understand, I'm sure,' said Will, 'that the theft of a corpse is a serious crime, punishable by death, so perhaps you could tell us firstly, why you did it and secondly, where we might find Lady Fairfield's corpse?'

'And the baby,' Nelly added.

Madeleine's fingers moved to the neck of her dress, olive green, with a cream collar and cuffs. Subconsciously, she made it a little looser.

The door swung open and Sophy came in carrying a large tray. She placed it on top of the table: a silver coffee pot, cream jug and sugar bowl. Fine bone-china cups and saucers; silver teaspoons. Upstairs, the floorboards creaked.

Sophy looked at Madeleine Avery. Some unspoken communication occurred between them.

Nelly glanced at Will, who was sitting, apparently at ease, but alert, like a dog with pricked ears. She knew, without it having to be said, that he believed them close to the heart of the matter now. It was simply a question of whether Madeleine Avery would tell the truth. And he was aware of the movement upstairs. He was as wary as she; prepared to react if they were threatened.

Sophy said: 'Shall I pour the coffee, Miss Avery?'

'Please do.'

As she passed a cup to Madeleine, Sophy suddenly exclaimed: 'I think we should tell them what happened, madam, for where we did wrong, it was for the right reasons and nobody should hang for trying to do right.'

'Not yet,' said Madeleine.

Sophy opened her mouth, then thought better of whatever she was about to say, and closed it again.

Nelly hardly dared breathe.

Please, she begged silently, *tell us.*

'Before anyone says anything more,' Madeleine said, focussing on Will and Nelly, 'I need to know in what capacity we are talking to you. Will you give me your assurances that anything that is disclosed in this room, today, is strictly between us?'

'With respect, Miss Avery,' said Will, 'it is impossible for us to answer that question until we know what you are going to say. We know that serious crimes have been committed. We cannot reasonably be expected to cover them up simply because you have told us the truth.' He paused. 'Neither, I would add, would we wish to add more harm to that which has already been done.'

Nelly glanced at him. He often behaved as if he didn't know what he was doing, stumbled over his words sometimes, but nobody could have spoken more clearly or directly.

There was a noise from upstairs, a creaking sound; Nelly recognised it. It was the runners on a rocking chair going forwards and backwards over the floorboards.

'Who is up there?' she asked.

Sophy looked again to Madeleine.

'Wait,' said Madeleine. She was becoming less composed. 'You have to understand that Sophy is not responsible for any of what happened. She is innocent.'

'Your loyalty is commendable, but we still don't know what you did,' said Will.

'Were you working with Sir Edward?' Nelly asked. 'Did you conspire with him to solve the problem of Lady Fairfield and her infant?'

'I? Conspire with Sir Edward? Of course not!' said Madeleine, with some vehemence. 'I'd rather work with the Devil himself! All this... everything we have done... was done to thwart my stepfather.'

A door opened upstairs.

'Who is up there?' Nelly asked again. 'Is it Sir Edward?'

She glanced at Will. His eyes were wide behind the lenses of his glasses.

'Shall I stop her?' Sophy asked.

Madeleine shook her head. 'Let her come.'

'Her?' cried Nelly. 'Who?'

Now the footsteps were descending the stairs. The door opened. Framed by the doorway, was a tall, well-built young woman with dark hair and broad shoulders. She was wearing a chemise and a dressing gown. In her arms was an infant, perhaps two weeks old, wearing a knitted bonnet that was too big for him, wrapped in a white shawl. He stared at the visitors with bright, dark eyes.

'Good morning,' the young woman said. 'I am Priscilla Fairfield and this is my son, Henry. I believe you've been looking for us.'

66

Priscilla sat on the sofa besides Nelly, holding the child. Madeleine reached out from her chair and smoothed the baby's cheek with the backs of her fingers.

'Aren't you sweet?' she whispered to little Henry. 'Aren't you the most darling little man?'

Nelly could not stop staring at Priscilla: the woman in the photograph come to life.

'Are you surprised to see me?' Priscilla asked her.

'I am happy to see you,' said Nelly sincerely. 'For the past two weeks, I have believed you murdered, and your son too.'

'As you see, we're both alive and well,' said Priscilla, kissing the child. 'Who told you we had been murdered?'

'Eliza Morgan, the seamstress.'

'Dear Eliza. I read in the newspaper that she had drowned.' She paused. 'Was my husband behind her death?'

'I think so,' said Nelly.

Priscilla's expression darkened, as if a cloud had passed over it.

'Poor Eliza,' she whispered, 'she was the kindest soul.'

The baby mewled, throwing back his little head, screwing up his eyes and making fists of his hands.

Priscilla lifted him to her shoulder. He tucked his head into the crook of her neck, and began to suck his fist. His mother rubbed his back with the utmost gentleness. Nelly, watching, felt a maternal tug, so strong it was painful.

'Miss Brooks and Mr Delane have come looking for explanations,' said Madeleine.

'Of course, they have.'

'I'll see to the dogs,' said Sophy.

'No, Sophy, don't go. We might need you.'

'But I...'

'Stay.'

Madeleine indicated an empty chair, and Sophy perched on it, looking nervous.

'What would you like to know?' asked Madeleine, looking first to Will and then to Nelly. Her gaze was gimlet-sharp.

'Everything,' said Nelly, 'if we are to see the full picture.'

'Where should I begin?'

'With whatever event initiated the chain of events that led us to this point.'

Madeleine thought for a moment, then sighed.

'I suspect that would be when my mother met Sir Edward.'

'Then that would be an excellent starting point,' said Will. 'How old were you, Miss Avery, when they first knew one another?'

'I was thirteen.' Madeleine picked a tiny fragment of lint from her skirt.

Will and Nelly waited while she gathered her thoughts.

'Mother was rather swept off her feet by Sir Edward,' she said at last. 'My father, long since deceased, had been a vicar, we were poor as church mice. Sir Edward bought my mother roses. He showered her with gifts. He said he wanted a family. A wife and children. Sons. Mother had birthed two boys, before me. They both died in infancy, but she was capable of bearing male children. It seemed a good match. They married. The first few months were bearable. After that...' She tailed off.

'She didn't have another son?' asked Nelly.

'She had no child of any description. She never even came close to it. With each day that passed, Sir Edward became angrier, and behaved more cruelly towards her. I used to be in the room when he beat her. Sophy tried to protect her, but he would hit Sophy too. He called my mother "desiccated" and "barren". He went to his club and met with his mistress, and came home smelling of her perfume, and still Mother was expected to lie with him. If she refused, he would attack her. I truly believe he took pleasure in hurting her.'

Now Priscilla reached across and touched Madeleine's arm, a gesture of support and empathy.

'His brutality was destroying her,' Madeleine continued. 'Sophy and I both saw it, didn't we, Sophy? Mother couldn't think straight any more. She was not herself. And then she did something that was apparently foolish but really was an indication of her desperation,' she paused. 'She pretended she was with child.'

'Why would she do such a thing?'

'For some peace, Mr Delane. She'd been to a woman who sold her medicine "guaranteed" to make her conceive; perhaps she thought if she believed it enough, it would come true. But it did not. And when Sir Edward found out...'

Nelly waited, with bated breath.

'He drove her to drink poison,' said Madeleine.

'You know this?'

'I heard him taunting her. I believe that in the end she

thought the poison was a better option than another day with him.'

Madeleine raised her hand to her eye and wiped away a tear. Sophy passed her a handkerchief and, as Madeleine took it, squeezed her hand in sympathy.

'It was reported that your mother died of a weak heart,' Will observed gently.

'My mother's body was attended to by the physician, Mr Thorpe-Thompson, who decided upon that explanation with Sir Edward. They thought a suicide verdict might reflect badly on Sir Edward and his political career.'

'Dear God.' Will was shocked.

'I hated my stepfather,' Madeleine said. 'I hated him with every ounce of my being. I was twenty-four years old and I was obliged to stay with him, to run the household. You can imagine my gratitude when he told me he was taking another wife. Although my relief was short-lived when I discovered the identity of his intended.'

She looked at Priscilla, then continued.

'Priss was only seventeen when Edward started "courting" her. I could see the revulsion in her eyes every time he paid her a compliment.'

'Compliments I was obliged to accept because of my father,' said Priscilla, 'he being massively indebted to Sir Edward, and in thrall to him. Although he died a few days before the wedding, my father was happy that I was to become Lady Fairfield. He believed my future was assured, and that of any children I might have.'

She looked at the baby in her arms, stroked his back. The child was dozing on her shoulder, one eye closed, the other half open.

'Is that coffee still warm, Sophy? Would you pour a cup for

me? Thank you.' She took the proffered cup and drank, taking care not to hold the cup over the baby, and gave a small sigh of pleasure. 'After I became Lady Fairfield, Madeleine was at liberty to return here, to her own home.'

'I should have stayed with you, Priss.'

'Nonsense. You did more than anyone could humanly have been expected to do. Besides, you knew I'd be safe with Sophy.'

'What would any of us have done without Sophy? She is our rock.'

Sophy touched her earlobe and blushed.

Priscilla picked up the story. 'Before my marriage, I expected to enjoy being mistress of Mordaunt Hall.' She laughed. 'What a fool I was!'

She is still only nineteen, Nelly reminded herself.

'Edward liked to show me off to his friends,' said Priscilla. 'The more important the man, the more attention Edward expected me to pay to him. He made lewd comments about me, to them. He implied I was a silly child, lascivious, foolish and expected me to laugh with him. He disgusted me. I disgusted myself.'

'Was one of these friends the Prince of Wales?' Will asked.

Priscilla nodded.

'Tell us about him,' Nelly said gently.

Priscilla held her baby close.

She sighed. 'I had a new gown made for the evening I first met him. Sophy spent hours helping me get ready. I sat next to him at dinner and played the ingénue. Bertie was easily charmed and Edward was pleased with my performance.'

And that, thought Nelly, *is the beginning of Henry's story. That's where it started. With a giggle, a compliment, a confidence, a warm glance.*

Nelly took the bee pendant from her satchel. She passed it to

Priscilla. 'I'll explain how I came by this later. But it is true, is it not, that you and the prince were lovers?'

Priscilla tried to hide her discomfort. 'I'm ashamed to say that we were.' She paused, then said: 'Bertie was attentive. He saw me for who I really was, at least, I thought he did. He was sweet. He made me laugh. And, God, after Edward I needed some happiness.' She exhaled shakily.

'Was your husband aware of your alliance?'

'He had his suspicions. Before he left for India, he forbade me to see the prince in his absence.'

'But you disobeyed him?'

'How does one refuse royalty when it arrives at one's doorstep demanding hospitality?'

Sophy was staring down at her hands. Her cheeks were flushed. She must have seen and heard everything. She must have been terrified of the consequences.

Priscilla cupped the baby's head in her hand and moved him back down onto her lap.

'When I discovered I was with child,' she said, 'I did not know what to do. Bertie hadn't been married a year and his own wife was also expecting. I wrote to Edward and asked him to come home at once, although I could not tell him why. If Edward did as I asked, I might have been able to persuade him, and others, that the child was his. But he couldn't leave the business or didn't want to abandon his mistress. Anyway, he would not return.'

Priscilla looked down at the baby. 'The last time Bertie visited, he insisted we were intimate and when he saw me unclothed, he realised I was in a delicate condition. He gave me a warm kiss, and the necklace as a token of his affection. "It has been a pleasure being acquainted with you, madam," he said.' The memory evidently pained her. 'He didn't return to Mordaunt

Hall after that. I thought he harboured genuine affection towards me. Evidently, I was mistaken.'

Nelly could hardly bear to imagine how hurtful that must have been.

'And then your husband came home...'

'Yes.'

Nelly waited.

The strain of remembering told on Priscilla's face.

'It was clear to him what had happened,' she said quietly. 'And he could not see a way out of the situation. He thought that when my infidelity became public, which was inevitable, the unavoidable scandal and the accompanying salacious tittle-tattle would be the undoing of his career; the ruin of the Fairfield family name. Any future sons he conceived would be tainted by my disgrace. He'd be a laughing stock in parliament, and, as a couple, we'd be social pariahs. He tried to beat the baby out of me with his belt, but Sophy stopped him with no consideration for her own wellbeing.'

All those assembled looked at Sophy with awe.

Sophy blushed.

'Then Priscilla had her first accident,' said Madeleine.

'I fell from my horse,' Priscilla said. 'The saddle slipped. But it was no accident. The girth had been cut.'

Nelly recalled Sir Edward recounting this event to her, claiming it was a figment of Priscilla's tortured imagination. Deep down, she had known all along that he had been lying.

'Who do you think was responsible?' she asked.

'Why, him, of course!' Priscilla said. 'Edward. My husband.'

67

There had been other 'accidents': a loose carpet on the stairs; a broken rung on the library steps; and, when Priscilla had gone out one evening to take the air, she had almost fallen into the coal cellar: the door, which Betty swore had been closed after a delivery, had been reopened. Sophy had been so concerned she'd summoned Madeleine, who had returned to Mordaunt Hall to protect Priscilla in the final weeks of her pregnancy.

'It was as if we were playing a game,' Madeleine said, 'one that we could not afford to lose. We always had to be one step ahead, predicting where the next "accident" might happen.'

Sophy raised a hand. 'We were concerned about the food being tampered with,' she said.

'Indeed we were,' said Madeleine, 'to the point where I used to go down to the kitchen and oversee the preparation of Priscilla's supper myself.'

'And I was becoming paranoid,' said Priscilla. 'I was losing trust in everyone, suspecting foul play whichever way I turned. Edward insisted I was insane, and I began to wonder if he might be right. I wrote everything down in my diary, and gave it to

Eliza. If anything were to happen to me, I told her, she should use my words as evidence. I knew the diary would not be safe in Mordaunt Hall and trusted Eliza to take care of it.'

Will's eyes were growing wider and wider. Nelly wondered if he was imagining the newspaper story all this would make.

Priscilla continued: 'I offered to leave the country if Edward would give me a divorce, but he said that was out of the question. And then I heard him talking with his most trusted friends, one evening, in the billiards room.' She tailed off miserably.

'What did you hear exactly?' asked Will.

'They were discussing the fragility of mothers and infants in the hours after childbirth. The doctor, Mr Thorpe-Thompson said if a man wanted rid of his wife, that was the time to finish her, because death in childbed was so common that nobody would question it.'

She paused as the baby squirmed, and held him close to her.

'The police inspector, Mr Vardy, said suffocation was the best method for post-partum murder because, if done quickly and cleanly, it is the hardest to detect. Mr Thorpe-Thompson said poison was more effective. "But wouldn't a post-mortem examination detect poison?" asked Mr Vardy, and Mr Thorpe-Thompson said, "There would be no need for a post-mortem if the attending physician, declared the deaths to be due to natural causes."'

Everyone was silent after this last statement. Remembering had taken its toll on Priscilla. Nelly was recalling the letter Sir Edward had shown her.

'A woman is so vulnerable in childbirth,' said Sophy. 'She cannot run. She is physically disadvantaged. She and her child are at the mercy of the people around them.'

'We knew we must be especially vigilant when Priscilla began to labour,' said Madeleine. 'We drew up a plan, didn't we, Sophy?'

'I would be with Lady Fairfield for as much of the time as I could be, while Miss Avery watched Sir Edward,' said Sophy. 'Violet, another of the maids and a sensible woman, was also going to assist at the birth. Our lady would not be left alone for a moment.'

'And then,' said Madeleine, 'we had a marvellous idea!'

Priscilla looked up from the baby with a small smile on her lips.

Madeleine continued: 'We thought, why not let Edward and Mr Thorpe-Thompson believe that they have succeeded? Persuade them that Priscilla and the baby are dead! Priscilla killed by the poison, the baby too weak to survive. Edward would not come searching for a dead woman. He would not seek retribution on someone in whose murder he was complicit. Priscilla would be free. Forever.'

'Wasn't that a terribly risky thing to do?' asked Nelly.

'It was less risky than letting Edward murder Priscilla, which I have no doubt at all he would have done if we hadn't intervened,' said Madeleine sharply.

'We worked it all out beforehand,' said Priscilla. 'We knew Mr Thorpe-Thompson would attempt to administer poison. All we had to do was convince Edward that I had taken it. Madeleine would say that the child was sickly, and had not survived, and Sophy would confirm the story.'

'And then we must remove the "bodies" quickly,' said Madeleine, 'and arrange a funeral.'

'We did not think Edward would want to see my corpse,' said Priscilla, 'knowing that he had helped bring about my demise. But if he did want to see it, we'd have staged it, somehow.'

'It was fortunate there was an unclaimed, female body in the city mortuary the very day you needed one to take to the undertakers,' said Will.

'It felt like a miracle when we saw the article in the newspaper,' said Madeleine, with such sincerity that Nelly did not doubt that this part of the plot had been improvised. 'And we did not think that anyone would be harmed by us claiming the unclaimed body for our own.'

'We had intended to visit the workhouses to see if any poor woman had died recently,' said Sophy, 'but that would have been a terrible task.'

'And it didn't come to that, because we had the girl with the scar on her chin,' said Madeleine. 'She was close in age to Priscilla, and similar enough in stature and looks for us to be confident the undertaker we used would suspect nothing. And we brought the shrouded doll to the coffin at the last minute, knowing that the lid was about to be closed.'

'So there was no murder,' Will said.

Priscilla shook her head. 'I am no ghost,' she said. She put one hand on the infant. 'Nor is this little man.'

'I went to Mordaunt Hall,' said Nelly to Priscilla. 'I found the sealed phial in the drawer by your bed. It contained strychnine.'

The three women, Priscilla, Sophy and Madeleine, stared at one another, appalled and at the same time completely vindicated.

'They really meant to kill me,' said Priscilla. She raised a hand to her lips, trembling, and then held the baby closer. She looked directly at Nelly. 'They meant to kill us both,' she said.

'I knew it,' said Madeleine. 'I knew!'

68

'So now we have told you everything,' said Madeleine.

'Not quite everything,' said Priscilla. 'On Saturday, we're travelling to Liverpool to board the steamship to Australia. Nobody will know us there. We shall start afresh.'

'You should leave as soon as you can,' Will said. 'If Sir Edward becomes aware of your deception, this is the first place he will look.'

'We could move into a hotel this afternoon.'

'That's what you must do,' said Will. 'But don't stay in Clevedon or Bristol. And don't turn to any of your usual allies.'

'This is all too much. I need a drink of water,' said Priscilla. 'Would you hold Henry, Miss Brooks?'

She passed the baby into Nelly's arms before Nelly had chance to refuse.

Nelly, who had never once cradled her own daughter, looked down at the miniature boy she was holding, and she marvelled at the courage of his mother and her allies to do what they had done. To have beaten Sir Edward at his own game. To have won.

She touched the back of Henry's tiny hand with her finger. She smiled at the serious expression on his little face.

'Oh!' she whispered, 'aren't you perfect!'

Now Priscilla was out of earshot, Madeleine looked anxiously from Will to Nelly.

'We have given you the truth, will you collude with us to protect it?' she asked, 'Not only now, but forever?'

Nelly glanced at Will. His eyes said: *This is your story. How it ends is up to you.*

'I would never do anything that would jeopardise your safety,' Nelly said to the women, 'nor that of the infant.' Her words were heartfelt.

'But not everything is settled,' said Will. 'What about Mr and Mrs Skinner? The parents of the girl in the coffin.'

'We will ensure they are compensated.'

'No amount of compensation will make up to them for the loss of their daughter.'

Priscilla came back into the room, and sat beside Nelly.

'We must, somehow, return the body to them,' she said.

'We will think of something,' said Madeleine. 'We cannot undo what has been done, but we will ensure everything is resolved going forward.'

'What troubles me,' Nelly said, 'is that if no story is printed, and Sir Edward is free to continue his political career, and to marry again, he and the doctor have got away with murder.'

'But there was no murder.'

'Eliza Morgan was killed at Sir Edward's bidding.'

'I hope her spirit haunts Edward to the end of his days,' said Priscilla, 'but if it cannot be proved she was murdered, then how can he be brought to justice?'

'Can some good be done in Eliza's name, if justice is impossible?' Sophy asked.

'That is a most excellent proposal,' said Will.

'I am sorry, Miss Brooks, that you will not get your story,' said Madeleine. 'But you have proved yourself to be a clever and determined newshound. I have no doubt that other truths-waiting-to-be-told will come your way.'

Will cleared his throat. 'Unfortunately, Miss Brooks has been suspended over her initial trespass into the Fairfield family crypt,' he said. 'She may well lose her position at the *Courier*.'

'Ah,' said Madeleine. She thought for a moment. 'Miss Brooks, you may not be able to tell this story in the newspaper, but now you know the nature of Sir Edward, and the men with whom he connives, can you not write a different exposé? For once the truth is known, surely any disciplinary measures you have endured will be revoked? We will, of course, assist you in any way we can.'

Nelly looked to Will who pushed his glasses up his nose.

'Yes,' she said. 'I can do that.'

69

THURSDAY, 1 DECEMBER 1864

Sam knocked on the partition at the side of Nelly's cubbyhole. She looked up from the feature she was writing about different styles of curtain pelmets – she was struggling to find four hundred words on the topic and was glad of the interruption.

'Hello, Sam.'

'Morning, Miss Brooks. Mr Boldwood would like a word with you.'

'What have I done now?' Nelly asked.

'I don't know, miss. You tell me.'

Pinned to Sam's jacket was the medal George Boldwood had presented to him for excellent work, for his saving the lives of Nelly and Will. Mr Boldwood had also put ten pounds into a bank account that Sam could access when he came of age, to give him a good start to adulthood.

Nelly stood up, picked up her notebook and pencil and walked across to the editor's office. The door was open.

'Come in!' said George Boldwood. 'Sit down, Nelly. I have a job for you.'

'Winter fashions?' she guessed.

'No. The tenants of the housing blocks in Bedminster have formed a committee. They've made a list of complaints against their landlord, Obadiah Scarrat, and they're holding a public meeting this afternoon. The chair of the committee, one Mr Albert Skinner, has requested you cover it.'

'Me?'

'Yes, you. You've made something of a name for yourself following the undercover exposé of the Venus club. The tenants want to ask Mr Scarrat why he can afford to give hundreds of pounds of donations in support of the political campaign of Sir Edward Fairfield, yet cannot pay for the most basic of improvements to his squalid properties.'

Nelly felt a thrill of anticipation. 'Will Sir Edward be present?'

'I doubt it, but we can deal with him later. If we put enough pressure on Scarrat, I reckon he'll turn on Fairfield. His sort always do. When you return, I'd like you to dig as deeply as you can into Scarrat's affairs, Nelly. Find out how far the corruption goes. We won't stop until we've exposed all those whose greed and selfishness taints the integrity of the city.'

***

The meeting was charged with emotion and a desire for change. Nelly was given her own small table and chair, to make her notes.

She observed the watchman, standing beside Scarrat, shuffling a deck of cards on his lap, and in daylight, in a crowded room, she saw that he was not the monster of her imagination, but a man in late middle age with a chronic cough and without the capacity to make his own decisions in life. He did as Scarrat told him, as Scarrat obeyed Fairfield. Little fleas on the backs of bigger fleas, as the saying went.

The grief about Eliza Morgan's death, and the anger at the unfairness of it, still rankled with Nelly, but now was not the time to challenge the watchman. When Fairfield and Scarrat were brought to account, then those beneath them might confess to the crimes they had committed in their employers' name. Justice would come, in the fullness of time.

Afterwards, she spoke briefly with Mrs Skinner, who was handing out leaflets. Mrs Skinner told her that just as they'd given up all hope, Gerty's body had turned up at an undertaker's on the Commercial Road. It had been given a wonderful funeral at Arnos Vale 'horses, plumage and all', all paid for by an unknown well-wisher. A beautiful stone angel had even been commissioned to stand lovingly over Gerty's grave.

'Miracles do happen sometimes,' said Mrs Skinner.

Little Archie, on her hip, reached up his face and kissed his grandmother on the cheek.

* * *

Nelly returned to the *Courier* offices late, but Will was waiting for her.

'Shall we go to Pierre's for supper?' he asked.

'Oh, Will, I'm sorry!' said Nelly. 'I promised I would accompany Mrs Augur and Eveline to the seance this evening.'

'And what am I to do without you?' Will asked.

'Visit Maud and Sam,' Nelly replied. 'You know they will be delighted to see you.'

* * *

It was a rush for Nelly to get home, and there was no time for supper before she and the Augurs departed for the spiritualist church. Nelly wore the green velvet shawl around her shoulders although she did not explain its significance to Mrs Augur or Eveline.

They arrived just as the doors were closing, and were hurried through into the main hall, which was laid out as it had been before, to take seats towards the back, the only ones still available.

Almost at once, Mrs Chauncey's assistant, Ursula, who was at the piano, changed the music to a more sombre tune, and Nelly settled down to watch the spectacle unfold. She removed the shawl from her shoulders and folded it on her lap.

The seance progressed in a similar way to the previous one, the same mixture of high drama, interspersed with periods of rising tension. Then, shortly before the curtain was due to fall, Mrs Chauncey, dishevelled and unsteady after all her exertions, suddenly stood and turned to face the audience.

'I have a spirit with me who cannot find peace,' she said. 'She is lost; she does not know which way to turn. Someone here knows this precious soul, and can help guide her towards the light of solace, but I sense a resistance to belief.'

Mrs Chauncey signalled, and the house lights went up. She gazed across the assembled faces of the audience.

'Whoever you are, open your heart. Let this poor soul in; reassure her that all is well, and that she can rest.'

Nelly sat still. She was afraid to open her heart for she did not wish to reveal the shame, and the pain within, yet she wanted to help Eliza.

She put her hands on the green velvet shawl and tried to summon Eliza to her.

All is well, Eliza, she whispered. *Lady Fairfield and the baby are alive.*

Nelly did not know if Eliza's spirit was present, nor if it could comprehend her, but she had tried.

We do our best, Nelly thought. *It is all we can do.*

* * *

The seance was over. It was time to join either the long queue for refreshments, or the even longer queue for the privies.

Nelly wrapped the shawl tightly around her shoulders, and stood waiting for a cup of coffee, with Mrs Augur and Eveline. As she did so, she became aware of Mrs Chauncey's assistant, Ursula, hovering behind her.

Nelly turned to face her. Ursula seemed flustered. 'Excuse me,' she said, each word spoken with her strong, northern European accent. 'I had a friend who had a shawl exactly like the one you were wearing.'

'This is the shawl that Eliza used to wear, if Eliza Morgan is the friend to whom you refer,' said Nelly.

Ursula looked at Nelly properly. 'You are Nelly Brooks, aren't you?'

'I am.'

'And my name is Ursula Schneider. Ushy to my friends.'

Nelly felt a satisfaction as the last piece of the puzzle fell into place.

'I suppose you know how Eliza came by the shawl,' she said.

'Indeed. And I knew she intended to tell you about the murder of Lady Fairfield and her infant, although I warned her not to. I feared she would bring trouble to herself and to you.' She shook her head resignedly. 'She was right to be afraid, wasn't she?'

'She was. I believe Eliza was murdered by the watchman,' said Nelly.

'So do I.'

'That's why you gave me the note warning me to beware?'

'Yes.'

Nelly passed the shawl to Ushy. 'Eliza would have wanted you to have this.'

'Thank you,' Ushy said, holding the fabric to her cheek. 'I shall treasure it.'

'One last thing,' said Nelly, 'did you know of any cause that was close to Eliza's heart? Did she perhaps support a church or a charitable organisation?'

Ushy thought for a moment, then she said: 'She was very concerned about the fate of the donkeys that haul the carts around Bristol docks. What will become of them when the harbour railway opens and they no longer serve a useful purpose?'

'I have access to a trust fund set up in Eliza's memory,' said Nelly. 'Perhaps we should open a donkey sanctuary in her name.'

70

SATURDAY, 17 DECEMBER 1864

Nelly turned left at the top of the hill and paused to catch her breath. In front of her was the newly opened Clifton Suspension Bridge.

God, it was beautiful!

The flags that had been raised along its length were gone now, as were the temporary stands arranged so that the maximum possible number of spectators could witness its official launch. There had been a parade, music, city-wide celebrations. The *Courier*'s commemorative supplement had sold in its thousands and prints of Mr Roscoe's pictures had been snapped up.

The Prince of Wales had not come to the opening. He had cited previous commitments; whether or not his reluctance to attend had anything to do with his hearing the news of Priscilla Fairfield's tragic death, nobody but he would ever know.

But with or without the prince, the bridge was open, connecting Bristol and Somerset. Nelly could walk across if she wished. She'd avoided doing so, being afraid of the depth of the drop, but today she was determined to overcome her fear.

She breathed in; the air up here, in Clifton, was more refined than that in the city below. On the far side of the bridge, the winter blackness of Leigh Woods was interspersed with the dark greens of the holly trees, of ivy winding its way up the tree trunks, and the yellow of mistletoe leaves amongst the higher boughs. When the snow came, Nelly promised herself, she would go into the woods and walk.

She would make the most of every second of being alive.

She thought of Madeleine, Sophy and Priscilla. They'd be well on their way to Australia by now. She tried to imagine what it must be like to be on a ship, crossing to the other side of the world, reinventing themselves, knowing they would never come back.

If they had the courage to make that journey, she could walk over the bridge.

Nelly walked past the tower and onto the span. Hundreds of feet below was the River Avon. The tide was out, so there were no ships on the river, only the pewter-grey water and the sloping mudflats, busy with wading birds. Above the water, but below Nelly, white gulls circled, tracing spirals in the air, and she heard the mew of a buzzard nearby.

Nelly felt a combination of joy and exhilaration at seeing the world from an entirely new perspective.

To her right, the river followed a meandering route through the gorge towards the Bristol Channel, and from there to the Atlantic Ocean. And to her left was the city, its roofs, church spires, great buildings and factories looking toy-like from here; smoke curling up from a thousand chimneys to settle in a blanket of smog over the city.

Her city.

The city that had taken her in, given her a room in which to live, and a job to do.

The city that had provided her with knowledge, and drama, and colleagues and friends.

* * *

Nelly had been back to Holywell, to visit Constance Parr. Angel had accompanied her and after a painful hour spent in the company of Constance, a trembling wraith who could barely speak, the two Brooks women had repaired to their hotel. There they had drafted a plan to extricate Constance from the asylum. Angel had managed to liberate Nelly; the two of them working together were determined to rescue Constance. It was useful that one of Angel's current admirers was a respected London solicitor.

* * *

Will had helped Nelly compose a letter to her parents. It was a mystery to Nelly how he, an orphan who had never had to navigate the complications of family life, had instinctively known what Nelly should say to appease her mother and father, and soften their attitude towards her without denying her true self.

She had expressed gratitude for all they had done for both her, and her daughter. She asked for their forgiveness for her 'juvenile recklessness'. Finally, she asked if they might meet to discuss Harriet's future: a future with Nelly in it.

Nelly wrote:

I should like to visit Harriet from time to time. I am not the child I was when she was born. I am an adult woman, with a home and a career. Perhaps I could visit Harriet in Switzerland, or, if you prefer, I will wait until she is returned to England. In the meantime, would you allow me to correspond with her, as a family friend, perhaps, or as a cousin?

I will, of course, respect your wishes and abide by the narrative you have told to Harriet.

The last sentence had hurt her to write, but Will had pointed out that her mother and father had all the power over Harriet's future, and if Nelly was to be openly involved – and she really did not wish to have to skulk around as she had been doing – she would have to make concessions. She also acknowledged, with Will's gentle encouragement, that her parents had only ever acted in what they believed were the best interests of the family. They had never wished for a daughter like Nelly; they had not known what to do with her; they had done what they could.

Nelly had not yet received an answer to her letter. But Will had told her not to worry. There was plenty of time for other approaches, other letters.

'It will work itself out,' he told her. 'Be patient, Nelly. You have the rest of your life, and Harriet's, ahead of you.'

Nelly did not know when Harriet would be returning to England. She had heard, via Angel, that her daughter had made a full recovery from the scarlet fever, and that she was thriving in the Alpine air. Harriet's wellbeing was more important than Nelly's feelings.

In two years, Harriet would leave school and be adult enough to make her own decisions about who she had in her life. Perhaps, by that time, Nelly's career and her wages would have grown sufficiently for her to be in a position to offer Harriet a real home, rather than a room in a lodging house, if that was what she wanted.

* * *

The crypt had been a strange place for a confession, but, as well as the confiding, there had been something else: a kind of redemption. By telling Will her story, Nelly had seen it through his eyes, and his understanding of what she had done, and its consequences, was accepting. There had been no shock, or distaste, only empathy.

Not all people regarded the world as Nelly's parents did.

Not all people were the same. Life was like the river. How you perceived it depended upon your viewpoint. And what you saw, like the automaton wren, was not always the truth, because truth was not absolute; it had its own nuances.

It was not as if Nelly had shed the burden she carried inside her, simply by being honest with Will. But the burden was lighter. She had found a crack in the armour. She had started to forgive herself. And with the forgiving came another feeling: an acceptance that Nelly was not, perhaps, the wicked person she'd been told, for most of her life, that she was.

Will had asked what became of Sidney, and when Nelly had told him that he too had been sent away, and that she often thought of him, and hoped that he was thriving, Will had said they should attempt to find him. There would be records somewhere. And Sidney, no doubt, wondered about his child, as Nelly did.

If Sidney could be found, the circle would be joined, and there would be catharsis.

Nelly Brooks leaned over the handrail of the Clifton bridge, and dropped the winter rose she had brought for her daughter. She watched it spin as it fell, before it disappeared from sight. It would be caught in the water, and the tide would take it, spinning, out into the channel, then into the ocean, and it would drift amongst waves as big as houses, and who knew where it might end up?

She stayed for a few moments, looking down, then she straightened. She could see Will now, walking over the bridge towards her, a wide smile on his lovely face. He waved, and she lifted her hand in response, and she headed back to the surety of him, feeling lighter with each step, inhaling all that she could see as if it were some kind of elixir. Until now, this was a view afforded only to the birds, and here she was, Nelly Brooks, at liberty to enjoy it whenever she wished.

My God, thought Nelly, *I am so glad I can do this. What a time this is to be alive!*

* * *

MORE FROM LOUISE DOUGLAS

Another book from Louise Douglas, *The Sea House*, is available to order now here:

https://mybook.to/TheSeaHouseBackAd

ACKNOWLEDGEMENTS

The biggest, warmest, most grateful thanks go to Isobel and Sarah, for their encouragement, support and input into making this book the best it could be. You are amazing and I know how lucky I am to have you on my side.

Special thanks to Sue and especially Rose, for skill, help and patience.

Thanks to the entire Boldwood team, for every little and big thing you do.

Thank you also to Marianne, Pat, Vikki and associates for everything.

Thank you to the book bloggers, the sellers, the publishers, promoters, marketeers, librarians, teachers, festival organisers, reviewers, social media allies and to everyone fighting in an increasingly difficult climate to keep authors in work and to celebrate books.

A heartfelt 'thank you' to everyone who reads.

This story is set in Bristol in 1864, the year the Clifton Suspension Bridge was opened. I have tried to be factually accurate concerning the setting, although some places etc are fictional. If there are errors, they are mine alone. I have retained some of the language and terminology used in the mid-nineteenth century around the subject of mental illness. Although it is shocking and offensive to the modern reader, it reflects the attitudes of the time.

I am indebted to many sources for information about this

period in history, but two books in particular, which I highly recommend:

The Mysterious Case of the Victorian Female Detective, by Sara Lodge.

The Five: The Untold Lives of the Women Killed by Jack the Ripper by Hallie Rubenhold.

Both are packed with details about how women lived in the mid-Victorian period and the attitudes and struggles they faced. Edward Fairfield is named after a senior civil servant quoted in *The Five*, a man with a 'slightly dissipated' personality who spent a significant amount of time at his club.

Other characters have been named after real-life and fictional characters from books read as part of the research.

This story was inspired by the lives of two women. First, the American journalist, Nellie Bly, born in 1864, who pretended to be insane in order to be committed to a notorious asylum from where she reported, undercover. And secondly, Harriet Moncreiffe, who married baronet and MP Sir Charles Mordaunt when she was eighteen. Harriet was involved in a sensational divorce case in 1869, following the birth of a child who was almost certainly not her husband's. During the case, it was revealed that the Prince of Wales used to 'regularly visit' Harriet while her husband was absent. Following the trial, Harriet was declared insane. She spent the remaining thirty-six years of her life in asylums.

The *Courier* is a fictional newspaper.

ABOUT THE AUTHOR

Louise Douglas is an RNA award winner and the bestselling author of several brilliantly reviewed novels. These include the number one bestseller *The Lost Notebook*, and the *The Secrets Between Us* which was a Richard and Judy Book Club pick. She lives in the West Country.

Sign up to Louise's newsletter to get a FREE short story!

Follow Louise on social media:

facebook.com/Louise-Douglas-Author-340228039335215
x.com/louisedouglas3
bookbub.com/authors/louise-douglas

ALSO BY LOUISE DOUGLAS

The House by the Sea

In Her Shadow

Your Beautiful Lies

The Secrets Between Us

The Secret by the Lake

The Scarlet Dress

The Love of My Life

Missing You

The Room in the Attic

The Lost Notebook

The Secret of Villa Alba

The Summer of Lies

The Sea House

The Emerald Shawl

Letters from *the past*

Discover page-turning historical novels from your favourite authors and be transported back in time

Join our book club Facebook group

https://bit.ly/SixpenceGroup

Sign up to our newsletter

https://bit.ly/LettersFromPastNews

Boldwood

Boldwood Books is an award-winning fiction publishing company seeking out the best stories from around the world.

Find out more at www.boldwoodbooks.com

Join our reader community for brilliant books, competitions and offers!

Follow us
@BoldwoodBooks
@TheBoldBookClub

Sign up to our weekly deals newsletter

https://bit.ly/BoldwoodBNewsletter

Printed in Dunstable, United Kingdom